THE PC
CONNECTED

ANDREW SHARP

Disclaimer:
This is a work of fiction. All characters, locations, and businesses are purely products of the author's imagination and are entirely fictitious. Any resemblance to actual people, living or dead, or to businesses, places, or events is completely coincidental.

prologue

Taken

Sara screamed, a high-pitched frightened scream. They had finally come for her, the day she had always feared was today.

Jeb, her younger brother by a couple of years, had opened the door without asking over the door communicator who was outside; at nearly sixteen he should have known better. Then he had stepped back and let the six men and women into their home without challenging them. They all wore smart dark uniforms, not the grubby type worn by grounders, on their left breast each had an embroidered symbol of a golden bird; these were people from the privileged lofts.

Sara looked for somewhere to run. Their home was made from two metal containers, one stacked on top of the other. There were no windows and only one door in and out and that had one of the intruders guarding it. The other five fanned out as they approached her.

She looked for something to throw or use as a weapon but the sparsely furnished front living space had little to offer. The main furniture was fixed to the shell of the room and the few items that weren't were of no use to her situation.

Feet hammered down the stairs behind her. Sara felt a moment of hope, her mother was coming to save her. Then she panicked again, her mother couldn't fight these people alone, if she did she might get hurt or worse. They more than likely wanted her alive but her mother and brother probably had no value to them.

Sky, Sara's mother, charged into the living space dressed only in a knee-length nightdress and without pause rushed past her daughter and leapt on top of the nearest intruder with her fists flying.

Sara looked to Jeb for help. He was tall, close to six feet, strong and his dark skin was contoured with toned young muscle, but he was just standing there watching his mother fighting. Sky was thrown to the floor but she was instantly up on her feet again attacking.

A punch smashed into the side of Sky's head and she dropped limply to the floor. Sara screamed again as she turned and ran upstairs. Hands snatched at her, narrowly missing as she escaped. She went up the stairs and into the bedroom she shared with her brother but before she could close the door a man and woman raced in behind her. Following her mother's example, Sara leapt at the nearest, swinging punches wildly. They all wrestled around the room for a moment before Sara landed hard on her back as the man slammed her to the floor. The air in her lungs expelled in a violent rush leaving her breathless. Before she could recover the woman had shackled her wrists together. They had her.

Lying still for a moment, as her breathing came back

to normal she noticed her cat peeping out from under a pile of dirty clothes. She willed it to stay still, not knowing what the uniformed men and women would do with it if they caught the cat; she didn't want them to find it.

The woman yanked Sara to her feet, pulling her up by the shackles that bound her wrists in front of her. The man clamped a strong hand on the back of her neck and they led her from the room.

Downstairs Jeb had remained standing by the door. Sky was prone on the floor and not moving. Two of the downstairs assailants grabbed Sara by an arm each and the woman holding the shackles let go, as did the man whose hand was clamped to her neck. Then she was pushed and dragged outside through the doorway.

They all marched a short distance down the main route before entering one of the side alleys. They snaked through a few more alleys, dragging Sara who was still resisting being taken. She had seen Jeb behind her a couple of times but he was tagging along freely.

"The mother is following us," said one of the men behind Sara.

"Take care of it," ordered one of the women.

chapter øne

Teaming Up

Scallion looked at the clock: 20:00, Friday 03 03 2923. The shift was changing on the flight dock. They would find the bodies soon, if not already. He had perhaps a four-hour head start on the authorities, but much less on the bounty Ninety-Six would place on his head. If he were lucky, the contract would be for alive, but he was never that fortunate. He looked around his miserable small dwelling pod, which was littered with old food packaging, empty alcohol bottles, and the remnants of used drugs, one last time to make sure that he had everything. The scarred holdall in his left hand held his entire life's worth and fortune. Inside, the ballistic handgun and a small amount of ammunition were illegal but necessary in his line of work. The drugs were recreational, and he needed them, as he did the half-bottle of cheap whiskey, if he were to get through any given day. The few credits were all he had now; the last guaranteed winning bet he had placed had just about cleaned him out. He had managed to stuff a single change of clothing in the bag, but that was all he could fit in alongside the package.

He scanned the frayed, stained and worn cot that doubled as a sofa, opened the three empty tiny cupboards on the opposite wall checking for anything he needed, but knowing he wouldn't find anything. The cracked wall screen, hit by a liquor bottle recently and pretending it was a window, caught his eye. The displayed mountain scene with clear blue skies was his favourite.

"Mirror."

The screen switched to show his reflection. He was three days unshaven, his shoulder-length brown hair almost black with grease. The left eye was dark, puffy and partially closed, and across his top lip was a smear of dry blood. He spat on his hand and rubbed the stain away. He still wore the badged, dark blue flight dock overalls of a loader, but he couldn't afford the time to change. His face looked haggard. Drugs, alcohol and bad women had added ten years to his existing forty. He was fit and healthy, though; he needed to be in the violent grimy underworld of crime and deception he passed through.

"Get a grip. You've no time for nostalgia, you prick. They're coming for you. Door open." He stepped outside to the filthy walkway beyond the room he had called home for six months.

He needed to disappear, and quickly. Getting to another station was his best hope for now, and that in itself would be difficult, if not impossible. He didn't know anyone that had tried to do that successfully. For starters, he would need more credits. The town was his only option for that. There, he could either steal the credits or find them in other nefarious ways. He looked up to the star-veiled hangar ceiling far above, mimicking a sky. The lights had dimmed to bring on the false concept of nightfall. The domicile pod he occupied was on the southern edge of Station Six's town. He could reach the dense population and be hidden in the narrow, gloomy routes and the maze of filthy alleys in minutes, but did he still have that long?

Scallion bounded down the rickety stairs two steps at a time, from the fifth floor to ground level, rapidly growing more aware that his capture, or worse, might be imminent. He looked back and upward for any sign of pursuit, checking the impoverished twenty floors, each lined with twenty-eight identical pods. He was lucky in that he hadn't needed to share. Others had to cram two adults and kids into a space only large enough for one. Why people still had kids and coupled up together with someone he couldn't fathom. That was a lose–lose situation. Less space, fewer credits to go around more mouths, and the kids could turn blood-sick anytime in their first year and cramped up like that their parents could only be food. Happy that no one was following or watching him, he moved on.

At the base of the stairs, he found a couple of run-down and battered shuttles. He mounted the nearest, taking the torn double bench seat facing forward.

"Town, Arent Square."

The vehicle lurched into motion, the engine complaining as it turned the shuttle around, with wheels squealing on the black pitch-coated metal surface.

"Piece of shit. Can't you go any faster?"

The small, open-top, four-seater carriage had no vocal responses, but he needed to vent his frustration. Running would be quicker, but he immediately discounted it. A man fleeing the tower pods at speed would be memorable to witnesses, and he couldn't afford to give his inevitable hunters any help.

Ten painfully long and desperate minutes later, he crossed the town's perimeter. An old, faded and tarnished sign stated: Welcome to Station Six, Population 109,674. The white numerals were freshly updated. *Who the fuck has that cushy job*, wondered Scallion for a moment, angry at the prospect that someone had it more comfortable and better than he did. *Does that include the tower pods and the lofts too? I doubt it. One lot's too poor to be counted, and the others are too rich to be simple numbers.*

The centuries-old, block-on-block prefabricated structures of the town were in no better condition than the ageing tower pods on the outskirts. Metal, mainly windowless, containers, every one the same dull grey colour, were attached together to create buildings. At least they were better homes, with several rooms, than the single box of the pods. Here there were also stores, bars, the brothel, the gambling house and the service buildings too. None were taller than six storeys; this was why they could be more spacious, as they supposedly had less weight on top. He didn't believe that, however. He believed it was just something people above in the lofts said so they could avoid spending credits to extend them upwards.

The shuttle stayed to the main routes as it passed buildings, mainly homes, but with stores and bars peppered in among them, all stacked one on top of the other and side by side. People were outside in low numbers, the darkness of night keeping most decent folk inside. Some of the bar doors slid open as he passed, revealing gloomy interiors. Some played music, others were virtually empty, while the more popular ones erupted in raucous noise until the door slid closed again. Stray dogs were a common sight, wandering where they liked, ignored but accepted. The numerous alleys were too narrow for shuttle passage, as although they were just wide enough for one vehicle, the stairs up to the higher levels and trash bins and junk littering them made it impossible for travel. On the main routes, two could narrowly pass each other while still allowing some room for pedestrians.

The motion stopped, and he faced the centrepiece of the circular square. Another decomposed old relic, once a tall fountain depicting fish and women pouring jugs, but no water had flowed from it in centuries.

Now where? Old Bob's? No, those cutthroats would try and take me themselves once they heard of the bounty. Valerie's? She had no love of Ninety-Six, but she needed the brothel to survive, and I wouldn't be worth any sacrifice on her part.

"Get out of the open, stupid." He knew he didn't have time to sit where he could be seen and remembered.

Going left, for no particular reason, he entered the darkest alley. The smell of trash and general waste was stronger here than on the routes. *Getting out of sight has to be my first objective, but after that?* He stepped in something slick and slippery but caught himself before he fell. *Probably someone's shit, literally.* Then he heard a soft moan, and for no specific reason, he decided to look closer.

It was a body, discarded between two large trash bins. The shit he had slipped on was blood. Stooping closer for a better look in the murky darkness, he saw it was a woman, savagely beaten, maybe stabbed, or shot. He didn't have time for this, and so he moved on.

Agitated, muffled and raised voices ahead caught his attention. *Are they looking here already?* The paranoia was now messing with his mind. He needed a drink, a fix, sleep, any escape. Trying to flee the unavoidable was screwing up his head. *The woman! She must live somewhere. If I save her, take her home, I'd be off the routes and alleys in a random location and out of sight.*

"Hey, you all right?" It was a stupid question and he knew it.

"Do you need help?" Another fucking stupid question.

"I'm going to pick you up." He grabbed her and started to lift her. "Look, if you need me to help you, you have to help me. Try and stand. I need you to tell me where to take you."

"Corgon Route, eighty-nine." Her voice was weak, but he had heard her.

He cradled her in his arms. She wasn't walking anywhere. Her last effort had been to give the address, and now she was gone, but he could feel her breathing; not dead yet then.

Corgon Route was close. It would be quicker on the main routes, but there he was more likely to be seen, and so he took the alleyways, hoping she'd still be alive when he got there.

The last alley exited close to his destination, but not so close that he could remain out of sight. He was more exposed moving down the route, and not inconspicuous with a blood-soaked woman in his arms. He also appreciated that it was that time when most people were either at home or in the bars, brothel or gambling house, so the way was relatively quiet.

"Hey, what are you doing to that woman?"

Scallion was paces from his goal: number eighty-nine on the ground floor of the blocks. The short, scrawny young man in front of him was the last thing he needed.

With the woman in his arms, he had no other option but to kick. The ball of his right foot hit the interfering man hard on the upper lip and under the nose. He dropped instantly beneath an erupting shower of blood.

"Fuck, fuck, fuck," cursed Scallion as he took the last steps to reach number eighty-nine.

"Woman, wake up." He shook her, rattling her as best he could without putting her down. "Wake up. I need you to open your fucking door if you want me to help you."

"Door open." She didn't seem conscious, barely alive, but she had spoken loud enough that the door slid open.

Scallion stepped inside immediately but then halted at the entrance. The man left out in the open was a risk, a marker for the hunters. Now he had access, he dumped the woman uncaringly across the threshold to hold the door open should it close. Then he went to retrieve the fallen man, scanning furtively for any witnesses, but he saw no one.

Finally, the door closed and he was inside, but with the added complication of two unconscious bodies. The man would recover, a little battered and bruised, but other than that fine. The blood-soaked woman was another matter.

The sound of a metal-framed chair scrapping across the floor woke Scallion. His mind was foggy, but as the realisation of his current predicament returned, he fully woke with a start. He was sitting on the floor and waved his gun indiscriminately around the room. An empty whiskey bottle rolled off his lap and clunked to the floor before rolling a short distance.

The man was conscious, tied and gagged to one of the

table chairs. He was trying to escape but was only succeeding in moving the chair across the floor. They were in the kitchen. The woman was laid out on the small dining table, not moving, her legs dangling over the edge. The man's eyes were wide with fear and panic. He was trying to scream but then started to choke as the gag in his mouth, overlapped by another tied around his lower face, began to restrict his throat.

Scallion watched initially, wondering whether to save the man or not. His prisoner started to turn blue; he couldn't breathe. Deciding it wasn't worth letting the man die until he knew if he had any worth, Scallion stood slowly and walked over to him. Waving his gun in the prisoner's face, he clumsily untied the top gag with his free hand before pulling the second from the bloated face.

The coughing stopped, only to be followed by floods of tears and begging. "Don't kill me. Please don't kill me."

"Shut the fuck up."

"Please don't kill me."

"Fuck this." Scallion struck the bound man across his temple with the butt of his gun. The silence that followed was calming. Now he had time to think.

He glanced at the beaten and wounded woman, a knife slash across her gut. She was lucky. The blade hadn't gone deep, but it had sliced a long wound across her abdomen. She would more than likely live, provided she hadn't lost too much blood. He had found a medi-kit in one of the cupboards. Inside had been a laserseal-pen, and so he'd been able to close the wound. There had also been several anti-infection-healing cartridges and a delivery-needle pump, and he had administered two of those as well. A third he had used on himself to resolve his swollen eye and other bruises.

With both his captives once again silent and him up on his feet, he needed to plan his next move. First, he replaced the gags on the man, but this time with less stuffed inside his mouth. Next, he searched the dwelling. He didn't need to be discreet or hide from outside observers, as the two blocks that made up the home had no windows. Very few did; it was a luxury and risk that few could afford. The front living space had been the scene of a struggle and a fight. The few items of cheap furniture not fixed to the shell of the room had been upturned and scattered. A quick rummage found there was nothing of value worth stealing. The same disarray existed in the kids' sparsely furnished bedroom upstairs. The woman's bedroom hadn't been the scene of a disturbance. However, the bed cover was on the floor, as though she had exited in a hurry. Again, nothing worth stealing.

Where are the kids? Is she a good worker? Good enough that someone would come looking for her? Looking at the clothing scattered about and the filter masks, it looked like she worked in the ore mine. From the evidence, the kids, a boy and a girl, worked in the factories, older teenagers too. The man, he guessed, worked on the farms. *Too soft for the mine. Would anyone be looking for him?* Time to wake them up and see if they have any value.

Lifting the well-wrapped sealed package from his holdall, he placed it to one side. It was a foot and a half long and ten inches wide all around. He had no idea what it was inside but figured it had to be valuable given the trouble it had caused. Under the package, lying loose in the bottom of the bag, was his drug stash. He selected a strip of shrink-wrapped pink smilers and popped one. It wasn't for him. It was a stimulant, and he needed to force it down the woman's throat. The sink was behind a panel on the wall. "Sink." The unit slid out, exposing a tiny basin with no drainer and a water tap. He opened a cupboard to find dry ration packs, and the next had some tinned goods. The third had some metal plates, bowls and cups. Taking a cup and filling it with water, he poured some down her throat as he massaged the smiler down. The rest of the water he threw in the man's face.

The woman suddenly sat bolt upright after only a few seconds but then collapsed back to the table, groaning. Good, she hadn't screamed. The stomach wound must have healed well, and her facial bruising had disappeared too. He would need to watch her though as he hadn't bound or restrained her, but he doubted she would have the strength to stand or fight. The scrawny man, young, maybe only nineteen or twenty, was staring wide-eyed at the gun and Scallion.

"No sudden movement from either of you or I will shoot you." He had no desire to fire. Not because he cared about their lives, but the noise of the ballistic weapon would be audible outside the building. "No shouting or screaming either and I won't hurt you. I'm going to remove your gag. Don't be stupid."

The woman had rolled over to face Scallion. She was conscious enough to talk. "My kids?"

"They're not here, but that's nothing to do with me." Scallion flitted his gaze between the two watching for signs of a threat.

"Who's he?"

"He saw me carrying you home. So now he's here."

"You didn't take me to the authorities, and you've kidnapped him. You're on the run."

Clever bitch. Not stupid this one.

"Yes. So that means I'm desperate, and if I have to, I will kill you both," he countered quickly.

"But first you want to know if…" She coughed, then took a moment to compose herself. There was no blood in the saliva running from her mouth. Another good sign that her abdomen wound wasn't severe.

"What the fuck have you given me?"

"A smiler. I needed you awake."

"Wow, I'm definitely awake." She forced herself up into a sitting position with her legs now dangling comfortably over the edge of the table towards Scallion.

"Don't do anything stupid. The smiler might let you think you're invincible, but you've lost a lot of blood and you were slashed in the gut when you were beaten."

She examined the wound through the tear in her knee-length nightdress. It had been sealed. There might be a slight scar, but it would be faint. "Good work."

"I've had lots of practice."

She checked that her knickers were still on through the rip of the gown.

"I didn't look or touch down there."

Scallion had thought about it. She was pretty. Nice tits: he had looked at them. She was maybe thirty, ebony skin. A brunette too, his preference. She had beautiful legs. Shorter than him, maybe five foot eight. He liked them shorter and smaller. He was six foot two, but there were still many women taller and bulkier than him.

"What do you need from us?" asked the woman.

"First tell me what the fuck happened here? Are the kids coming back? Will anyone come looking for you when you miss your shift?"

"Someone took my kids. I tried to stop them."

"Why would anyone take your kids?"

"Sara is a connected."

"Fuck, how've you kept that a secret so long?"

"We hide it. For nearly eighteen years we kept it a secret. We didn't want to be separated."

"The boy?"

"Jeb. No, he's not connected."

"So why did they take him?"

"No idea. Leverage against Sara? Maybe they think he is too?"

She slid off the table to stand. Scallion stepped back and raised the gun to her.

"Don't do anything foolish."

The man tied to the chair was sobbing now.

"And you shut the fuck up. Grow a pair. I'll be asking who you are next."

"I need to get my kids back."

"That's not going to happen. They'll already be up in the lofts. They're gone."

"Then I'm going to the lofts too."

"You won't get up there. They'll kill you before you even get close. No doubt they think they left you for dead already."

"Rich, pampered bastards took my kids, and I'm going for them."

"Look, lady, I've been a career criminal all my life and even I wouldn't risk the lofts."

"You need to get out of the station, don't you? What are you going to do, walk across the Scorched Land? You need a means of transport. The lofts might be an option for you too."

"You trying to recruit me to your cause?"

"As you said, I've no chance alone."

"Fuck that, you've got a death wish. Anyway, answer my fucking question. Will anyone be looking for you? Partner, boss, anybody?"

"No, no partner. He died years ago in service. Work won't come looking for a day or two. I'm not that important."

She stepped forward, straightening fully upright as she moved.

The gun snapped to her. "Nothing stupid."

"I need a drink." Then she shuffled towards the sink.

"So who the fuck are you?" said Scallion to the young man.

The young man had stopped crying but was too frightened to speak. He was still wide-eyed with fear.

"You'd better start talking, or you're no good to me."

"I'm Poppy. I work on the farms. I look after the groff plants. You know, the ones they can use the seeds from to make smilers."

"Will anyone be looking for you?"

"My husband might. But he's home with our son. We argued yesterday, and I stormed out, so he might not bother looking for me for a day or two."

A repeating tone came from the living space. Someone was calling on the wall screen.

"Ignore it."

"If I do that they might come knocking," said the woman.

"Who the fuck is it?"

"How should I know unless I answer it."

"Ignore it."

"You're the boss."

The call tone stopped.

"Husband? So you're one of those religious freaks."

"Matrimony is the only way two people should be together."

"Fuck that. There's no fucking gods, and if there were they wouldn't be here in this shithole."

"Mother sees all and is everywhere."

"Well she ain't with you now, is she?"

"She's always with me."

"What about the farm, will they look for you?"

"They might. I'm a head grower. If the crop has a problem, they'll need me."

"Head grower, eh. So you've got credits?"

The slight-built man was short, maybe five foot tall when standing up, skin colour light yellowish-brown and almond-shaped eyes, maybe of drich origin mix. His clothes were brighter than the average person would wear. A yellow jacket, trousers and similar matching shoes and shirt, all spoiled now with flecks of his blood. He didn't look important.

"Not with me. But yes, at home. If you take me there, you can have what you need to run."

The woman started walking towards the living space.

"Where the fuck are you going?"

"To get dressed. If we're going to the farms, I need to put some clothes on."

"Who says we're going to the farms?"

"You need credits. He has them. As a head grower, his domicile will be on the farm. They keep his kind close to the crops. I need someone like you to figure out how I get into the lofts."

"Look, lady, I'm not helping you find your kids.

They're probably already halfway to the Device already."

"Then that's where we're going."

"Fuck you, lady." But he didn't stop her from leaving, and once she was out of sight, he turned back to the bound man on the chair.

"I won't do anything stupid. I swear on all that is holy. I just want to be back with my husband and son."

"Fuck, fuck, fuck!" What choice did he have? There was no doubt that by now there was a bounty on his head. As soon as he stepped outside, the authorities, bounty hunters and every other lowlife would be looking for him. He needed to get out of this station fast.

Leaving Poppy tied to the chair but without the gags, Scallion went to look for the woman. He found her in her bedroom pulling on a short black leather jacket over a tight blue vest top. She was already wearing a pair of figure-hugging trousers with knee-high laced boots.

"What the fuck is that?" He pointed his gun straight at the animal on the bed. "Where did that come from?"

"It's a cat."

"Fuck off, there are no cats. Not for a hundred years or more since the last great food shortage. And if any survived that, the grumbles wiped them out when they breached the perimeter fences a few decades back."

"It's an OD, an ore-drone."

"Fuck off, now you're taking the piss. How the fuck do you afford an OD?"

"Do you have to swear in every sentence?"

"What if I... do?" He stuttered past the swearing that was on the tip of his tongue.

"Sara made it."

"Fu... really! That's one gifted kid." He would try and

watch his swearing for a while because she was pretty, and he fancied his chances later.

"Where'd she get the parts?"

"I stole them bit by bit from the ore mine, and anywhere else I could scavenge them. It took her two years to build it, and she finished it only last week. It's still young, still developing and learning."

"She couldn't make a dog. Something less conspicuous?"

"Too big, more parts. And she liked the thought of a cat."

Scallion assessed the OD. Black fur, sleek body, long tail, bright green eyes with dark slit pupils; it looked real, alive. It was lying on the bed, making a soft rumbling noise.

"Why's it making that noise. Is it broken?"

"That's a purr. It means it's happy."

"Where'd you get the ore to power it?"

"Again, stolen like the parts. I'm not a thief, but she was so clever, talented, gifted that I had to find something to keep her occupied and challenge her. I stole ore dust, chip fragments and small components a little at a time. Nothing so large that it would get noticed by the scans. And if I was caught, it was just like dust or a part that might have accidentally drifted into a pocket."

"What can it do?"

"I don't know. So far, it's just been a cat. We've kept it hidden most of the time."

"So it has power ore, intelligence ore. Does it have comms ore?"

"I suppose so. I managed to get hold of all three. Sara said that's what she needed."

"We're taking it. It's probably worth a good few credits."

"You're not selling my cat. And yes we're taking it."

At that, the woman slung a slouch bag over her shoulder and picked up the cat. "Stay inside and be quiet," she said as she placed the animal inside the bag. Then she reached under her pillow and pulled a blaster pistol.

Scallion levelled the ballistic in his right hand, but the woman didn't turn around and instead dropped the pistol into her slouch bag beside the cat.

"Where the fuck did you get a blaster?"

"My partner was a security operative on the dock. When he died, they gave me his stuff. The pistol came with that."

"Don't think that should have happened."

"Neither do I, but I didn't give it back."

"Why didn't you use it when they took your kids?"

"It was hidden then, and I didn't get a chance. I'm ready now," she said as she turned. "My name is Sky, and you are?"

"Scallion."

"Well, Scallion, let's get you ready too, shall we?"

Poppy hadn't even tried to escape. Thirty minutes he had waited alone before the woman showed up again. They were probably shagging. More than likely at gunpoint too, as he doubted the woman would be willing, but he had seen the lust in the ruffian's eyes.

The woman entered the kitchen, strode over to the holdall, and took the man's clothing. She didn't even acknowledge Poppy before she left. Ten minutes later, the thug and the woman came back. The man had changed into a dark knee-length jacket over a black shirt and trousers with matching dark ankle boots. The change of clothing wasn't why Poppy's mouth hung open though. The man was clean-shaven, and his long dark greasy hair was now washed, cut noticeably short in length and blond; he barely recognised him as the same man that had kidnapped him.

"So, we're leaving now, Poppy. This is Sky, and I'm Karl," lied Scallion. "Are you going to give us any trouble?"

The bound man shook his head.

"Right, I'm going to let you loose and then we're going straight to your home."

"You won't get past security. You don't have the right clearance," Poppy challenged.

"We won't be using the security point," replied Scallion.

"There's no other way in?" questioned Poppy

"The maintenance conduits."

"But they have botdrones and defences."

"Leave them to me."

Outside, the ceiling was daylight bright. Holographic clouds drifted over the lighting cells to cast soft shadows on the ground and surfaces below. In the stark light of day, the slum they called town was even more squalid. Litter drifted down the main routes. Botdrones were supposed to collect such waste, but they were few in number and the waste relentless. People of all types and colours were out and about now. Most would be going to or from a shift at the ore mine, the factories or the farms. Others worked in stores, the bars or on the service provisions. All children attended school from the age of three and then everyone over the age of seven had a job allocated to them.

"Hold my hand," said Scallion, throwing the straps of

his bag over one shoulder before grabbing Poppy in a firm grip. "Don't try anything." He pulled back his coat just enough to show the handgun tucked into his belt and trousers.

The three of them strolled casually down the route and were initially ignored. Most people kept their heads down; no one wanted to stand out, to attract any attention from the patrolling authorities or the criminal elements lurking in many of the shadows. The gangs and lawbreakers were left alone unless they made themselves a particular nuisance. The station's security forces focused on protecting and policing the flight dock, ore mine, factories and farms. These revenue streams, much of which went off Devil's Rock to Eden, were all critical to the wealthy, up high in their lofts. The grounders were just commodities to labour for them, a population they needed to keep alive and relatively healthy but not at any great expense.

A dog barked and Scallion looked in its direction.

"Relax," said Sky. "You'll attract attention."

He was sweating, even though the controlled temperature was moderate. He was nervous, and he hadn't had a drink or any drugs since he'd finished the whiskey. However, Sky was right, and he had to keep calm. *How is she so calm?* They had a forty-minute walk to the right conduit access point, and they were going to pass many people along the way.

Scallion knew the town like the back of his hand. After all, he had lived there all his life, like everyone else. Anyone hunting him would assume he was looking for a way out of the station. They would be monitoring all the possible exits. He wondered for a moment how much his bounty might be. No one would be expecting him to be going to the farms, surely? He was confident this detour would buy him some time to think about how he was going to get out of the station.

The robust service shed was cordoned off by sturdy, thick meshed fencing on all four sides and above. It was located midway down an alley, with only domicile blocks on each side. The place was quiet, with only a solitary dog rummaging through the trash. A combined numeric keypad and a card swipe secured the gate. Scallion produced a palm-sized transparent tablet from his pocket. Lights danced across the clear surface of the utility device and seconds later the lock popped.

"Neat," commented Sky. "Bet that wasn't cheap to come by."

"I got it for free. The last owner didn't need it anymore."

The same type of lock barred the shed door.

After closing and locking both the gate and the door behind them, they were inside the shed. Space was a little cramped for the three of them, especially as they were avoiding the floor hatch should it suddenly open. Dark panels lined one wall from top to bottom. Scallion touched all four surfaces and they blinked into life, each displaying a holographic keyboard and requesting an access command.

Scallion typed a command into the first and the screen turned amber. "Shit, wrong code."

"Won't the utility device help?" asked Poppy.

"Not on these. They change the code every couple of weeks. But in truth, there are only four command codes they use. I just have to put the right one in next, or the panels will lock out for an hour and alert one of the control rooms."

"And you know all four codes?" asked Sky.

"Yes, everything has a price, and everyone is corrupt. So that makes everything available if you can pay the asking."

"So which of the three remaining are you trying next?"

"Ssshh! I'm thinking. They're always used in order, and I last used one three weeks ago… so… got it."

He typed in another code and the panel came to life displaying readings of the services flowing through the conduit tunnel. With one panel accessed, he entered the same code at the other three and all became active with illuminated holographic dials, graphs and wave-bars.

"I can disable the lasermesh and the filters. They might send an engineer or reset them from a control room, but I doubt that will be quick," said Scallion.

"No, not filters." Poppy almost screamed.

"They won't think anything is down there, any person at least if the filters are off. They might also think the tainted air has tripped the lasermesh in some way."

"That tainted air will kill you in less than an hour, and after thirty minutes your lungs won't be able to recover, and you'll have weezies for the rest of your life." Poppy showed real fear on his face.

"Look, there are filter masks over there. We each take one and move through the conduit as quickly as possible before they reset everything. The control rooms are lazy, and this shit is all old and fails regularly. No one will be bothered. They can ignore minor glitches like this for days. Trust me. You work outside every day on a farm, so why are you so worried."

Scallion touched a screen one more time, and the floor hatch unlocked and slid open, revealing a ladder descending thirty feet. Sky collected three filter masks, complete with eye visors, and they each put one on.

The illuminated conduit was wide enough that they could walk abreast if they chose to, but they formed a line with Scallion at the front and Sky at the rear. There was plenty of headroom and running miles in both directions were a multitude of different coloured and sized cables, pipes, valves and small dark service panels. Ladders descended randomly, well distanced from each other and centrally onto the deckplate. Other conduits crossed at an irregular frequency. Scallion drew his handgun and they set off towards the farms.

"Karl, look."

"I see it, Poppy. It won't bother us. It's here for the grumbles."

Ahead was a botdrone hovering three feet above the deckplate. A two-foot diameter globe armed with four small laser-bolt turrets giving it the ability to fire in a three-hundred-and-sixty-degree arc on every axis.

"How do we get past it?" said Poppy.

"We walk. It's used to ignoring engineers," replied Scallion. "We're too big to register on its targeting sensors. Don't you know anything?"

"Farming, that's all I know. I rarely leave the farm."

"So what were you doing in town last night?" asked Sky.

Poppy ignored the question. "Look, it's moving."

A fat grumble dropped suddenly from the ceiling just feet ahead of them and Poppy screamed the high-pitched scream of a young girl. The botdrone targeted instantly and fired. The six-inch bolt of blue light splattered the creature in a wide radius of showering blood, bone fragments and flesh.

"Gross," said Sky.

Scallion looked at his feet and trousers where the fragments had reached him. "That stinks."

They moved past the botdrone, which was moving in the opposite direction.

"How much further?"

"Nearly there, Poppy. Keep your shit together."

They had seen several other grumbles scampering across cables, pipes and the deckplate, and it was quite apparent that Poppy was phobic about the creatures. The vermin kept away from people. They feared dogs, and that was why so many strays were allowed to roam freely. They had invaded every station over fifty years ago. Suddenly they had found a way out of the Scorched Land, under the perimeter walls and into the towns. No one had been concerned at the invasion, even though the grumbles were larger animals than the rats and mice, and remarkably similar in appearance. They differed not only in size but their fur was bright blue and they were fanged; they were bloodsuckers first and foremost, but they devoured every mouse and rat in every town. They were so successful that both rats and mice had become extinct. Now they fed on each other, forming gangs, and controlling territories. Their numbers were few, compared to what the extinct prolific breeding rats had been, and most people considered them a better swap over the lost rodents.

"Shit! Run." Scallion set off at pace as the dark-screened dormant service panels were lighting up. Someone was resetting the systems.

Sky overtook Poppy, who fell behind, breathing heavily.

Scallion reached the ladder first, a much longer ladder than the one they had climbed down. At the top, he opened the hatch and entered another service shed identical internally to the previous. Sky was only seconds behind him, but they had to wait for Poppy. A bloodcurdling scream came from below just before they saw Poppy grabbing the ladder's frame. The skinny young man climbed slowly, making hard work of his progress, showing no signs of any urgency.

"Aaahh!" Sky gasped as Poppy crawled off the ladder onto the floor, where he collapsed whimpering.

Scallion sniggered, and finally not able to hold it, he laughed aloud as he closed the hatch. A crisscross of welted burns covered the frail young man's back. His shirt and pants were shredded where each line ran. The scorch lines across his arse looked particularly sore and still smoked slightly. The smell was like cooked chicken. A lasermesh had caught Poppy. He must have almost passed through it as it came back online. The burns were painful, but a person could jump through lasermesh and only take minor burns, as they were designed originally to only kill rats. The laser beams were visible, interwoven across the width of the conduit, avoiding the pipes and cables but covering any space in a close-knit mesh. The wounds were nothing that a laserseal-pen couldn't knit back together and heal, but they would sting until treated.

Sky removed her facemask and took Scallion's before hanging them on the shed wall with a collection of others.

"It's not funny," whimpered Poppy, head buried in his arms, face down on the floor.

Scallion tried to stop laughing and slowly regained his composure. "It could have been worse."

"How?"

"Lucky it's your back and arse and not your dick and balls."

"Oooh." Sky winced at the thought.

"Outside, we'll be in the plant farm's control zone. I'm fairly sure we'll be close to the groff fields because of the seed smuggling that goes on, but Poppy you'll need to guide us to your home quickly. The quicker the better if you want your wounds healed."

Leaving the service shed, they entered a different world. Gone were the filthy alleys and littered routes, replaced by clean white corridors. A hovering botdrone passed them as they exited the shed door. It moved along the wall slowly, shining a beam on the nearby surface that both removed dirt and any possible bacteria. B23, in large red print, was marked on the wall opposite the shed.

"We're close," said Poppy. "This way. We need to be in B twenty-six."

Along the corridor, there were occasional doors in both directions, but other than botdrones, they met no one. They passed a viewing window, and Sky and Scallion couldn't resist looking outside. Below them was a large groff field. The dense red bulbous fruits, lying on the ground, looked ripe and ready for picking. Each groff was surrounded in a swathe of broad purple leaves. Ahead of them, high above the crop, was another service corridor like the one they were on. Pipes were attached beneath the corridors, running both ahead of and behind theirs, linking the corridors together and on occasion giving controlled bursts of water spray, cleansers, germicides or growth agents as required. Intersecting service runs also connected one corridor to another.

"I've never seen the real sky."

Scallion looked up, following Sky's gaze. The groff was an outside crop as they needed the tainted air for growth. The world outside had a permanent orange tint, almost imperceptible, but it was there, and it became more crimson as night fell. The sun was high in the dull beige-orange sky behind pale grey broken clouds. The old stories said that the sky had once been blue before the Destruction, but no one knew for sure.

"Come on, my back's sore," said Poppy. "We need to move."

Reaching B26, Poppy touched the small panel beside a door, and they waited until the lift arrived. Inside the tube was a circular platform, and when the door closed, they went downwards.

"Let me do the talking, and no guns, please. I don't want to frighten Carlu or Sunshine."

The door slid open, and Scallion drew his handgun immediately. Sky produced her blaster a moment after.

"How old's your son?" asked Scallion.

Poppy couldn't speak. The nicely furnished white living space ahead of them was in disarray and blood was splattered everywhere, including a handprint in blood slapped in the middle of the window looking out towards a crop field.

"Less than twelve months I'd guess," stated Sky. "We need to go back up."

"We can't. We need his credits, and he needs a medi-kit. Stay close."

Stepping cautiously out of the lift, they swept the room with their weapons.

"These things are fast. Shoot first, don't wait until you see it."

Something toppled over on the far right of the room. Scallion fired two rapid shots into the vicinity.

"Shoot first," he reminded Sky, who nodded nervously. She had turned pale, and this was the first time that Scallion had seen her not looking confident.

Something was disturbed in another area of the room. Two more shots and this time Sky fired too. The red six-inch rod of light burned a hole through the back of an upholstered chair. This time they heard the soft snarl of something wild and threatening.

"It's definitely in here. You only had one kid, right?"

Poppy nodded.

The scream was unholy, frenzied and primal, as the small child leapt from behind the nearby overturned sofa with his mouth open wide and two large fangs protruding from his upper gums. The blood-smeared infant had eyes like hot burning coals as he flew through the air towards Scallion. He fired, and the baby exploded like a ruptured bag of meat: blood and flesh splattering across the room.

Poppy fainted.

"Look for survivors," ordered Scallion, moving across the room with his gun before him. Sky followed, and they crept slowly to the far door, which slid open as they approached. Beyond was a glass dining table and six matching chairs. Two of the walls were entirely glazed, looking out across crops of groff, and all the surfaces were smeared with bloody handprints.

"Watch the stairs. I'll check the kitchen."

The door slid open, revealing a large, well-equipped kitchen complete with a circular food preparation island.

"It's clean here," he called, as he swept around the stand and returned to the dining room.

He took the lead, and they climbed the blood-stained stairs. There was a short landing at the top with three doors, each smeared with blood.

"Bedroom open."

The first room was for the kid, with a cot against one wall and a small bed on the far side. A holographic mobile danced about the ceiling displaying cute dancing animals, and a soft lullaby was playing; the room was clean. The next room had a large circular bed that was rotating slowly at its centre, but that too was clean. The final room was a luxurious bathroom, complete with a deep tub, a walk-in shower cubical, bidet and sink. This room wasn't clean.

The half-devoured body lay on the floor with the belly and chest ripped wide open, and all the vital organs were missing. "Ravenous little bastard." Scallion relaxed and lowered his handgun. "An open cot. Idiots. They should have had the runt caged, and the door locked when it slept."

"First-time parents. Probably couldn't believe their child would get blood-sick."

"Well, Poppy's life's about to change. No more fucking luxury domicile for him."

"We'd better go see if he's okay."

They woke him in the kitchen, one of the clean rooms and where they had found the medi-kit. Sky had treated his wounds, and he hadn't flinched during the process, so far had he retreated into his mind. It had taken some effort to rouse him. Having not wanted to waste a smiler on him, Scallion had slapped his face red-raw before Poppy's eyes opened.

Conscious now, he was sitting in a corner, head down,

not making a sound.

Scallion had ordered a meal from the preparation stand where he was sitting, and the serving area in front of him showed a countdown for the two minutes it took to prepare. The unit pinged. The meal was ready, the cover slid back, and a plate rose to the surface with roast bovine, vegetables, tuber-fries, and gravy. His stomach grumbled at the sight of the food. He couldn't remember the last time he hadn't eaten from a tin, a ration pack or another package of long-life processed food.

"A real fucking meal. Fuck, you had it good, Poppy."

"Do we have time for this?"

"Relax, Sky. He needs to get his sense back, and I'm hungry. I couldn't find any alcohol and this unit won't produce any, so I'm eating. When I've finished the meal, he'll give me the credits one way or another and then we can leave."

Sky went over and sat on the floor in the corner with Poppy.

"I can't imagine how you're feeling. I lost my partner, but I still had my kids. You've lost both."

There was no indication that Poppy was listening.

"Look, I'm guessing you served the seed that fertilised the egg and your husband carried the baby for the full term. If that's how it was, then you'll be classed as a carrier. The only way you'll be able to resume your life here is if you had nothing physically to do with the kid's creation, but I doubt that. They'll not only sterilise you, but they'll drop your classification, and you won't be head of anything ever again. You'll have to go live in the town with the rest of the farm workers and the rest of us lower classifications."

There was no movement or sound from the curled-up

man pressed into the corner of the walls.

"Look, if you're listening, Scallion will want the credits you promised him. He won't ask nicely. Your best chance is to come with us."

"Recruiting for your cause again," called Scallion with a mouthful of meat. "He won't come with us. He won't last two minutes away from this life."

"You probably don't care if you live or die at the moment, but my kids are still out there, and the longer it takes to catch up with them, the less likely that I'll find them. Please, I need your help."

Poppy stayed frozen in place. The soft sound of his breathing was the only indication that he was still living.

"It wasn't your fault. There are no signs before they turn blood-sick. It just happens. There was nothing you could do."

"I wanted to cage Sunshine, but Carlu said no. He could always get his way with me. That's why we argued and I left. It sucks that I was right and he was wrong and I can't tell him to his face."

"Come with us unless you want to be sterilised or, worse, thrown into a grubby town domicile. That's assuming they don't just stick you in a pod on the outskirts."

"He's right. I won't last two minutes on the run."

"You're smart. You have to be to become head of anything. Smarter than either of us. He's the thug, I'm the diplomat, and you can be the brains."

"Who are you calling a thug. I'm more than just muscle, lady… diplomat indeed."

"I don't know where to start looking. The lofts, the Device. I've no idea what we're going to do next."

"The people that took your kids. How were they dressed?"

"Smart. Uniforms."

"Not grounder uniforms?"

"None like I've ever seen before."

"Probably elite from the lofts. Did you notice any insignia on their left breast area?" Poppy tapped the area on his chest to indicate where he meant, and he lifted his head now as he spoke directly to Sky.

"Yes. Now that you say it, yes. They all had a bird or something with wings. Gold-coloured," replied Sky.

"An eagle. They belong to the governor of bovine, Governor Frisk. He doesn't reside here in Station Six. Only his envoy will be here, and a small number of his elite. He's from Station Eight. If he took your kids, they would be on their way to Station Eight. Assuming no one has hijacked them along the way. Connected are valuable, and other governors might look to acquire them for themselves."

"How the fuck do you know that?" interjected Scallion.

"Do you know anything about who lives in the lofts, Karl?"

"Rich fucks."

"You have no idea, do you. There's a hierarchy, a structure. The groff I grow here doesn't belong to Governor Jerim up in the lofts here. He's governor of poultry. There are only so many stations, and the governors have to share the resources. The governors report to head office. That's how they refer to their seniors. It's all a class system. You're at the bottom, Karl."

"Fuck you, Poppy."

"See, you're smart. We need you. I need you. Please?" said Sky.

"I might not last two minutes on the run, but I'll last a lot less if they put me in a tower pod. I might want to die just now, but I've not got the strength to do anything about that. I think I need you now, just as much as you might want me."

"About fucking time. So where are the credits," said Scallion.

"I'll get changed, get the credits and I'll be back in a few minutes."

"I'd stay out of the bathroom if I were you," called out Scallion as the door started to close behind him.

"One of us should maybe go with him."

"Good idea. I'm finishing my food, so not me."

"We'll wait then."

Ten minutes passed, and Scallion was visibly nervous that Poppy might have done a runner, or called the authorities, but he was trying not to show it. Sky could read him though and knew that he was worried, and he knew that she knew. *Too fucking clever, she is. She's going to be a real pain in the arse.*

The kitchen door slid open and Poppy returned. He wore an expensive pink jacket with matching trousers, shoes, and a colour-coordinated top.

"Fuck me. Not exactly inconspicuous are you."

"I'll wear what I like. This is my favourite suit, and I'm not changing."

"Fuck, all right. Where are the credits?"

Poppy slid two transfer cards across the top of the surface of the food-prep island to Scallion.

"How much?"

"Enough."

Scallion put his thumb on each of the cards to see the

totals they held, but nothing happened. "They're empty!"

"No, just locked." As he passed the preparation station, he picked them both up again. Reaching Sky, he handed her one of the cards after he had unlocked it with his print. He indicated that she should imprint her thumb on the card, and she did.

"Now one card is locked to me and the other to Sky."

"Fuck it. I'll just cut your thumbs off."

"They are biometric and not the simple cards you're used to. Our thumbs will need to stay attached; we'll need to stay alive and our vitals remain normal, as any stress, such as if you tried to force us to use them, and they won't work. If we die, they won't work. Now, if you want credits, you work for us."

"What the—?"

"Looks like you're on Team Sky and Poppy now and coming to find my kids."

"No way. I'll find another way out of this station."

"Go ahead."

Scallion paused, unsure what to say or do. "How much is on your card?"

"Wow! Enough," Sky said after looking.

"We were savers. Wanted to ensure Sunshine had a good place in society. I've emptied our accounts though. Everything is on these two cards. A withdrawal like that will get someone's attention, so we'd better get moving."

"Where are we going then, brains and diplomat?"

"I know someone who will help us," replied Poppy. "You need to get us back into town, and I'll get us somewhere safe."

"Fuck it." Scallion pushed his empty plate away. "So where's your bags?"

"I'm not taking anything. I don't want any memories to haunt me. I'm barely holding it together now." His last words quivered as he spoke and a single tear rolled down his left cheek.

"Great, a pink softy, and a pain in the arse bitch in charge. What the fuck could go wrong."

The three of them returned to the living space, heading for the lift, ignoring the mess and the blood that coated everywhere, especially the area splattered with the baby. They were halfway across the room when the lift door slid open.

They froze.

A humanoid OD exited the lift. It looked like a humanoid botdrone, but the seamless shell, entirely matt-grey, and fluid movement declared that it wasn't. The right thigh opened, and a heavy blaster pistol slid out and was taken by the OD.

"Stay where you are," a strong, confident male voice said.

Scallion dropped his bag, pulled his weapon, and fired. The bullets hit the ore-drone, two in the chest and one in the head, but they were deflected and ricocheted off its armour plate.

Two blaster bolts scorched the OD's shell, but other than leaving dark splayed ring patterns, they had no detrimental effect.

The OD pointed its blaster to the window and blew it out. Tainted air rushed in, and the three humans felt their throats become dry and coarse almost immediately. The ore-drone was unaffected.

A dozen strategically located facemasks, mouth-covering only, dropped on tethers from the ceiling. The humans each grabbed their nearest masks and dived for protection behind furniture. Both Scallion and Sky fired rapidly at the OD to provide them cover as they hid. The ore-drone remained stationary, blocking the path to the lift, allowing the bullets and bolts to bounce off its shell.

"Scallion. Where is the package, and you will be allowed to live," said the OD.

Three blast shots ripped through the furniture extremely close to each of them. The OD was demonstrating that their barriers were ineffective.

"My sensors have the tracker located in this room, but I need to know that you still have the curio too," continued the OD.

Another blaster shot, and Poppy screamed. A thud followed as he fell to the floor. One of Poppy's pink legs was sticking out from behind the overturned chair, and Sky could see one of his arms lying motionless.

"I will kill the woman too. Unless you reveal yourself and the curio."

The dining room door slid open, and Sky watched Scallion flee, leaving her behind.

She waited for the blaster shot. She had no value to the OD, so she was expendable, but the shot never came. She heard gunshots from the dining room. *What the hell is he shooting at in there?*

There was a loud crash in the living area as something substantial fell to the floor. Silence. Then more shots from the dining area.

Sky very cautiously stood up and looked around. The OD was face down on the floor, motionless, and sitting on its back, licking its front paws, was the cat.

"Now that I wasn't expecting."

Sky crossed the room, picking up her slouch bag from where she'd dropped it, and continued to the dining room. The door slid open. Scallion aimed his gun at her but didn't pull the trigger. She surveyed the room. The glass in the two window walls was damaged where he had been firing bullets at them in an attempt to shatter them. His escape plan hadn't worked.

The confusion and questions on Scallion's face were a picture, and she took great pleasure in not answering his unasked queries.

"I've taken care of the OD. Now we need to get out of here quickly, but you need to lose that package, whatever it is. I'll see if Poppy is still alive."

Scallion put his holdall on the dining table and pulled out the package. It was wrapped and sealed tight, but he had a pocketknife in the bag and started stripping away the layers of wrapping. Uncovering a tin box, not locked, and he flipped the lid. Inside, the tracking disc was obvious, but he had no idea what the curio was. Picking it up he examined it. A shiny cylinder, not metal but something remarkably similar, capped at both ends and full of different-sized holes. Inside the outer cylinder were other cylinders also covered in holes. It was more substantial than it looked, eight pounds he guessed, twelve inches tall and six inches in diameter. He put the cylinder back in his holdall, deciding to work out wat it was later. It was a curio, and he had handled one before so had no fear of the superstitions surrounding them. If he could find a buyer for it, he wouldn't need Sky or Poppy anymore.

"A little help." Sky was half carrying, half dragging Poppy

into the room. "Get him on the table and I'll fix him up."

The blaster bolt had narrowly missed his head, scorching across the top of his right shoulder and the right side of his face. He was conscious but partially stunned as they stretched him out on the glass table.

"You smell like cooked chicken again," said Scallion as he let go.

Sky took the medi-kit from her bag. She had acquired the one they had used earlier in the kitchen, thinking that it might be something useful to have.

She got to work with the laserseal-pen. "Give him a couple of healing cartridges," she ordered Scallion, who picked up the delivery-needle without question.

While Sky worked on the wounds, the air purified around them and they were able to remove their masks. The automatic systems had kicked in, filling the breached window with a bonding foam as the extractor fans purged the taint.

"Finished."

"How does it look?" asked Poppy, now recovered from the shock and the ringing in his ear.

"The shoulder's good. The face too…" Sky hesitated.

"What?"

"You've lost half your ear. The bottom half. The lobe and a bit more. Looks good I think," said Scallion, grinning. "You don't look such a softy now."

"No, no."

Poppy pushed himself off the table and raced to the screen in the living space. "Mirror," he shouted. "No, no. Fuck, I liked this suit."

chapter two

No Escape

"Okay, so we're back in town. Where next?"
Scallion didn't like it that he now answered to
both Poppy and Sky. He had thought about
cutting them both loose and going it alone on the whole
journey back to the service shed, but they held the credits.
He also had no idea what he was going to do next, and
both of them seemed to have a plan. These two were
usually the types of people that he would have robbed,
beaten up and generally intimidated. They considered him
a lowlife and a petty criminal, which he was, but he didn't
need them reminding him of the fact. Poppy had acquired
the OD's heavy blaster pistol, and that should have been
his. The softy had claimed it and now carried it in a pale
blue purse slung over his shoulder. The little drich had
changed from his pink suit to a blue one before they had
left, and that matched the purse.

"Valerie's," said Poppy.

"No way. The brothel? She'll turn me in without a
second thought. Probably not even a first."

"Valerie's," repeated Poppy.

Scallion sighed, *the brothel then*. He just hoped this plan, whatever it was, would work. If not, he would dump them both and go it alone.

"Keep the curio out of sight," added Sky.

He wasn't stupid. He knew that having it with them made both Sky and Poppy nervous. Not because they had any superstitions, as many did about such devices, but because it was valuable enough for someone to send an OD to retrieve it.

They left the service shed and entered the dark alley as nightfall began; the lighting was slowly dimming as the stars were coming out. Poppy took the lead now, and Scallion found himself wondering once again how things had changed so quickly.

"Not that way," said Scallion abruptly, spotting some people up ahead, and he turned sharply into the alley on his right.

His companions stopped on the route, hesitant about following him.

"Get off the route now." Scallion's request sounded urgent, so they complied.

"What are you doing?" asked Sky.

"That's Demic ahead. The loud one with the others. She's a bounty hunter, a killer for hire and generally not a nice person."

"You think she's looking for you?" asked Poppy.

"I don't want to find out."

"Okay. We'll cut past them through the alleys." Poppy again took the lead.

Once they had passed the threat, they came back to the route and continued walking.

"Where are you going? The brothel's that way." Scallion pointed to their left.

"I know," replied Poppy, without answering Scallion's question, as he headed in the other direction.

"Door open," commanded Poppy as they reached what was his destination.

The ground-level domicile wasn't near the brothel. It was a couple of routes behind it.

"Why are we here? Who lives here?" Scallion's questions were once again ignored. He didn't like it that neither of his companions was telling him anything about what was going on.

"Who does live here?" asked Sky.

"No one lives here, but it's registered to someone, so it's not a vacant block," answered Poppy.

The living space was sparsely furnished. The layout matched that of Sky's domicile, but the dust covering everything indicated that no one had been there for some considerable time.

In the kitchen, Poppy knelt and put his face to the floor. They heard him mutter something, but they couldn't catch the words. A hidden hatch slid open, and there was a dark hole in the floor of the room.

"What the fuck. Who are you, Poppy? This shit isn't something a dumb farmer knows."

Again his question was ignored.

"It's dark down there. There's no lighting. But the passage is clear, and we just need to follow the walls to the other end," said Poppy.

They climbed down the ladder together, one after the other, and before they reached the bottom the hatch above them shut, enveloping them in complete darkness.

"Put your hand on the wall and keep walking until we reach the other end," instructed Poppy

Scallion had been last off the ladder. He held his hand up, and soft light emanating from the small utility device revealed a little about where they were. All the surfaces were smooth. There was a little spare headroom, and if he reached out with both arms, he could stretch across the entire width of the passage. Behind them was a wall, and so there was only one direction to go.

"There are no secret tunnels in town. It's impossible. The network of maintenance conduits and the station's foundations make digging impossible," said Scallion.

"Yet, we are here," answered Sky.

Keeping the soft light on for the entire walk revealed nothing new until they finally reached a ladder at the other end of the passage.

"Where are we?" said Scallion.

This time he got an answer. "Valerie's," said Poppy.

At the top of the ladder, a hatch opened, and they climbed out.

"Light," commanded Poppy, as the hole in the floor shut and their small cell became illuminated. The confined box where they now stood had no visible exits and no control panels. The light source was all about them, but with no visible lighting cells to provide it.

"Where are we now?"

Once again, he was ignored.

"We can't get out now from inside. So we need to wait for someone to let us out," said Poppy.

"So we're trapped."

Again he was ignored.

The three of them managed to sit down, but in such

a small space, their legs often became intertwined, and Scallion was getting short-tempered and cramped. The other two hadn't answered any of his questions. How long would they have to wait? Who were they meeting? Why were they here? And many other similar queries had fallen on deaf ears. He rummaged in his bag, and his hand came out holding a strip of green screamers.

"You're not taking that in here," stated Sky, grabbing the drugs.

Scallion managed to keep them from her.

"What are they?" asked Poppy.

"Screamers," replied Sky. "They're hallucinogenic. Some people call them Nightmares, as not everyone has a good trip with them."

"I don't get nightmares, and I could do with a distraction," said Scallion.

"Give me them." A scuffle began in the small space as Sky attempted to wrestle the drugs from Scallion, and Poppy tried to keep out of the way.

Suddenly the door opened.

Everyone froze in the new intrusion of fresh light, and they each looked up from their entanglement.

Valerie stood outside, framed in the doorway. She ran the brothel, and every other flesh-peddling woman, man and child in the station worked for her. She took no shit from anyone. Her small army of protectors ensured that her house was always under her authority. For such a powerful woman she was small, just under five foot tall. A drich with a very slim figure and small breasts. The tight slinky, shiny dresses that she wore exaggerated her flat outline. If her face hadn't been so very feminine, set against flowing blonde hair, she might have passed for a young boy. For although she must have been in her fifties, no one knew her real age, and she looked no older than twenty. Natural looks or cosmetic enhancement? Again no one knew.

"Get straight to it, or you'll stay in there until you die."

She was unarmed, with no visible weapons showing, and alone. Her outstretched arm was held over a control mechanism.

"Carlu and Sunshine are dead. Blood-sickness," stated Poppy. His statement was enough, and Valerie moved aside to let them clamber and crawl out into the room beyond.

They were in a storeroom, with all types of liquor bottles and canisters stacked in a multitude of shelf baskets and racks.

"Who's she, and why are you with a scumbag like Scallion?" Valerie asked Poppy.

"Who's Scallion?"

Valerie indicated.

"That's Karl."

"No, that's Scallion."

"We're on the run. She, Sky, is trying to find her kids. At least one of them is a connected, and Governor Frisk has taken them. He's got a bounty on his head… Karl, or whatever his name is. I did wonder why that OD said Scallion. We need to get out of this station."

"I've not heard of any bounty on him, and I'd know. A connected kid? Not heard anything about that either. The last one of them found here, in this station, was a few years back, and it's longer still since the one before that. Don't put your hand in that bag."

Scallion froze. The tone of Valerie's last words wasn't a polite request. A blaster had appeared in her hand, and it was pointed straight at him. Where she had hidden the weapon in such a tight blue dress was a mystery, but he was in no doubt that she would kill him if he so much as twitched.

"I was just putting these away," he pleaded meekly.

"Just drop them. I won't have that kind of shitty drug in my house."

Scallion let them fall to the floor as he stood up. Poppy and Sky were already standing.

"You two put your bags on the floor and move away from them." As she spoke, she stepped back and moved Poppy behind her, waving her blaster between Sky and Scallion until they complied.

"Now, from the top. Tell me your stories, or you won't leave this room. What—?"

"It's an OD. A cat," explained Poppy, as the black animal appeared over the rim of the slouch bag.

"Dangerous?"

"No, I don't think so." Poppy moved forward and picked the animal up, cradling it in his arms before he once again went behind Valerie.

"You first." She trained the blaster on Scallion.

"I was in the dock. I was going to steal a valuable commodity that was being stowed away in a container. I was early. I meant to turn up after it had been stashed and simply walk away with it. Then these security guards turned up to hide a package in the container. Finding me surprised them. I took advantage and shot two of them immediately. Then I fought with the other two. I recognised one of them as being on Ninety-Six's payroll,

47

so I couldn't leave any of them alive. Then more guards showed up, and I ran. I figured because I'd fucked up one of Ninety-Six's smuggling operations that he'd have a bounty on me, and once the bodies were found the authorities would be after me too. So I ran."

"How did you end up with Poppy?"

"He kidnapped me," said Poppy, interrupting. "And he has a curio with him. Must be important too, as someone sent an OD to collect it."

"Where's the OD?" Valerie glanced over her shoulder to the storeroom door, as if expecting it to suddenly show up.

"The cat incapacitated it," Sky said.

"What?" Valerie moved further back, now almost at the doorway, to bring the small black animal into her vision.

"My daughter made it. It's just been a cat so far, but somehow it took out a biped OD."

"Why did you kidnap Poppy?" said Valerie, her attention returning to Scallion.

"He saw me in the route carrying her. She was covered in blood, and I couldn't leave him to alert anyone where I was."

"Why was she covered in blood?"

"They took my kids, Sara and Jeb, teenagers. I tried to stop them and failed. They left me for dead, and he saved me."

"He doesn't save anybody. So why?"

"I needed to get off the routes, and her place seemed a good place to hide."

"Show me this curio. Carefully."

Scallion took it from his bag.

"Any idea what it does?"

"Not got a fucking clue."

"Right, put it away. So, how's Poppy caught up in all this."

"He wanted my credits, so we went home to get them," said Poppy. "When we got there, it was already too late for Carlu. Sunshine attacked us. He was blood-sick, but he shot him. If I'd gone home alone, I doubt I'd be here now."

"Wow, you've changed, Scallion. You're saving lives now instead of taking them. This something new you're trying? Stay here. Don't come out and stay quiet. I'll send someone for you shortly. And Scallion, take any of your shitty drugs or touch any of my merchandise" – she waved the blaster at the liquor – "and you won't see another day. If they do anything stupid, Poppy, shoot them," continued Valerie, and she made to hand over her blaster.

"I've got my own." He took the heavy blaster pistol from his purse.

"You do keep surprising me." Valerie smiled as she left.

"You going to shoot us?" said Scallion.

"You maybe. Sky no," Poppy replied as he handed her the cat.

"How the fuck are you in so tight with Valerie? She doesn't like anyone. Everything is just business with her," said Scallion.

Poppy ignored the question.

"Are you both always just going to fucking ignore me?"

"Yes," came the synchronised reply.

Several minutes later the door opened and in stepped Tianee, Valerie's second. Not a working girl, not muscle either. She was a curvy redhead in her late thirties, pretty, and she managed the floors and bar in the brothel. Scallion had once seen her cut a man's throat at the bar without flinching, and without fear of repercussion.

"Put these on," she said, and she threw each of them a bundle. "I'll take your bags and weapons too, and the cat."

Poppy and Sky received client's robes, long hooded gowns that hid a person's identity if that was preferred, or what they were wearing, or not wearing, as they moved through the brothel.

Scallion held a red leather studded thong and a matching full-face mask. "I'm not wearing these!"

"Strip. Put them on. It's not a request."

The others gave him no privacy as they all watched him strip naked. He struggled to get the thong comfortably up the crack of his arse and around his balls but managed, and then finally he put on the facemask. There were two peepholes for him to see through and a large circular opening at the mouth.

"Not too shabby," said Poppy, grinning. "For an older man, you're in good shape. "Maybe a little more length is needed, though."

"Fuck off," came the muffled response.

"Poppy, take them to Valerie's office," ordered Tianee.

The brothel comprised four levels of block modules, all stacked and laid out together to make one large complex. The ground floor had no interior doors in the public area, and the four massive industrial blocks created a square formation that allowed anyone to walk freely around the inner walls where the blocks met. Each of the four spaces had a different theme. The entrance area was the bar, with a long counter serving a large variety of drinks; drugs were also available, but only the type Valerie would permit on her premises. Another area was always in shadow, with soft red light cast over private booths, where lap dancing and the odd blowjob took place. The other two, each decorated differently with erotic art or paraphernalia, were a mix of low booths and different-sized tables where anyone could mingle. It was late at night, and the place was busy. No one paid them any particular attention as the three of them came out from behind the bar and moved on towards the stairs. The hired muscle at the foot of the stairs let them pass without question.

The next two floors were domicile-sized blocks for private room hire. The top floor had restricted access to Valerie's apartment, office and her other private areas. More muscle, two men and two women, all visibly armed, guarded that entrance, but they let the three pass without question.

The office was luxurious and fully carpeted. Carpets were a rare commodity in the town. The antique wooden furniture was comfortable, elaborate, and framed with beautiful upholstery.

Valerie sat on the edge of a dark wooden desk by the far wall. She indicated a sofa in front of her. "Take a seat."

"Did I say you could take that off," she said, chastising Scallion as he began to remove his mask. He stopped what he was doing, not sure if she meant that or not, but taking the safe option.

"Take it off and cover-up." She tossed him a client's gown.

"What'd you put me in this outfit for?" he asked sheepishly.

"You forget, I know you, Scallion. The only way to make sure you're not armed or carrying any contraband is to have you butt-naked. Plus it amused me, and I don't have reason to be amused very often."

He muttered something under his breath, glad to be ignored this time.

The door opened behind them, and Ninety-Six entered. Scallion went pale quickly. Sweat suddenly ran down his spine, and there was no hiding the fear he showed.

Ninety-Six was so named because that was how many people he had needed to kill personally, and with his bare hands, to climb to the highest rank in the station's criminal fraternity. Nothing illegal had happened over the last twenty years in Station Six without his express authority. He was a brute of a man. Seven-foot tall, exceptionally wide at the shoulder, and always wearing a tight vest and shorts to show off his extreme muscular definition. He was scarred across his bald head and over his right cheek. Both of the scars could easily be removed, but he wore them proudly.

Valerie made the introductions. "You know Poppy and Scallion, and this is Sky. Sky, this is Ninety-Six, and in case you don't know who that is, he's basically in charge of all crime in the station."

"Scallion…" Ninety-Six said the name so sinisterly that Scallion felt himself squirm. The big man perched on the opposite corner of the desk to Valerie. "I'm told you think you've upset me. Is that true?"

"No. I don't know. I didn't mean to if I have."

"So you were trying to steal from me? You think that was going to work?"

Scallion didn't reply.

"Well? I asked a question."

"I didn't know it was yours. It was supposed to be a simple pickup. They hid it, and I took it. Easy job. In and out without any trouble."

"They weren't smuggling anything for me, and I have no idea why they were there or who was trying to get that curio out of the station and to Eden. And I have no idea where it came from. Someone cleaned up your mess before the authorities got involved, and that wasn't me either. That's a lot I don't know, and I'm not happy about that. Can you remember anything else about the security guards that you killed or those you ran away from?"

"Like what?" Scallion looked directly at Ninety-Six for the first time.

"Think, stupid. Anything at all?"

"They were just regular dumb guards."

Sky shot him a scathing look. *Shit.* He remembered that her partner had been a flight dock security guard killed in service. *Fuck. Is there any chance I've killed her partner?* The recent ones weren't the first he had needed to take care of.

"So you have nothing that helps me! However, it does seem that your stupidity resulted in you saving Poppy. All be that unintentional."

Scallion glanced over at the softy, dressed in his pale blue suit under a client's gown. *Who the fuck is this guy? Why are both Ninety-Six and Valerie so concerned about his welfare when they supposedly hate each other?*

"Grig," said Scallion sharply as he suddenly remembered that detail.

"What?"

"I heard one of them say the name Grig. Grig

wouldn't be happy about this, one of them said. I was on top of some containers, hiding when they went past me."

Ninety-Six looked to Valerie, who shook her head.

"Are you sure they said Grig?" said Ninety-Six.

"Yeah. It stuck now that I remember it because I wondered who the fuck Grig was."

"Grig's a pretty common name, Scallion. How did you find out about the package?"

"I overheard Torgon discussing it in a bar."

Valerie slid off the edge of the desk and indicated that Ninety-Six should follow her. They left the office together. It was a bizarre sight: the giant of a man being escorted out by the comparably diminutive woman. Two beefy guards stepped inside to watch over the three of them in their absence. Ten minutes later, Valerie and Ninety-Six returned, and the guards went back outside the door.

"Okay, you can both go. We will look after Poppy from now."

Poppy made to object, but a stern glance from Valerie silenced him.

Tianee entered the office carrying Scallion's and Sky's bags, which she dropped in front of them.

"Everything's there. Now go. Get out of here. Tianee, show them both off the premises," ordered Valerie.

That was the end of any discussion. Scallion removed the thong and got dressed as they moved through the floors; his clothes were in his holdall. Then they were outside in the darkness of night.

He could feel her penetrating judgemental gaze boring through him, even though he was avoiding looking at her.

"How many security guards have you killed over the years then?"

There it was, the question that he knew had to come eventually.

"I only killed corrupt ones."

"How can you be so sure?"

"Look, can we get off the routes. I've still got the curio, and someone wants this badly."

"They let you keep it?"

"You've still got your cat. Your OD. I can hear it purring."

"Why'd they let us go?"

"We aren't a problem. Someone else is. This Grig guy, he's their problem. I wouldn't want to be in his boots when they catch him. Look, your domicile is probably still a safe place. Let's go there and work out what we do next."

"I'm not going anywhere with you."

"Don't you still need to find your kids?"

"Yes. Of course."

"I'll help."

chapter three

Leaving

"That OD knew your name," said Sky.

They were both sitting in her kitchen, drinking a mid-morning hot drink. She had let Scallion sleep on her sofa in the living space, while she slept in her bed.

"It didn't know yours, and your cat took it out of service."

"But we don't know if it was killed or just stunned. It might still be looking for you."

"It was looking for the curio, not me. I left the tracking disc back at Poppy's. Whoever wants the curio has no idea we're here. That gives us time to come up with a plan to get to Station Eight."

"How do we know that's where they are?"

"We don't, but do you have any other options?"

"The Device," suggested Sky.

"If Governor Frisk took the kids because they're connected, then he will want to see evidence before he sends them to the Device. It's going to be easier to get inside the lofts at Station Eight than even getting close to the Device."

"But you said getting into the lofts was suicide."

"We have no other option, do we? First, we find a way to get to the station, and work the rest out from there."

"We need Poppy," said Sky.

"That's not going to happen. Whatever deal he has with Valerie and Ninety-Six, he's with them now. They need to make him disappear. New identity unless they hand him over to be sterilised."

"Okay, what do you suggest?"

"The train."

"Have you ever seen the train?" asked Sky.

"No, but they run to and from all the stations."

"But it runs overland in the tainted air, and the loading yards are outside too, manned only by botdrones. I know the ore containers are transported to the yards by botdrones because they're outside, and then there's the beasts out in the Scorched Land and the mutants."

"The train's all I've got. The lofts have shuttles, but I can't fly a shuttle, can you? And I don't think even if we could fly one they'd let us land at another station. They'd shoot us out of the air," said Scallion.

"What do we do when we get to Station Eight? How do we survive? Do you think all the stations are the same?"

"Probably, but I don't know."

"There's a train schedule at the mine. I need to go back to work to get a look at it," said Sky.

"Will that be easy?"

"No. But I've got used to sneaking around where I'm not supposed to be. That's how I got the parts and ore for the cat."

"I can't help, can I?" said Scallion.

"No. You'll just have to stay here and stay inside. If you go out and someone sees you, that might lead whoever is after you to us. I'll confirm when my next shift is on the screen and then get ready."

Sky turned up for her next shift dressed in her coverall work uniform and carrying her facemask. The access point to the mine was on the eastern side of the station. She walked past the tower pods to reach the security point, and there she joined one of the ten queues of people passing through.

Reaching the front of her line, she stepped into the cylindrical booth embedded in the wall, and the door closed behind her.

"Name and role," was requested over the internal speakers.

"Sky. Sorting clerk."

The booth scanned her biometrics and checked for any illicit items. As her security clearance was processed, she put on her full-face mask. Mine masks were marginally larger than regular devices as they carried a bigger filter because it wasn't only tainted air they needed to keep out. Clearing security, the exit door slid back, and she stepped out into the ore mine.

There were no filtration systems in this part of the station hangar. The unrelenting rock dust that swirled around in thick clouds was too much to cope with. Hence every person here wore masks at all times. The sky above was always daylight; there was no day and night cycle here as every hour was a working one. No holographic clouds either, but the billowing dust had the same effect, casting moving shadows across the surfaces below. A small dust devil blew across Sky as she stepped out of the booth, obscuring her vision, and she waited for it to pass before moving forward.

A humanoid security botdrone holding a blast rifle was several yards ahead observing everyone that came into the mine area. It was one of ten lined up alongside a couple of human security guards in front of the checkpoint. Similar botdrones patrolled everywhere in the ore mine.

She walked past it towards the industrial blocks, three tiers high, forming three rings radiating out from the central lift housing. Her place of work was in the outer ring. There, she sorted through rock fragments for ore that the processing plants on the inner block ring had missed, either because they were too small or still encased in dense rock. No humans worked in the actual mine, that was the sole domain of mining botdrones – worm-like devices with drilling heads and matching tails and storage canisters along their length suited to burrowing through the rock several miles below searching for ore deposits. They only returned to the surface to offload their cargo, and then they dived again with another set of empty canisters. There were no structured tunnels down there, and only the one large lift shaft that descended into the darkness; how deep the lift went she had no idea. It carried the botdrones up and down continually. She could see the worms beyond the blocks, three feet in diameter and ten feet long, moving between the lift house and the processing plants.

"Keep moving." A passing security botdrone challenged her when she stopped to look towards the lift shaft. It was a regular occurrence, but keep moving and they could be ignored, unlike the human guards, who were more inquisitive. However, the human security presence was minimal, but she would have to avoid them more than the botdrones. She, like everyone else, had heard the story of the man that had refused to move on. He had sat on the ground instead. The story went that the botdrone had shot him with a laser rifle, killing him on the spot. No one she knew of had ever made the same challenge or looked to disprove the tale.

The inner ring was automated and serviced by botdrone engineering units. There were a few trained humans there too, but they were minimal, and she had no idea what they did. The outer ring was predominantly human, and where the vast majority of people worked. They spent their four-hour shift standing in front of a conveyor sorting rock and dropping any ore they found into a canister by their side. When the canister was full, it drove off, and another took its place. The middle ring was the control section, along with the maintenance and repair sections. Again this was mostly automated, but humans there monitored service screens and mine drone output readings, adjusting or recalling underperforming or damaged worms. On her first day, many years ago, she had been given a very brief tour of the whole mining process from start to finish, but after that, she had never ventured beyond the outer circle until an opportunity accidentally presented itself and she started acquiring parts for her daughter's project by visiting the middle ring. There, in one of the control room modules, she would find the trains' schedules.

Sky didn't go to a workstation. Each work slot was a random allocation, to fill gaps in the lines, and so initially she wouldn't be missed. Instead, she went to a cleaning point. Inside the point were a filter bank, a uniform vendor and the toilets. A botdrone stood outside the doorway, but only humans ventured inside.

Others were there using the services, and so she joined a queue. Reaching the first stage, she removed the filter cartridge from her mask and inserted it into the slot on the wall. An adjacent slot issued her a replacement. The old one would be scrubbed and recycled back into circulation. The next stage was the uniform vendor. She stood before a blank screen and it scanned her face before dropping a clean uniform in the shoot for her to take. From there, she moved on to the changing cubicles. They were allowed enough dignity that they changed behind a closed door, both for personal protection and security; only one person was able to enter any cubicle at a time.

Inside, she stripped off her sorting uniform, and beneath that was a controller's coverall. That came off too, and she reversed the uniforms with the clean sorting clerk's coverall beneath the controller's. She deposited the dirty uniform for cleaning and recycling back into use and then left the cubicle. Toilet stalls were available just before the exit, but most people avoided them. Unlike the changing cubicles, more than one person could enter these, and behind those doors, many things happened that did not include urination or defecation.

It was a little over two years ago that the uniform vendor had dropped the wrong uniform to her, and so it was looking a little grubby now, but no one had yet noticed that. Suitably disguised, she crossed over to the middle circle of modules. On the ground level were the repair areas, and this was where she had picked up the parts to make the cat. The next tier housed the control rooms.

What was above that she didn't know.

The working environment here wasn't a very social place. The random allocation of workstations, and the botdrones discouraging any loitering, meant that seeing new faces was a common occurrence for everyone. So as Sky wandered through a series of control stations with people lined up and sitting before an arrangement of holographic screens, she was unchallenged. Seeing what she needed over the shoulder of one of the controllers, she stopped. He was sorting a shipment manifest of containers and allocating them by dragging the holo-shapes to zones on the train. She knew from experience that the last stage of his work displayed the train's departure time, which he needed to accept before moving on to the next manifest.

"Keep moving." She hadn't noticed the botdrone walking up behind her. She needed a few more seconds.

"Keep moving." Sky had never waited to hear a second warning, and she had no idea how long the botdrone would give her before enforcing the command.

"Final warning." The soft click of the trigger easing, and that was the safety released.

She glanced nervously between the botdrone and the holograph data. It hadn't yet raised the rifle towards her, but that would only take it a fraction of a second when her time ran out.

The weapon came up and she moved on, turning her back on the botdrone, wondering if she'd left it too late.

Scallion was bored already, and Sky had only left an hour ago. She had taken all his drugs and flushed them down the toilet. A condition if he was to stay there. She still had possession of Poppy's credit transfer card, and she had used that to enforce her demand. There was no alcohol in the domicile either, and he had searched everywhere just in case there was a stash.

"Fuck it." He picked up his gun and grabbed the few credit chips that he had and went outside. He knew he would be able to return, as Sky had given him voice access, a trade-off alongside his surrender of the drugs.

It was late afternoon, and there was a store not too far away. Finding drugs on the routes was too risky, as most of the dealers knew him, but alcohol from a nearby store was feasible, he calculated.

"Scallion. A new look. I almost didn't recognise you with blond hair. You trying to hide or something?"

He had taken the winding path through the alleys, bought two bottles of very cheap whiskey and was on his way back. He turned, and behind him were Fichal and three of his goons. He didn't owe the loan shark any credits, but he had punched him in the face recently at a bar when he'd been high and drunk. Fichal wasn't the type of person to forget that.

"I think we have some unfinished business, don't you?"

Scallion thought about reaching for his gun, but he had a bottle of whiskey in each hand and would need to drop one. Then there was the fact that two blasters were already pointing at him.

The goons spread out behind Fichal, two of them aiming the blasters and the third producing a long blade.

"Oh, don't worry about them. This is personal."

The loan shark was younger, bigger and stronger than Scallion. One on one, Scallion still thought he could take him, but if he fought back now, he didn't doubt that the goons would more than even the odds. He could run, but where? He couldn't lead them back to Sky's, and where else could he go? Should he take the beating? That would leave him in a bad way, probably unconscious and wounded in an alley. Maybe even dead.

"Hi, Fichal. I'm going to a party, want to join me?" He held up the two bottles in an attempt to support his lie.

"No, I'm good. Think I'm going to get my kicks here." And he laughed, knowing that Scallion's options were limited.

Scallion took the first punch without blocking. He stepped away from it to reduce the impact, but it still hurt and dazed him a little.

"That's the one I owe you."

Scallion thought for a moment that that might be it, and everything was over.

"However, as you know, I charge a high rate of interest."

It was not over.

The next two punches missed as Scallion ducked and weaved. He knew how to fight, but he couldn't avoid Fichal every time.

"I'd stay still if I were you. Trigo…" One of the goons fired his blaster, and the charge struck inches away from Scallion's left foot.

The next three punches hurt, every one of them to the face, and finally came the kick that landed him on his arse. Nevertheless, he still held on to the whiskey as he curled up in a tight ball with the bottles pulled to his chest.

The kicking started. Then, suddenly, it stopped.

"I wouldn't do that."

Demic. Scallion recognised her voice.

"What's it to you? This is my business."

"Well, I think your business is concluded."

"Trigo."

A blaster fired and then silence. Scallion uncurled slightly and took a look. Trigo was dead on the floor, and Demic had her weapon pointed at Fichal.

"Now your business is my business. I don't like it when someone gives the order to shoot me."

"It was a misunderstanding, Demic. I got carried away because of Scallion here."

"Nobody move." A patrol: two route security guards were checking the scene.

Scallion felt sorry for the guards. Neither Fichal nor Demic were the sort to run away from a couple of guards.

"What the fuck!"

Scallion saw it too. What had caused Demic to curse had dropped in behind the two guards. A policing botdrone. A larger version of the grumble terminator in the maintenance conduits, four feet in diameter with six heavy blaster turrets.

"Drop your weapons," the botdrone demanded.

Fichal's backup with the blaster turned and aimed at the guards. He hadn't seen the botdrone, and it took him out instantly. Panicking, the other thug started to run. The botdrone took him out too.

The concussion grenade was deafening, and accompanying the noise was a blinding flash and a fast-billowing cloud of smoke.

Scallion felt Demic grab his arm and then he was being dragged away from the alley, barely on his feet but managing to keep his balance as they fled. A door opened, and a young couple were exiting their domicile. Demic pushed against them, forcing them back into the room, ordering them to remain silent under the barrel of her blaster. She was intimidating enough without the blaster. Six foot four inches, sharp angular features, attractive in a quirky way, green hair tightly cropped to the scalp, broad and muscular. She had another two stones of lean weight over Scallion. The couple showed no sign that they were going to argue or shout out.

Outside, the guards could be heard talking rapidly between each other and asking the botdrone which way to go. The botdrone made no response; it had lost them. Scallion wondered what might have happened to Fichal, but other than a desire for revenge, he realised that he didn't care.

"I've not seen a security botdrone in the routes for two or three years now," said Demic. "That's unusual. I wonder what's brought that out now?" The guards and the botdrone had moved off outside. Demic had holstered her blaster, but the young couple still held tightly on to each other, afraid to move. "We need to stay out of sight for a while in case it's identified us. You have somewhere to go?" She pointed at the two whiskey bottles.

Sky opened her kitchen door and couldn't believe what she saw. Scallion was naked on top of a naked woman having sex in the middle of her kitchen floor. He rode her from behind while she was on all fours facing the door. The table was on its side and the chairs scattered. There was an empty whiskey bottle on the floor, another one less than half full and partially empty strips of drugs, along with the scattered contents of the medi-kit.

"What the fuck!"

"Quiet, lady, he's almost there."

"Aagh, agh, aaagh…" Scallion came.

"Aw, disgusting. I'm never going to be able to unsee that fucking look on your face. Gross."

"Now who's fucking swearing," said Scallion, laughing as he withdrew and stood up, his penis shiny wet and dripping semen.

"Aw, put it away. You're a fucking animal. I leave you for a few hours and you… you…"

The kitchen door shut, and Sky was gone.

Demic and Scallion got dressed, picked up the table and straightened the chairs. Demic collected her drugs, while Scallion poured half of the remaining whiskey into the other bottle and handed it to Demic. Then they both sat at the table and carried on drinking.

"Where do you think she's gone?"

"Well, if it was me and this was my house, I'd be getting my blaster to shoot you in the fucking dick right now."

"She does have a blaster."

The kitchen door opened and Scallion dropped off the chair to the floor to hide under the table, which offered him no concealment.

Demic roared with laughter.

"Who the fuck are you anyway?" said Sky.

"I'm Demic, and I don't like having a blaster pointed at me."

Sky lowered the weapon. "You're the bounty hunter, the gun for hire. The 'generally not a nice person' according to him."

"Oh, that's how he describes me is it!" And she kicked

him hard while he was still under the table.

"What are you doing here? How did you find him?"

"He was getting the shit kicked out of himself in an alley, and I decided to give him a hand."

"You were outside when you know you have an OD looking for you… and God knows who else. You're a fucking liability, a moron. Why the hell did I think you could help me find my kids?"

"It's not a bad plan he has. And with me helping, you might just pull it off."

"What! He told you what we're doing?" She raised the blaster again, and Demic slid her chair back to be sure that she wasn't in line with the weapon.

"I know he's an arsehole, but you will need him to get to the train. He's good at getting into places he doesn't belong. I don't care, but I wouldn't shoot him if I were you. Just saying?"

"Aaagh!" Sky lowered her blaster. "So what's in it for you?"

"Credits. He tells me you have enough credits to pay my fee and any expenses. The Pink Softy, I don't know who that is, by the way, apparently gave you enough to get out of the station."

"I don't have another choice, do I, and the train leaves tomorrow for Station Eight. There's one tonight, but that's going to Station Four. I don't know how often they go where, so we have to be on the one tomorrow. I must be stark raving mad!"

"I'll need half my credits upfront."

"Twenty-five per cent."

"Forty."

"Thirty."

"Done." Demic produced her transfer card to receive the funds.

"I'll be back. It's hidden. I don't trust that sniffling shitbag under the table."

Later that day, early evening, Demic and Sky went out for additional supplies. Scallion had outlined his plan for getting to the loading yards and for getting on the train. He admitted they would need to adapt as they moved because he had never seen the train, nor been to the loading yards; he had never been outside the station. Nevertheless, he was reasonably confident they would succeed, and if not, there would be a few moments where they would be able to abandon their choice and return to town. However, he also had to admit that it was going to be extremely risky. No one he knew of had ever tried what they were about to attempt.

The moment came to leave the domicile for the final time. Each wore a medium-sized backpack and hidden beneath long coats they wore a stocked utility belt and bandoleer along with a selection of weapons. Most of their new equipment wouldn't have been possible without Demic's contacts or Poppy's credits. They were now well prepared for any eventuality that they could foresee, and maybe a few they couldn't.

"Someone's following us," said Demic after they had been on the move for several minutes.

They may have seemed a little out of place with long coats and sporting backpacks, but other than the occasional odd glance from some they passed, no one else had given them any out of the ordinary attention. "Slow down and keep going," she said, slipping off the route and into an alley.

A few minutes later, as Scallion and Sky passed another alley, they heard Demic call them. Leaving the route, they followed the call and entered the alley.

The bounty hunter was standing by a trash bin, her blaster aimed at someone or something behind it.

"Poppy." Sky's enthusiastic reaction caused Demic to holster her blaster.

"You know this guy?"

"This is Pink Softy, as Scallion referred to him. This is Poppy. It's his credits that have funded us."

"So what's he doing following us?"

"Poppy?"

"I'm running away. I was going to knock at your home earlier, but I saw this big woman, and I didn't know who she was or if things were still safe for you. I was going to call out to you at some point. I just hadn't picked the right moment."

"What are you running away from?" asked Sky.

"Look, we don't have time for this," interrupted Scallion. "We're on a timetable, remember?"

"He's right. Go back, Poppy, to wherever you came from," said Demic, as she moved away to resume their walk down the routes.

"Can't I come with you?"

"It not safe what we're doing, Poppy," advised Sky. "We're leaving the station, and it's risky."

"I don't care. I want to come."

"We need to move now," insisted Demic.

"What we are doing is extremely dangerous, Poppy. You might die."

"I still want to come."

Sky looked the small man over. He was soft, unfit, and

not a physically strong person. He wore a plain dark suit with a purse over his shoulder, and so wasn't dressed or prepared for what they were attempting. Even she had to admit he would be a liability, but he was clever, and they wouldn't be where they were without him. "Stay close and don't ask any questions. Come on, we need to move."

Demic shook her head, but she wasn't the one calling the shots. She was simply the hired gun.

A few minutes later they moved off the route and down an alley to locate a service shed. Scallion bypassed the locks, opened the panels and studied a layout plan of the conduits before shutting down the lasermesh. They each took a filter mask from the wall before descending a ladder, even though they had left the filters below on so the air would be breathable.

After a short distance, Poppy screamed and the other three drew their blasters trying to identify the threat. It was a grumble, sat on a pipe above them to the right.

"Really," scoffed Demic. "And you brought this guy along."

They moved on, almost jogging, conscious that time was against them. Poppy was already slowing and struggling with the pace.

"How are you so unfit?" Demic asked as she grabbed the small man and started to drag him.

"This one." Scallion identified a maintenance conduit going off to their right. They had passed a few junctions already.

"Are you sure?"

"Yes. The layout map indicated this one as our best route."

Demic grabbed Poppy, lifting him from the floor,

tucking him under her arm, and they all raced down the deckplate.

"Demic, you're up."

The bounty hunter moved to the front and took a quick look around the corner of another junction.

"Clear. No botdrones. That's a promising start."

The next run was short, only a couple of hundred yards before they came to a solid doorway blocking their progress. The pipes and cables ran through glands in the bulkhead around the door, providing services beyond.

"Masks on," said Scallion. "Demic, you ready?"

The big woman drew a ballistic pump-action shotgun from beneath her coat.

"Are you sure that'll stop a botdrone?" asked Sky, looking at the long wide-barrelled weapon that was half the length of a rifle.

"Yes. It has before."

The others drew heavy blaster pistols, Poppy producing one from his purse.

"You know how to use that?" Demic asked Poppy.

He nodded.

"You need to hit a security botdrone with more than one blast with one of them. The closer grouped the shots, the better chance you have of penetrating their shell and putting them down. You got that?"

Poppy nodded again, and Demic turned away from the small man while putting her mask on.

"Ready?" Scallion looked to Demic. He was about to open the door ahead of them, and they had no idea what might be waiting.

The door slid open, and at the same time Scallion disabled it so it couldn't be closed again remotely, a precaution should they need to make a quick escape back the same way. Facing them stood a humanoid security botdrone.

The shotgun's explosive bullet took it centrally in the chest as it started to raise its rifle, and a smouldering hole appeared in the armour before the botdrone fell.

Demic moved quickly, picking up the botdrone's rifle and checking it for possible damage from her shot. It was still in order. Undoing one end of the strap on the shotgun, she slipped the weapon from beneath her coat and handed it to Scallion.

"We keep moving," she said.

The slightly increased difficulty in their breathing alerted them to the fact they were now breathing tainted air.

They moved slowly now, crouched and as silent as possible. Demic moved while looking down the scope on top of the rifle to see as far ahead as possible. She stopped, steadied her weapon, and fired. A botdrone at a ladder dropped as the bolt penetrated its head.

"How far?" she asked Scallion.

"We need to go up the next ladder ahead."

Demic picked up the botdrone's rifle and handed it to Sky as they passed the fallen target. Then she repeated her shot as they approached the next ladder, and that rifle she handed to Poppy.

A whirring of drives starting up around them indicated that the maintenance conduit filters in this section had been turned on. The tainted air had reached the maintenance conduits behind them through the open door.

The four of them hung on the ladder as Scallion

opened the hatch above. Demic was at the back, the last to climb should they be followed. Anything waiting for them beyond the hatch Scallion would need to deal with. The hatch opened, and there were no blaster shots as the three ahead of her climbed and exited. She followed.

They were outside now in the Scorched Land. Stacked and spaced containers surrounded them. The freight transporters varied in colours and marking, but the vast majority of the containers were of standardised dimensions. The three most common sizes were twenty feet and forty feet, though there were exceptions, with specialised units both smaller and larger. All the standard containers were eight feet wide and had a standard height of eight-foot six inches. These regulation sizes allowed them to be stacked high and butted together in large numbers to maximise the use of storage space. It also meant they couldn't see any great distance ahead or behind and were lost in a giant warren of towering structures.

"Which way?" asked Demic.

"I don't know." Scallion looked up to the open sky above and the wisps of orange clouds drifting slowly along. He was in real daylight and feeling the warmth of the actual sun for the first time.

"Don't look up," warned Poppy. "Keep your view forward and low. Follow the ground. Looking up will make you dizzy and upset your balance because you're used to inside. Many new farm workers fall over, even fall sick, when they first step outside. It can be disorientating."

"We need a direction, Scallion," urged Demic.

A massive mechanical foot fell close behind them. High above, a massive carrier botdrone was collecting a container, straddling the stacked tower to their right.

Another foot landed ahead of them as another carrier collected another container. Lifting their respective loads, they both set off in the same direction.

"Follow them," ordered Scallion. "They've got to be heading for the train."

"Keep one eye above too," warned Demic. "If one of those feet lands on you it's all over."

They ran along following the carriers. On more than one occasion they narrowly missed being crushed as feet slammed down around them with multiple carriers collecting or depositing their cargo. Then they reached the edge of the towering blocks, and there before them, three hundred yards away, was the train.

It was a vehicle of connected flatbed trucks with containers stacked eight high, twenty long and four deep. The truck beds were themselves six feet off the ground and mounted on a series of heavy-duty robust-looking caterpillar tracks. They counted thirty carriages in all, and at both the head and tail of the train was a powerful engine. Not all the trucks were filled or being filled with containers. Two shorter flatbeds housed a pair of cannons each and a brace of turret guns. Three others each had a large cylinder running their length, and another three looked like tall sheds with multiple side doors running both horizontally and vertically.

Lined up at the foot of the train along its length were security botdrones.

"Now what?" asked Sky.

"Now you pay me, and I find a way back inside," responded Demic.

"That's not what I meant."

"My job was to get you to the train."

"I don't agree. Your job was to get us safely on the train, and we're not on the train."

Demic didn't argue and turned to look ahead.

"So how do we cross the open ground and where do we get on the train?" she asked Scallion.

"We have to get inside one of the sheds. Out of the open."

"Which one?"

"I have no idea. I did say there were gaps in the plan if you remember."

A klaxon sounded.

"Is that an alarm?" cried Poppy. The fear was evident in his voice.

Then came the sound of heavy metal moving, grinding, whining and complaining at being disturbed.

Part of the massive three-hundred-foot wall beyond the train was moving. A gate was opening. The train was going to leave. All the botdrones lined up alongside the trucks turned their backs to the yard and started climbing up the containers, mounting the train.

"Run," called Scallion, and he started to race across the open ground.

Demic gave Poppy no warning as she swept him up under her arm and gave chase beside Sky only paces behind Scallion.

They reached the heavily shadowed side of the nearest shed-truck without being fired upon, either from above or behind. Scallion clambered up the caterpillar track and started work to open one of the shed's doors. In seconds it slid open. "Get in."

Poppy flew past Scallion and landed unceremoniously on the deck. Then both Sky and Demic were in behind him while he closed the door and suddenly they were in darkness. Sky switched on a torchlight. Poppy screamed. Standing in front of them was a humanoid service botdrone. Demic reacted with lightning speed and darted towards it, taking the botdrone in a headlock before ripping the head clean off with an almighty tug.

chapter four

Beasts and Mutants

"That was impossible," repeated Scallion for the umpteenth time.

They had been in the container section for just over thirty minutes now.

"Adrenaline, or maybe it was faulty," repeated Demic.

"But you ripped the head clean off."

"But it was inactive. Maybe it was broken."

The shed section's cargo was inactive botdrones. They weren't like any most of them had seen before. Demic, however, referred to them as loft botdrones.

"How do you know they are loft botdrones?" asked Poppy.

Demic did not reply immediately, and only when she noticed everyone staring at her, waiting, did she reply.

"I've seen one of them before and so assume because the rest are unfamiliar that they must also be loft botdrones."

Everyone accepted the response and Scallion moved to the service panel. Using the utility device he was able to hack into it. There was a soft hum as the compartment's air filtration system came on and then the lighting. Everyone removed their masks.

"Anyway, I'll take my full payment now," Demic said, addressing Sky. She was changing the subject from the botdrone incident, but she also wanted her payment.

"Why are you here?" asked Sky.

"You were right. The contract was to get you onto the train. I've not failed a contract yet. This wasn't going to be my first."

"But now you're here with us?"

"There was no way I would have been able to get back to the cover of the loading yard without at least one security botdrone on top of the train seeing me. This was my only option."

"Does she eat?" asked Poppy. He was stroking the cat, curled up in his lap.

"No. Well, not that I've seen," replied Sky.

"It's so real. Warm like a real animal."

Sky held out her transaction card for Demic to tap hers to it.

"Appreciated," said the bounty hunter once she confirmed the transferred credits. "But now I'm off the payroll I'm going to get some rest." She moved over to an area away from the others.

The shed section was thirty feet in length, twenty wide, roughly half the width of the flatbed carriage and ten feet tall. Inside were secured ten assorted botdrones, including the headless one, with the largest the size of a double bed and a similar shape to one, and the smallest a one-foot diameter sphere. The unused space left plenty of room for the stowaways to get comfortable.

"I wonder what these do in the lofts?" asked Scallion to no one in particular. "Maybe we should try and activate a couple to find out?"

"Don't you dare," warned Sky. "They might be dangerous or raise the alarm."

"One of them might also give us a way into the lofts at Station Eight."

"It's not worth the risk. Let's just get there first, and we still have to work out how we get off the train unseen."

"This one has lots of ports. Maybe I can open a few to see what's inside."

"Scallion. I'm warning you. Don't mess with them. Don't keep being such an arsehole, or I'll shoot you myself."

He looked at Sky and decided that she probably meant it. So he moved away from the three-foot diameter sphere and found a spot to sit.

"How long will we be in here?" asked Poppy.

Silence. No one knew the answer.

"Oh! Do we have food and water at least?"

"Yes," replied Sky. "That we brought."

For the next half-hour, Sky busied herself taking select supplies and equipment from Demic, Scallion and herself and redistributed them to Poppy.

"Were you expecting a war?"

"Yes," Demic replied from where she had bedded down.

Poppy looked at the array of supplies and equipment before him. Food rations – basic but they would keep him alive for a week. Water, a torch, a filter mask and spare cartridges. A six-inch knife. A small blaster, to go with his heavy pistol. Two concussion grenades and two explosive grenades. He scooped them all up and put them in the canvas satchel that Sky had also provided. He had noted that the others were still much better equipped than he was, but they hadn't expected him, and so he appreciated them sharing, knowing that neither the bounty hunter nor the thug would have shared willingly without Sky.

Scallion was pacing now and fidgeting with the botdrones. Sky knew he would be craving alcohol or drugs or both. Demic was asleep or appeared that way. She was avoiding the rest of them as best she could in the restricted space. Poppy was also drifting in and out of sleep, with the cat still curled up with him.

"Can you open the door a little?"

"Why?" asked Scallion. He was trying to open one of the ports on the spherical botdrone.

"None of us have seen the outside. The real outside, not the farms. It might be something we never get the chance to do again."

"Okay. Masks on and I'll try." His curiosity was aroused.

He worked on the service panel and the door slid wide open. The first thing to hit them was the noise. The caterpillar tracks were rotating at considerable speed and churning their way across the ground beneath them. They hadn't realised the terrain nor their velocity until now as the carriage felt practically motionless due to the suspension system.

The outside surprised them all. They had all expected a bleak, barren, dusty, rocky terrain. Instead, there was a carpet of green and yellow tall grass between an array of multicoloured vegetation and a myriad of different tree species, both tall and small, dotted in clumps and stretching out to the horizon over a gently undulating landscape, all softly illuminated by the dawn's rising sun.

"It's beautiful," said Poppy, breaking everyone's stunned silence. "I never imagined this. I thought the world outside was still dead following the Destruction."

"Close the door, quickly." Demic's request was urgent, and when they followed where she was pointing, Scallion closed it immediately. Above them, flying along escorting the train, was a security botdrone remarkably similar to the one encountered in the alley with Fichal, but this one was larger.

"Can you maybe just crack the door a little for a while," pleaded Poppy. "The plant life is amazing. I never thought such things existed."

Sky's pleading look was something that Scallion couldn't refuse. He worked at the panel and the door opened a little more than an inch.

"A bit more?"

Another inch.

"If that botdrone pays this carriage any attention, let me know immediately. I'll close it again shortly though as we don't want to waste any filters unnecessarily."

Sky and Poppy stared through the gap in the door, pointing things out to each other like excited children.

"You got a moment?" said Demic to Scallion.

"Why? What you got in mind?" The smirk on Scallion's face, evident even behind his mask, implied that he was hoping for something sexual or drug-related.

"None of that," corrected Demic.

They took the spot where the bounty hunter had

located herself and sat close together.

"First of all, don't freak out and don't make a scene." Her voice was low and guarded. She looked over to the door to make sure the others were paying them no attention.

"Why, what are you going to do?"

"I'm going to do nothing unless you force me to. I'm going to tell you something that… Well, let's see how it goes."

She took a deep breath, looking Scallion square in the eyes. "I'm an elite or was. I worked at Station Six lofts."

"Fuc—"

She forced her hand over the mouth of his mask and Scallion thought for a moment she was going to break his jaw; such was the intensity of her grip. Then she released him.

"I've known you for what, four years, and now you tell me this. How's that even possible? Are you telling me the truth?"

"Yes. They think I'm dead. No one is looking for me, but I always have to be careful when another elite is around. Your hair-brained scheme to get us out of the station sounded stupid and impossible, but if it worked, I would get out of the station too."

"So we helped you. Does that mean we get a refund?"

"Don't push it!"

"What exactly is an elite? I know you are the lofts' security but are they as special as they say? Why the fuck would you want to leave the lofts? Isn't it supposed to be all luxury and pleasure up there?"

"Yes, the conditions are far more privileged than a town, or mine, factories or the farms. Everyone eats real food and is well cared for. But it's still a class system up there too. Some get more than others, and they all still need to work."

"So why?"

"Why what?"

"Why are you telling me this now?"

"Station Eight is not the same as Station Six. I've only been to one other station, Station Four. I was part of a protection detail for one of the station master's officers."

"Who... what the fuck is a station master?"

"Later. Let me tell you what you need to know now."

Scallion nodded for her to continue.

"The stations are not all equal. They were all built the same centuries ago, with mining, flight dock, farming, factories and the like. But over time mines have stopped producing, crops have failed or been blighted, and there's been disease and riots and more, which means some stations are less productive than others. The stations, like Station Six that are still fully functioning, can make demands on the less fortunate stations. I heard that Station Eight has no mining and so no factories or repair abilities. I'm guessing that's why we're sending them botdrones. Most of the less fortunate stations rely heavily, if not completely, on the stronger stations sending them whatever they're ordered to produce. And then the strong redistribute it. The more profitable stations keep others less profitable, telling them what they can and cannot produce or do."

"But won't these rich governors fight back if their station is struggling?"

"The governors are all in it together. They live in different stations to keep their hierarchy working. Their shuttles let them move around as freely as they like. No matter where they live, no matter what station, they are well looked after."

"So what about Station Eight? Why are you telling me all this?"

"A few years ago, while I was still an elite, I heard that Station Eight had been overrun by mature blood-sick. Only the grounder population, but if that's true, I have no idea what we're going to find."

"And knowing this you let us go there? You came along?"

"No matter what we find there, I agree that her kids will be taken there. Probably by shuttle. If we don't get them back there, then they will most likely be gone for good."

"This is all fucked up. Fucked up." Scallion stood up and walked away, pacing, trying to rationalise what he had just heard.

"So why didn't I know all this before? Why doesn't everyone?" He had come close again, not wanting to attract attention.

"Information is power. No one, not even station masters, governors, no one is told anything more than they need to know."

"Who tells these station masters, the governors, what to do?"

"I don't know."

"Is it the head office?"

"How do you know about that?"

"Poppy mentioned it."

"How the fuck does he know about that?"

"There's a lot about Poppy that's not right. He's got

more secrets than any of us."

"Yes, it's head office, but other than the name I don't know any more than that."

"So what can we expect when we get to Station Eight?"

"I don't know. All I know is that they were all built identical originally, but they're not that way now."

"What are you going to do when we get there? You're off the payroll now," said Scallion.

"I've decided I'm going to stick with Sky. Get her kids back if we can."

"Why?"

"I just am. Let's leave it there. Now you know, what are you going to do? Following a cause. Those two. That's not your style."

"For now I'm sticking with you. Having your skills at my side might be useful. Are you such a powerhouse because of your elite training?"

"Yes, that and more. But what are you going to tell those two?"

"I'm not. You are."

After allowing them some time at the door while collecting his thoughts, Scallion closed it once again. No sooner were their masks off than he declared that Demic had an announcement.

The bounty hunter glared at him, but he shrugged it off.

A few minutes later, Sky and Poppy knew what Scallion had been told.

Everyone sat in silence for a while, absorbing the information.

"So you know how to get into the lofts?" asked Sky.

"No. I know the permissible routes, but we won't have permission."

"Elites are enhanced, aren't they?" asked Poppy.

"Yes."

"What's enhanced?" asked Scallion.

"They have an adapted skeleton. They are stronger, faster, than other humans."

"Not quite right. The stronger, faster bit, that's true. But adapted skeleton, that's a bit vague. We are selected very young. They feed us with all sorts of enhancing supplements and drugs, bone hardeners and more during our early years. Not all make it through even that stage. If it's not the training, even then, it's the cocktail of stuff they put inside us that kills us or sends us out of our minds or our young bodies just stop. Then they attach things to all our joints. The surgery kills more of us. The mechanical enhancements that are bolted and screwed to our bones add more strength and speed. As we grow, they need to be modified, changed, until we are fully matured. I'd say less than ten per cent make it through to be an elite."

"So, are you still human?" asked Scallion.

"Yes, still human. We're also not indestructible. Some always need to be on medication as their bodies constantly reject the implants. Others like me have no problem with them."

"So that's how you fucking ripped the head off that thing."

"Yes. Now you know."

"Well, I, for one, am glad you're here," said Sky. "From what you say, we're going to need someone like you."

"Me too," added Poppy.

The cat meowed, as though in agreement. Everyone looked at the small black animal, as that was the first sound it had made, other than purring.

The day dragged on. Scallion cracked the door one more time, and this time he took a long look too when they saw mountains in the distance. He had hoped to see the idyllic scene that used to be on his screen back in his pod, and other than a beige-orange sky rather than a blue one, he wasn't disappointed.

Night came and they all slept, comfortable for now that they were safe and undiscovered.

The crash into the train jolted them all from their sleep and prompted weapons to be drawn immediately.

Then silence.

"Are we there do you think?" asked Poppy.

Another crash rocked the train, and this time the carriage they were in leaned over.

They heard cannon fire.

"Open the door. Only a fraction," ordered Demic.

Not questioning the instruction, Scallion complied.

"More," commanded the bounty hunter. "I need a bigger arc of vision."

"Oh my!" Sky saw what Demic could see, and both Poppy and Scallion raced over to see too.

A monstrously large scarlet-red worm was breaching the ground. The head was thirty feet across, and its eight jaws opened, splaying out like eight-foot-long petals on the head of a flower, revealing row after row of spiked teeth and expanding the diameter of the mouth to over forty feet. Then it struck. The impact on the train rocked its entire length, and this time they saw several containers falling, crashing to the ground as the train raced on.

The blast cannons fired again, and a glowing globe struck the side of the worm as it was diving back beneath the ground. It was burrowing so fast that it might as well have been diving into water. The rattle of the ballistic turret guns fired explosive shells, creating a flowing arc of scorching shells as they flew through the air, peppering the worm as it disappeared below the surface.

Another crash rattled the train, and it leaned the other way. Another worm on the other side or something else? There was no way the four of them could know.

The worm rose again, keeping pace with the train, and its massive open jaws once again targeted it, its appearance triggering more cannon and turret fire.

They had dived for cover as the worm struck their carriage, and one jaw smashed against their door. The impact added momentum to the jump for safety and hurled them across the shed to the far wall. This time they thought the whole train was going to topple over, but it hung precariously for a moment before falling back to the horizontal.

Two more enormous impacts resulted in more falling containers and cannon and turret fire. Then the worm, or worms, were gone.

"The door won't close!"

While the others had been clambering for their masks in the tainted air, Scallion had raced for the service panel without his mask. Poppy, noting the predicament, found his mask and came up behind him, putting it on him while he was attempting to close the door.

Demic moved directly to the door and added her strength and brute force to the panel, trying to force it to move. It remained stuck. Sky lent a hand and then Poppy.

"The track's damaged and the door's bent." She pointed to the damage. "It's not going to close."

"We should have left it shut in the first place," complained Scallion.

"We needed to see what we were up against. And what if the impact had jammed the door so we couldn't open it? What then? Wait for botdrones to cut us free?"

"Look, we're alive. We have masks, food and water. There can't be too far left to travel, and we have plenty of filters." Sky was defusing the tension before it escalated. They listened.

"Look at this." Poppy picked up a broken tooth, six inches long with small sharp serrations along its length. "That would make easy work of any human or botdrone. I wonder what other creatures are out there?"

"Let's hope we never find out," said Scallion as he took a closer look at the damaged door. "If we had a hot-torch and a heavy hammer I could fix this."

The cat was pawing and meowing at the spherical botdrone with the closed apertures that Scallion had been trying to open.

"I think it wants that botdrone," Poppy suggested.

"What makes you think the cat wants that?" scoffed Scallion.

"It's an OD, remember."

Scallion felt stupid for forgetting the obvious. "Well give it the botdrone then."

Poppy released the straps that had been holding the botdrone to its cradle.

The black cat then started to sniff and rub itself against the shell of the botdrone, leaping on top and circling it as it did so.

Scallion wanted to say something sarcastic about the cat's behaviour or call Poppy's interpretation of what the animal wanted stupid, but he had already embarrassed himself once, so he bit his lip.

The cat found a port that it seemed to like and started to claw at it.

"What's it doing, Sky?" asked Scallion. Shifting his scepticism about the OD's actions to her. *Let her explain this.*

"I've no idea."

Then the port opened, and the cat started to climb inside, squeezing itself into an opening that looked too small, yet it managed to get inside, and the port closed behind it.

Nothing happened for a couple of minutes, but none of them took their eyes off the sphere. Then, suddenly, the three-foot ball came to life and floated up into the air.

"That's the OD, right?" asked Scallion uncertainly, as he picked up the ballistic shotgun and aimed it at the botdrone.

Demic shared his uncertainty and started to raise her blast rifle.

"It must be the OD," said Poppy, almost certain. "Sky, has it done anything like this before?"

"No. It's just been a cat. But it did take out the OD at your home."

"Do you know its programming?"

"I've no idea. Wouldn't know where to start. That's Sara's work. I haven't got a clue."

The botdrone drifted smoothly across to the damaged door, and from one of the ports appeared a nozzle, and then a scorching hot blue flame erupted. The heat was applied to the damaged area, and then the sphere rotated slightly. From another port, a blunt hammerhead burst out at force and clanged against the door; the panel gave slightly under the force. The heat was reapplied, and then the hammer clanged on the door on two more occasions.

"Try and close the door now," said a female voice from the botdrone.

"Scallion," prompted Demic when he made no move towards the panel, "it's talking to you."

The door closed. It complained a little as it dragged against the damaged track, but it closed properly, and the filters began to clean the air.

The botdrone landed back on the transport cradle, and the black cat re-emerged looking no different to when it had climbed inside.

"Do you know anything about its programming?" Poppy asked.

"Nothing. All she ever said was that it would look after us one day."

"Look, I know ODs are capable of cognitive thinking way beyond that of a botdrone, but that was way past anything I've ever heard of, and we have two ODs and a lot of botdrones working on the farms."

The cat meowed, brushing up against Poppy's legs, and without any hesitation, the small man picked it up and cradled it in his arms.

"Well, I'm just glad it's on our side," said Scallion.

An hour later, there was a deafening bang as a huge arrowhead punched through the door of their compartment. Poppy screamed, the others readied weapons and took defensive positions. Four arms sprung out from the arrowhead turning it into a grappling hook that began to pull on the door.

"Now what?" shouted Demic with her rifle raised.

"Do we open the door?" asked Poppy.

"I think someone is doing that for us," replied Sky.

The door was starting to buckle under the pull of the grappling hook.

"Take cover. Get behind something and get your masks on." Demic wasn't taking any chances.

The door finally broke from its tracks. It wasn't entirely ripped from the carriage but it was never going to close again. It had been torn back, creating a large hole, and the hook had gone slack. Outside there was the sound of blasters and ballistic fire over the sounds of the train.

A head and hands appeared over the rim of the damaged door. The features of the face were strange, the eyes blood-red. They were being boarded. Demic fired and the head ruptured beneath the shot, and the body disappeared, thrown from the train.

Another head and hands appeared and Demic fired again. No one else appeared, but the gunfire outside continued.

The others remained in cover, weapons ready, but Demic moved towards the door, wanting to see what was outside. Alongside the train raced a variety of vehicles, mostly ground-based, but there were a few hovercraft too. She quickly counted ten and assumed by the noise that there were more on the blind side of the train. The heaviest of the vehicles, of which there were three, carried the harpoon guns, and behind them was a trail of containers they had already yanked from the train. One of the vehicles was reloading a massive harpoon when a cannon took it out and it exploded. The other vehicles supported turret guns and raiders firing continually at the train. There was another explosion and Demic saw the flying security botdrone exploding in the air. Then all the vehicles trailed off and fell behind. They had what they wanted or had done enough. The train rattled across a bridge. Demic looked down into a deep gorge and a fast-flowing river, before ducking back inside the carriage.

"Raiders," she said. "They weren't human, so must have been mutants. Organised with vehicles and stealing containers. They took out one of the flying security botdrones, but they took losses themselves."

"Are they gone?" asked Poppy.

"For now. We crossed a bridge and left them behind."

"What did they look like?" asked Sky. They all knew the stories of the monstrously deformed mutants that walked the Scorched Land following the Destruction.

"Two arms, two legs, human-shaped, but I couldn't get any detail. They looked pale, gaunt, different."

"They didn't wear filter masks," commented Poppy. "They breathe the tainted air." His comment wasn't directed to anyone. He was just confirming the fact to himself.

chapter five

Station Eight

"That must be Station Eight."

The others joined Poppy at the damaged door. Ahead of them in the distance rose the high perimeter walls that went on for miles surrounding the gigantic central hangar that housed the station's grounder town, lofts, flight dock, factories, mine and farms. An expansive complex capable of housing several hundred thousand people across the distinctly divided areas. The closer they got, the more detail became evident: the three-hundred-foot outer wall had turret guns and cannons mounted on it. Beyond, once they passed the first gate, was an empty corridor of land four hundred yards in width before there was another three-hundred-foot defensive wall and gate. "A kill zone," Demic had termed it.

"These places are built to keep people out, that's for sure," commented Poppy as they passed through the gates.

"Or in?" suggested Sky.

"Now!" And they jumped.

The train had slowed as it passed through the gates. It

was still a risky jump from the moving vehicle, but they had decided this was their best option. Landing just inside the second wall's perimeter, they aimed to stay as close to the train as possible while avoiding getting crushed under the churning caterpillar tracks. Once on the ground, they picked themselves up and moved quickly to the cover of the shadow beneath the towering wall. Everyone, except Poppy, seemed to have landed without injury. The small man was limping slightly but insisted he was okay and to keep going.

Hugging the wall's surface, taking advantage of the shade that it cast, they moved along its length away from the gate and deeper into the loading yard. After a few hundred yards, Demic decided it was time to cross from the wall to the distant containers. They all knew that by doing so they were out in the open and exposed; they hoped that all the attention would be on the train.

They made it to the next cover without hearing any alarm or coming under fire, and they all sighed with relief.

"These containers are empty. They've been forced open. Quite some time ago too by the look of them." Scallion was initially concerned that with many of the doors open, anything could be hiding within them. Closer examination revealed that they all now seemed to be derelict and hadn't been used or entered for possibly years.

"They aren't stacked as high as Station Six. And there is most definitely less activity in this yard. Still, keep an eye out for the loader feet dropping," warned Demic.

They were looking for a maintenance conduit hatch so that they could drop out of the yard as swiftly as possible. They weaved deeper into the dark shade of the stacked containers, watching carefully for any sign of a threat. The tale that the station had been overrun by blood-sick was prominent in all their minds.

"The train's leaving," pointed out Sky. They could see it in the distance along a clear line direct to where the train had stopped.

"It doesn't look like very much was off-loaded or loaded," said Poppy. "That can't be a good sign?"

"I've found a hatch."

As Scallion opened it, Demic was ready to shoot anything either on the ladder or at its base. She was expecting a botdrone, but nothing was guarding the way. Cautiously she took the lead and descended.

At the bottom, Scallion attempted to access one of the service panels, but it was locked. He tried one of the four codes but was denied access. He wasn't willing to try another and risk raising any alarm.

"But what about the lasermesh?" asked Poppy, obviously remembering his last encounter with one.

"Looks like we're going to get a few burns."

As they headed into the station, the bounty hunter took the lead, scouting ahead through the rifle scope. They were surprised to find no botdrones guarding the conduit or the ladders. Another unusual fact was that the lasermesh was inactive. When they came to the boundary door separating the loading yard from the inner conduits, Scallion opened it. Demic was ready to take out anything on the other side, but again nothing was waiting for them.

"I'm not sure where we'll come up in the town, but if I try and follow the exit path in reverse to when we left Six, then we should exit on the town's perimeter somewhere. Assuming the stations are all laid out the same."

They had no better plan, so they followed Scallion's lead.

"No grumbles and no botdrones hunting them," Poppy pointed out, acutely aware of their absence because he was the one explicitly watching for them.

They left the service conduits and opened the shed door. Outside they found themselves in an alley not too dissimilar to those they had left behind in Station Six. It was daylight, and as Scallion unlocked the cage gate, the other three took in their surroundings.

"Looks much the same," commented Poppy.

"There's no clouds in the sky, just the ceiling lights," indicated Sky.

"It's noticeably quiet," added Demic.

"It smells different too..." Sky paused, trying to figure out why. "It doesn't smell as foul. It smells cleaner."

"There's less litter too, and less trash," added Poppy.

The gate opened, and nervously they left the cage, each ready to aim a weapon at the slightest disquiet.

"Do you think they're still here?"

The other three knew that Poppy was referring to the blood-sick, but as they had no answer, they remained silent.

Taking the route at the end of the alley, they headed towards the centre of the town. For the first several hundred yards they saw no one, but then they heard voices, and shortly after, they saw human faces. Their presence raised curious glances, due mainly to three of them wearing long coats and backpacks, but no one they saw seemed overly nervous at their presence.

"Not a lot of people about," commented Poppy.

"More than likely all working," suggested Sky.

"No. There should be more people," added Scallion. "We should find a bar or store and see if we can get more information."

There was a scream from the alley to their right. The few people about other than them chose not to notice it. Demic, however, reacted and went to investigate; the others followed.

Three men were holding a woman to the floor as they struggled to take her bags. She was fighting back, but she didn't have the strength or ability to dissuade her attackers for long. The men looked unkempt and harsh, and they were showing the defenceless woman no quarter, punching, and kicking her, forcing her to release the two bags.

"I wouldn't do that," said Demic, challenging them.

The three men turned their attention to the new arrivals, seeming unworried at the intrusion. One started to raise his blaster, and Demic's blast rifle quickly appeared from beneath the long coat levelled at the man. He froze, as did his two companions when the gate-crashers produced three more blasters.

"There's enough to share," suggested one of the attackers.

"I'm not the sharing type," replied Demic.

The three eyed up the four, estimating their chances, and decided that it wasn't worth the fight. They backed off slowly, making no sudden moves.

"We good to go then?"

Demic waved them away with the rifle. "Don't circle back. You won't get another chance."

The men walked backwards for about a hundred yards before turning to run.

"You going to rob me too then?"

"No." Sky had bent down near the lady and was picking up packets and tins of food that had fallen from her bags. "They were stealing food?"

"What else. This is two weeks' supply for me, and I was trying to get home without attracting attention. It looks like I failed twice on that account."

She was a mature woman, somewhere between fifty and sixty guessed Sky. There was a keen, intelligent glint in her eyes, and Sky could tell that she was trying to work out her next option and whether the newcomers were friendly or more trouble.

"We have our own food. You don't have to worry about us. Do you live close?"

"Why?" The woman stared at Sky, her eyes narrowing.

"We're new here. We're from another station, and we could do with someone, you maybe, answering a few questions for us."

"Another station? I doubt that. What are you after?"

"We are. We've only been here, in this station, for less than an hour. We came in on the train."

The woman looked the four of them up and down. She seemed understandably sceptical. The four of them would have reacted the same way should they have heard the same story back in Station Six. People did not move between stations.

"I'm sorry, but we don't have time to debate this. I'm here to save my children. We would like to get off the routes and out of the alleys and know more about what's been happening here. Will you help us?" asked Sky.

"Do I have a choice?"

"Yes."

It took the woman only a moment to decide. "I live close, follow me."

Her home was on the second tier of the blocks, only a

short walk from the alley. It was eerily quiet as they climbed the stairs to the walkway from the alley. The almost silence was disturbing. There was a distant hum in the air, and it took them a moment to realise what it was. They could hear the filters above cleaning the air, something they had never heard at Station Six.

"Why is it so quiet?" asked Demic once they were inside.

"There's a lot fewer people since the blood-sick raged through the routes."

"Are they gone now?" Poppy's voice indicated his fear and trepidation.

"Not seen or heard of one since. So I suppose so."

"When did it happen?" asked Demic.

"A little over four years ago now. You *aren't* from here, are you?"

"No," replied Demic.

"And you're here to save her kids?"

The home matched the layout of Sky's domicile, but with less furniture, and the surfaces were more faded, making it look older and sadder. She led them into the kitchen and started to put away her goods in the cupboards.

"I hear the mine's closed here?" Demic took the lead on the questions.

"Ten years now, give or take. They closed the whole section when it dried up. The botdrones became a little scarcer after that, probably because they weren't getting repaired or serviced regularly, maybe? Then the factories started to close. We still run a few, but only the ones that process the food into tins and ration packs. We don't make clothes here anymore. There are a few farms still running I understand, but what they're growing I don't know. Still, there's that few of us now that most of us still have a job. Then there's those, like the three in the alley, that just take from the rest of us."

"How many are left now?"

"I don't see many people and talk to even fewer. This whole block only has two other families and me in it. The rest are empty. But someone said recently at the factory that the town sign still gets updated, and it says, or said, twenty-one thousand or thereabouts. No one lives in the pods now, no need, with so many homes available in town."

"All the rest were killed by the blood-sick?"

"Oh, it was a slaughter. No idea where so many came from, and all at once. They ran wild through the routes, all sizes, men, women, kids, even babies. They ripped everyone apart. There were no botdrones to fight back, and people with guns and blasters of their own mainly ran for cover. Somehow they got into homes too. It went on for five days. Then the lofts sent down an army of botdrones that wiped out the blood-sick. That was another three days. When it was all over, the botdrones cleaned up the dead and life began again for those left behind. That was it. Since then, the shops stay stocked, some bars stay open and life just goes on."

"That's awful," commented Sky, with real empathy. "Did you lose anyone?"

"Partner was already dead. He was killed in service at the flight dock. I had two children, a boy and a girl, teenagers. The blood-sick got them. I was working, and when I eventually got home, after sneaking and running through the routes and alleys, they had both been slaughtered in their bedroom."

Sky looked towards where she knew the bedrooms were.

"No, not here," commented the woman, noticing the look. "I moved. Couldn't stay there. But these blocks are all so similar I still see them sometimes, playing, fighting, as kids do."

A tear rolled down Sky's cheek. Poppy's face was already a river of muted sobs.

"How do you go on?" asked Poppy, barely containing his emotion.

"I can't give up. I've thought about it, but my kids wouldn't be proud of me if I did. So I suppose I keep going in their memory."

"So, I'm assuming you know nothing about the lofts or what went on up there?" Demic brought the conversation back to what they needed to know now.

"Knew nothing about what went on up there before, and still know nothing. Can't help you with that one."

"Do you see elites down here?"

"No."

"Are there any security patrols?"

"A few humans and botdrones are working at the factory. I've not seen any in town for some time now, but I don't venture far. Work, shop, home, that's about all I do."

"There's no dogs? Is that right?"

"Yeh, that's right. What the blood-sick didn't kill, people caught and ate. Food was short after they'd raged through the routes. Grumbles were caught and eaten too. They all disappeared in the same way. I'm told that there was cannibalism for a while too until all the bodies had gone."

"I need to go for a wander in town," said Scallion. "Check out the bars, brothel and more. Assuming the brothel is still open?"

Everyone looked at him with surprise at his remark, except the woman, who simply answered him without any change in her tone or expression.

"Yes, that's still open."

"For information," defended Scallion, as the disdainful looks fell upon him.

"He has a point," conceded Demic. "Scallion and I should maybe check things out before nightfall. Any information might help us. We need to see how similar this place is to Station Six. We're against the clock on this one. If the kids came here by shuttle, they might have already left again."

Sky conceded to Demic's logic but warned Scallion to stay off the alcohol and drugs. They needed him now and might even depend on him to gain access to the lofts. The two left for town, leaving most of their equipment behind to better blend in with the population.

"Do you think he'll stay sober?" asked Poppy.

"He needs a drink. I can tell that. He may skip drugs if he has alcohol. Hopefully, he won't overdo it, and I think Demic will keep him on track. Even though I know she likes to party on occasion too," replied Sky.

"How do you know that about Demic? I thought you'd just met?"

"Let's just say that I've seen a whole lot of her in that short time, trust me."

Five hours later, a little after nightfall, the wanderers returned. Both Scallion and Demic smelt of alcohol, but they didn't seem to have indulged in any excess. They reported that Station Eight was practically the same as Station Six in structure, layout and design. There were obvious differences: no dogs, less population, less activity and cleaner, quieter routes and alleys. But in general, it was mainly the same. The credits chips were identical; Demic's transfer card had worked the same. There was the same proportionate mix of drunks, lowlifes and decent citizens, and the same type of information brokers, moneylenders and general riffraff. They had needed to ask about and attract a little attention, but they had finally found the sort of information they had wanted. It had cost some credits, more than they had expected, but both felt that it was worth the expenditure. Scallion more so, as it hadn't been his balance sheet getting reduced. Both Poppy and Sky offered to reimburse Demic, but she declined. She was no longer on the payroll, and they were now all in it together.

The owner of the brothel, a large fat man, and in every way distinctly different from Valerie, had shared information while they drank together. He had been very forthcoming, bragging that he supplied men, women and kids to the loft clientele on quite a regular basis, though none of them ever returned.

Poppy interjected at that point, remarking that Valerie had often done the same.

The useful part of that exchange had been the snippets of conversation the loft's agents had imparted. It seemed that the lofts too were substantially less densely populated at the station. Not for the reason that they had suffered any losses during the Blood-Sick Rage, but because there was less to do up there now. An engineer in one of the bars had also told them that many of the station's services had been significantly reduced. He worked in one of the control rooms, and some of the riser conduits had barely any services transferring along them. Scallion had been able to identify several of those little used now. A flight dock attendant told them that only one dock was currently operational, and there was only one flight per week to the Device. All this led them to believe that they thought they had a way into the lofts that would be unnoticed, and that the security up there had been decreased because of the reduced population. It still wouldn't be easy, and there would still be elite and botdrones to contend with, but they had a chance. More of a chance than they would have had at Station Six.

Agreeing that they all needed rest before moving on, they slept. Ista, the woman whose home they occupied, put Sky and Demic in the spare room on two single beds. Scallion and Poppy had to make themselves comfortable in the living space. The cat surprised everyone by choosing to remain with Poppy. They would rise early and follow Scallion's lead on how best to gain access to the lofts. They had a plan, but much like the one to leave Station Six, it wasn't complete in every detail, and there would be a significant amount of improvisation in its execution.

They woke to a morning meal, prepared in the kitchen by both Ista and Sky. The two women had struck up a friendship. Their shared past similarities – a partner working in the flight dock who had died in service and two teenage children – giving them enough in common to bond and reminisce over. They had combined their supplies, and everyone had to admit that, for rations and preserved food, it was a delightful meal.

Finally ready to depart, Sky wished Ista well and insisted that she accept some credits for her hospitality. There had only been a little soft stubbornness before the credits were accepted, and then the four of them left.

They took the routes, as they had no one to avoid by winding through the alleys. Their destination was a service conduit in the southeast area of the hangar. There, Scallion would gain access, leading to a riser that would take them to the lofts. They expected security, but as this was one of the risers identified by the engineer with little provisions running through it, they hoped that any obstacles would be minimal.

They took masks from inside the shed with them. It was more of a precaution than a necessity, as the filters were running in the conduits. It would also preserve their filters if they were required later. The lasermesh wasn't operational, and they soon reached the door barring their way to the lofts' riser. It took the utility device a little longer to hack the extra security of the door, and Scallion had to make a couple of adjustments to the device before his third attempt succeeded in opening it. Demic was ready, as were Sky and Poppy, to fire upon anything that waited there, but nothing was guarding the door on the other side. Beyond, there was an enclosed area with another door only paces ahead of them, and a hatch barring any ascent.

"Never dared even to attempt this before," stated Scallion. "I always assumed there would be botdrones every five feet or so along the way."

"Don't speak too soon," cautioned Demic. "As an elite, we always knew that the risers posed a potential security risk but knew that they were well guarded. We haven't encountered any security yet, but we will."

The hatch opened on the first attempt, the modifications he had made to the device previously improving the efficiency. Looking up, they followed the direction of the ladder, surrounded by pipes and cables, as it ascended through a narrow course. Using the rifle's sight, Demic scoped the way ahead.

"It's clear. I can't see any lasermesh, and there are no botdrones. There's another hatch at the top. If we're caught in this conduit, we'll have no escape and no cover. I suggest Scallion goes ahead with me, while you two wait here. If anything is waiting for us beyond that hatch, that will give you both time to escape and find another way."

"And what about our escape?"

"As I said, if we're caught in there, we have no cover and no escape."

Scallion hesitated. He wanted to make any excuse, suggest an alternative, but the voice in his head was able to discount every one of them before he even uttered a word. Finally resigned to the only option, he put a foot on the ladder and started to climb.

"We need to swap places."

Demic had to agree with him.

"I can set the hatch to open on a timer. Once the plates all roll back into their housing there will just be a hole, and you're better equipped to deal with anything waiting. I'll just be in the way."

"Set it for three minutes."

"I can't. Maximum is two."

"Then we're just going to have to make sure we don't get into any knots climbing over each other in this tight space. Set it, and then move quickly."

"Set. Go!"

There wasn't a fraction of a second to spare as Demic succeeded in climbing above Scallion just as the hatch opened. All in the same moment, Scallion screamed as he lost his grip and footing and fell down the conduit. Two rapid blaster shots fired as one, and then there was a deathly silence.

"A little help please."

The backpack had snagged on a bracket, catching Scallion, but his arms and legs looked awkwardly tangled between ladder rungs, pipes, and cables.

"Hold on. I need to clear the way first."

Demic climbed out of the riser into a wide circular chamber. Two biped botdrones had both been shot below their facial chins, taking their heads clean off. They lay crumpled on the floor beside their weapons. Pipes and cables curled out of the riser, along the floor, before running up the wall and out of the cylindrical compartment via ceiling glands, disappearing deeper into the lofts. A single door exited. Demic operated the panel and it opened.

The clean, well-lit corridor running left to right was empty. Closing the door, she turned her attention back to Scallion.

"You okay?"

"I think I might have broken my arm."

She was surprised at his uncharacteristic calm. She imagined he would have been screaming and cursing at such an outcome, but he wasn't.

"Painful?"

"Fuck yeah! If I thought it was safe to be screaming

and crying like a baby, I would be, trust me. Now get me out of here and get that medi-kit."

They closed the hatch and laid him out on top of it. Sky treated his injury by wrapping a splint-bandage around the break. It had been a clean break but needed a little straightening. Scallion clenched his teeth, fighting not to pass out from the additional pain and not to scream.

The splint-bandage, once activated, expanded to cover his left forearm like a second skin. It would hold the bone in place, relieve the pain and apply repairs to the fracture while it was in place. Depending on the severity of the break, the arm would heal in a day or two. Until then, it would provide enough support for the arm to function normally.

"Right," said Demic, "if the layout is the same, then Governor Frisk's apartments are not too far along the south-facing profile. He'll have elite guarding the entrances, along with botdrones, but once we're inside there should be minimal security. There will only be the governor, some of his aides, family if he has any and serving staff. There's rarely much trouble in the lofts, so they won't be expecting any. But don't let that make you too confident. The elite are dangerous and always looking for reasons to prove themselves."

"So, if there's not much trouble up here, you had it quite cushy then?" asked Scallion.

"No. There's always some powerplay going on, and sometimes we're the ones making it on behalf of a governor or a station master. One such incident is how I lost my place."

"Oh…"

"For another time, Scallion. We have a job to do now.

Stay close and kill anything that sees us. You won't get a second chance, but don't shoot unless necessary. We don't want to advertise."

Scallion armed himself with one of the botdrone's dropped rifles. The three removed and discarded their longcoats, as they were no longer needed to hide the utilities and weapons beneath.

"If we get separated, the way out, if you get a chance, is the way we came in. So pay attention to where we go."

Demic checked the corridor was clear and then they were on the move. The first thing they noticed was the smell: sweetly scented and fresh. All the surfaces were soft white, all backlit and easy on the eyes. The way was wide enough for all four to travel abreast, and they had feet of headroom above them. Demic took several turnings, passed multiple doors, and never slowed the pace. Poppy kept up this time. *Probably adrenaline. Scared stupid,* decided Scallion. But he also had to admit he was probably in a similar state.

Demic stopped abruptly, selected a nearby door and ushered them all inside. As the door closed, they heard voices approaching. Poppy raised his rifle to fire inside their space, but Demic grabbed and stopped him. The botdrone in the enclosure was dormant. A cleaning device that would only activate when necessary.

The closed door muffled much of the sound beyond, and so they waited until they were sure the owners of the voices had passed and gone. Demic checked the corridor, and they were off again at pace. There were more turns and they once again entered an enclosed space housing a dormant cleaning botdrone.

"The next point will put us under risk of fire. If the

patterns are the same, there will be at least two elite at the door. I'll take both and anything else there as I'm the surest shot. You don't shoot unless I miss. Once we're inside the apartments, though, shoot anything that threatens. Now check your weapons and kit and be ready. This is where it gets real very quickly."

They stopped at the corner, and Demic stepped around it alone. There were no shots, and everything remained quiet. The others, moving out behind her, could see the door ahead, but it was unguarded.

"We might be too late," said Demic. "No guards means the governor's probably gone. But they should still be there if his family's home. Something's not right."

"Or he has no family?" suggested Scallion.

"We have to find out for sure." Sky wasn't leaving without knowing if her children were here or not.

The bounty hunter moved forward more slowly and with greater caution.

"Scallion, the door."

He bypassed the security, and once the door opened, they entered. Inside, the immediate observations were the carpeted floor and the change in the lighting of the panels to a soft blue. There was a short corridor to another door and on the left wall a further door. Demic checked the first door: another dormant cleaning botdrone.

"Ready?"

Demic waited for each of them to confirm their commitment and then she opened the next door.

The room beyond was large, spacious and elegantly furnished. A large window wall on the far side looked out over the Scorched Land's greenery, stretching to the distant horizon. Plants grew in pots along the walls, pictures hung about the interior, and shelves displayed ornaments and other expensive bric-a-brac. Yet all that went unnoticed. What was notable, and demanding their full attention, were the ten uniformed elite lined up before them with raised weapons. The door behind them opened, and more elite flanked them; there was no chance of escape, and so they lowered their weapons and surrendered, allowing their weapons, utility belts, backpacks to be stripped from them.

"Razer. Well, well. I thought you were dead."

A bald man, middle-aged, fit, strong, healthy and in charge of the elites was speaking directly to Demic.

"Good to see you too, Harp. I was hoping you were dead too."

"It's here." One of the elite was holding up the curio from inside Scallion's pack.

"Get it up to the shuttle pad," ordered Harp, indicating an archway to the left of the room. "And bring in our guests."

From a room far to their right, passing under another open archway, walked Valerie and Ninety-Six. Both were shackled, bracelets on both ankles, connected by a chain to another pair of bracelets on their wrists.

"Who's Poppy?" asked Harp.

He stepped forward.

"Get over there with those two." And he indicated the chained prisoners.

"Sixteen of them. Be ready," said Demic.

Scallion couldn't believe that Demic was genuinely planning to do something. She had whispered as she passed him, moving towards Harp. He stepped back, moving closer to Sky.

"Be ready," he murmured, barely believing he was going along with Demic. *I must be fucking mad. But they're probably going to kill us anyway. This might be a better way to go?*

"Stop there, Razer. I know what you're capable of. Well, what you used to be capable of. But looking at your company now, you're probably not that good anymore."

"Want to find out?"

"You can't goad me. The three of you would already be dead once I had the curio if it wasn't you in front of me. I'm curious, where've you been?"

"So, brave as usual with men and women covering your back. I bet not one of them has ever seen you fight an equal that wasn't chained, bound or already wounded. Have any of you?"

Scallion noted that there was curiosity in the eyes of many of the armed elite looking at them. At least ten of them were focused on the exchange, and another two monitored Ninety-Six closely, his size probably identified as a potential threat. The others glanced between him and Sky and the developing situation between Harp and Demic. He wondered how many others in the room recognised Demic, Razer, and what they thought of her?

"I don't hear anyone backing you up, Harp. Why don't we give them a show? Something to talk about. The infamous Razer kicking your butt."

"Not going to happen."

"Oh, really. Then why haven't you killed us already? You know it's the best thing to do, and quickly. I've got out of worse situations. You know that. So kill us. The longer you wait, the sooner I'm going to, because you're a weak excuse for an officer and have no balls without backup."

Harp scanned the men and women under his command, their curiosity, their loyalty posing unasked questions.

I'd just fucking shoot us, decided Scallion. *Not worth the risk of not doing so. But then again I'm not full of pride, reputation and distinction like these dumb fucks.*

"Sarry, make sure none of the prisoners tries anything." Harp was undoing his belt to remove his holstered weapon.

"Yes, sir." The woman gave signals to the others, and they all spread out. Their attention was divided between Ninety-Six, Valerie and Poppy to the right, and Scallion and Sky, who were pushed back away from the two starting to square off against each other in the centre of the room.

Harp indicated a large sofa and a couple of chairs, and three elite lowered their weapons to move them, creating more open space. As they did, there was the dull clunking sound of something falling to the floor. Everyone looked.

A concussion grenade and two explosive grenades bounced onto the carpeted floor. Demic kicked them into the room and they exploded. She must have cooked them before dropping them as they erupted in early flight. The explosive blasts threw everyone that Scallion could see off their feet, while the flash and smoke obscured his and everyone else's vision a fraction of a second later.

Blaster pistols and rifles fired, their red and blue bolts visible through the billowing smoke. A few shots narrowly missed Sky and Scallion, but they were already moving to a new location. Scallion collided with an elite and struck him hard with a fist to his face, but the man barely flinched as he grabbed Scallion by the throat. Sky put a dagger through his throat, and the elite fell, gurgling blood. At his feet was a rifle, and at his hip a holstered blaster. Sky took the rifle and started to fire into the room. What she could see, Scallion had no idea, as his vision was still blurred from the blinding flash of the concussion grenade and all he could make out was smoke. Dropping to the floor, he drew the pistol and moved away towards Sky.

A powerful hand grabbed Scallion's neck and at the same time stopped him levelling the blaster.

"The room on the left. Now!" It was Demic. She released him and disappeared into the smoke.

Scallion kept low as shadowy figures slowly became visible. Two murky shapes fell ahead of him hit by blaster bolts. He had no idea who they were or what side they were on as he kept close to the floor and pressed on towards the left-hand room. Once inside, he stood up and turned back to the archway, covering his retreat. There was negligible smoke in the second room, and the fog in the first was starting to dissipate. He was alone, but he had no idea where to go next, so he waited with his blaster raised and ready.

Sky came through the archway next. He fired but diverted his aim at the last second. She shot him such a scorching look that he thought he was going to burst into flames. Then she too turned and covered their escape.

An elite wasn't too far behind Sky and raced into the room as she turned. Her aim was far from sighted on the pursuer, but Scallion was ready, and two blasts to the head saw him fall in a spread of blood, bone and brain matter. Sky nodded to him in appreciation.

Redemption from her fury for now. But it's not over yet. Where the fuck is Demic? How are we getting out of this shit pile?

The blaster fire stopped, along with the screams and cries of fighting.

Sky moved towards the archway and looked back. Scallion stayed well back, clear of any line of sight from that direction.

The look on Sky's face told him that whatever she saw in the room beyond wasn't pretty. However, she wasn't ducking for cover. *A good sign. Have we won? Fuck, won what! We're stuck in the lofts with no escape. All we've done is prolong the inevitable.*

She retreated quickly, just as Demic rushed under the archway carrying backpacks, some utility belts, and several rifles.

"That way," she hollered, indicating a stairway.

Behind Demic barged Ninety-Six, covered in blood, bracelets still on his wrists and ankles but broken from any connecting chains. Cradled in his arms was a body. Scallion didn't have time to recognise whom he was carrying as Demic turned him and forced him up the stairs, pushing his utility device into his hands.

"Open that fucking door now. They'll be right behind us. Lock it, jam it whatever way you can once we're through."

Scallion locked the door and encrypted the lock. He hoped that would buy them some time. When he turned around, they were in a hangar-shed. To his right was a walkway stretching out into the sky, leading to a circular platform. Demic had dropped all the equipment and was opening a cabinet on the far wall. She was ripping the door open having pounded on it enough to buckle it to give her a grip over an edge of the warped door. From inside she extracted a weapon unlike anything Scallion had seen before: a long tube, twice the length of a rifle. With that in her hands, she raced for the walkway and ran outside.

As Demic left the shed, her image shimmered as she passed through the curtain-field keeping the tainted air outside. He watched as she aimed at the sky with the weapon on her shoulder. In the distance was the outline of something in flight.

Must be a shuttle, decided Scallion.

Demic fired, and a vicious-sounding missile took to the air leaving a wispy trail of smoke in its wake. He lost sight of the projectile's flight, but when it struck the shuttle, the explosion was visible.

Demic ran back into the shed, gathered everything she had dropped and charged back outside, calling, "Follow me."

The door started to take a pounding beside Scallion. They were trying to break through. He looked around the hangar-shed but could find no other exits other than towards the distant Scorched Land. Ninety-six and Sky were already running to catch Demic. They all passed through the curtain, and he was alone.

Seeing no other choice, he ran after them. He passed through the curtain and immediately realised he was breathing tainted air. He looked over the walkway as he ran to catch the others. They were hundreds of feet above the ground and the platform ahead of them was suspended in open air beyond the perimeter walls, with no other access points.

'We're dead. We're running to a dead end in tainted air.'

As he reached the platform, Demic pushed Sky off the far edge to fall to her death below. Ninety-Six leapt willingly after her.

"Jump!" screamed Demic to Scallion.

He stopped. "No way!"

Then she grabbed him and threw him off the edge.

He screamed and looked to the ground that he was hurtling towards, but he wasn't hurtling. He was falling much more slowly than he should have been. Yes, the ground was coming quickly towards him, but not at a pace that seemed fatal. He landed as though he had fallen only a few feet, but his knees buckled, and he sprawled out across the grass.

"Get up. Run!"

Demic lifted him by the scruff of his neck and pushed him forward.

"Run. Run fast before they think to site the wall guns and cannons on us."

The memory of those cannons and turret guns seen from the train fuelled his flight, and ignoring the tainted air clawing at his throat, he ran and ran hard. He followed Sky and Ninety-Six, but he didn't gain any ground on them.

'Damn, that fucker's fast for a big man. And he's carrying a body.'

Demic overtook him and quickly passed Sky at the front, changing their direction towards a distant treeline.

chapter six

The Scorched Land

Demic stopped them once they were deep into the trees.

"They'll assume we'll keep running, so we don't."

"And what if they double guess your double guess?" asked Scallion.

"The governor's downed flight will be their priority. Harp might want to come after us, but he'll be overridden."

"What! He's still alive?"

"Most of them fled the room when it started. They assumed we were cornered and could come back with reinforcements."

"We were fucking cornered. Who the fuck jumps off a… a… what the fuck was that?"

"A shuttle pad. They extend from the hangar. While they're extended they have an anti-gravity curtain dropping from them, should anyone fall."

"You knew that before we jumped, right?"

"Not really. It's optional, might have been on, might have been off. But it was all we had."

"Fuck, fuck, fuck."

"Hey!" It was Sky. "Whatever! Break out the masks before we get weezies and give me the medi-kit. Next, before I get pissed off, tell me you didn't shoot down that shuttle with my kids on it without a plan?"

Ninety-Six hadn't said a word. He had handed Poppy over to Sky so that she could treat his wounds but had then sat away from them beneath a tall tree.

"You know who he is, right?" Scallion asked Demic.

"Of course. I worked for Station Six for years. I know who he is."

"What happened to Valerie?"

"Head blown off. He wasn't happy about that. The chains that bound him, he broke them himself and tore through every elite he could get his hands on. Tore them apart with his bare hands."

"Did you kill Sky's kids?"

"Unlikely, but possible."

"What does that mean?"

"If the shuttle had gotten away, we would have had no chance. They're fitted with safety features and survival devices. The missile would have downed it, but everyone on board should be alive."

"I'd tell her they're alive. She scares me more than you."

"Here, your curio's in the bag. Keep hold of it." She handed Scallion one of the backpacks before moving over to Sky.

"How is he?"

Sky looked at Demic as if she had a hundred questions

of her own but replied on the point.

"He's lost his left arm. He should be dead. The amount of blood loss might still do the job. If Ninety-Six hadn't held the wound so tight, he would have bled out for sure."

"Looks like you sealed the wound?"

"Yes, but there's nothing left in the laser-pen, and we're out of healing shots. All that's left in the medi-kit now is one fracture bandage."

"We're going to have to move soon. Can we move him?"

"He'll have the same risk lying here or being carried by Ninety-Six. Are my kids alive?"

"Yes. The shuttle crashed, but it will have saved anyone onboard."

"Everyone?"

"I don't know for sure."

"Then we need to get to them before your elite friends do."

"We're on foot. They will have vehicles and a tracker. We might need a better plan."

"I saw the filters. We have maybe three days maximum. We can't go back to Station Eight, so we have to get to the shuttle, right?"

"Then we have a plan. Now I need to talk to Ninety-Six. He's not looking very friendly, and I need to know what he's going to do."

Demic went to sit with Ninety-Six and Scallion moved over to Sky and Poppy.

"You know he must have sold us out in some way, don't you?" Scallion indicated the still form of Poppy when he spoke.

"I'm guessing so, but for now that's not important."

"How are you so relaxed and controlled about all this?" asked Scallion.

"I'm not. But what other choice do I have? My kids are out there, and that's all that's keeping me going and sane. Nothing else matters. I can panic and scream later."

"Good job on the arm by the way."

"I used to fix my partner's wounds and the kids' injuries. But I never thought I'd be sealing an amputated arm."

"He won't be happy, you know. That's another suit ruined."

Sky smiled at that. It was poor humour, but humour nonetheless.

"Okay. We travel due south." Demic was on her feet, and Ninety-Six stood behind her. "We divide what we have between us so that we each have the best chance. Ninety-Six will carry Poppy. But we need to move and keep moving. Rest will be infrequent and little. They will no doubt get to the shuttle crash before us. But the closer we are behind them, the better chance we have of getting to the kids and surviving the Scorched Land. So let's move."

The conversation was non-existent as they travelled. Demic set such a pace that both Sky and Scallion struggled to keep up. Ninety-Six kept moving like a machine: silent, expressionless and constant.

When they eventually stopped for a break, not long after nightfall, both Scallion and Sky dropped. They were spent, and Demic knew it.

"Sleep," Demic told them. "Get as much rest as you can. Tomorrow will be much the same pace as today."

Scallion woke suddenly. His filter was clogged. *Must be fucking faulty*, he cursed, realising why he had woken. He rummaged in his backpack for a replacement filter.

Demic stopped him. By the light of the moon, he could see her face behind the mask and knew not to resist as she held him quietly.

They had crossed grassland, travelled through trees and waded across a stream the day before. Now they lay beneath six trees that were the only shelter and cover for some distance in any direction.

Scallion followed Demic's gaze and saw why she was attempting to avoid discovery. Not too far away, silhouetted in the moonlight, was a herd or pack of large creatures. It was difficult to tell if they were grazing or following a scent trail, perhaps theirs? But not knowing what they were, he suffered the poor filter while they waited for them to pass.

Once they had moved on, Demic released her grip on his shoulder.

That will fucking bruise, as sensation returned to his arm after she let go.

As dawn broke, Scallion woke to the sound of sobbing. He thought it was a dream at first, but opening his eyes, he realised what it was. Poppy was awake and coming to terms with his loss. Ninety-Six was cradling the small man in his arms as one would a baby. Sky and Demic were already awake, and although conscious of the strange scene with Poppy and Ninety-Six, they were ignoring it as they ate cold rations.

The pace was slower than the day before. Poppy was

on his feet now, but he was not the only one to be blamed for the faltering pace. Neither Scallion nor Sky were good distance runners, and much of the time they slowed to a walk. They also needed to stop when they saw creatures around them. They had no idea what were predators and what were not. The whole landscape was alien to them. Birds flew, insects buzzed. Four-, two- and six-legged animals of all sizes, big and small, navigated the grass, trees, waterways and skies all around them. The Scorched Land was far from the dead, barren place they had believed it to be when they were in Station Six.

"Down!" Demic ordered them to lie flat in the grass as there was nothing else nearby for cover.

The others caught on seconds later as to why. In the distance was a vehicle. Mutants, elite, someone or something else? They had no way of knowing.

"Looks like a station vehicle, and it's coming towards us." Demic knelt and sighted down the scope of her rifle. "Yes. It's coming directly towards us."

It was a wheeled carriage, with a plate glass windscreen and side windows, that appeared to be empty of passengers. Even the central, front driver position was vacant. Demic kept scanning. It braked and stopped over eight hundred yards away. Demic waited, checking the position of a grenade on her belt should she need it, while never taking her eye from the rifle's scope. A side door opened. No one exited.

"What can you see?" asked Poppy. The others had each taken to looking through the scopes on their rifles, but he only had a blaster.

Dropping from the carriage, from the open door, they saw the black cat.

"It's the fucking cat," declared Scallion as he watched it jump up onto the front bonnet of the vehicle.

"She's brought us a vehicle," proclaimed Sky.

"How the fuck… Okay, don't answer that, she's an OD."

"Right, up and move," demanded Demic as she trotted towards the carriage with her weapon still ready.

It was a six-wheeled people transporter with three doors on either side leading to internal benched and backed, seats. There was a small flatbed storage space under the same roof, behind the final seat, and the front bench was split, divided by the driver's position. The carriage was high off the ground and suitable for rough terrain.

"Get in." Demic took the driving position.

"You can drive this I assume?" checked Scallion.

"All elite can drive. Just in case we need to come out here on a rescue mission."

"You've been out here before then?"

"No."

She adjusted the holographic display before her as she settled into the driver's position. "Got it. The shuttle isn't too far now, not in this. It's transmitting a detection pulse."

"I take it there are others closer than we are?" asked Sky.

"There's nothing on the scanners. I don't know. I would have thought they'd already be at the shuttle."

"Maybe they've been and gone?"

"Not helpful, Scallion," scolded Demic.

"Just saying."

Sky and Ninety-Six sat on either side of Demic. Poppy had the middle seats, with the cat, while Scallion had the rear bench to himself.

The vehicle equipment included filters, so they were able to remove their masks.

"So, did you sell us out?" They had been travelling in silence for a little while, glad of the rest to their tired legs. However, Scallion couldn't hold back any longer on questioning Poppy. He wanted to know what had happened, how Ninety-Six and Valerie were at Station Eight. Who *was* Poppy?

"No. He never sold you out, Scallion." Ninety-Six spoke for the first time since they had met again. "He was never with you in the first place to sell you out. He was looking out for Valerie and me."

Scallion paused before going on, as he had no desire to push Ninety-Six on the matter; he liked his arms and legs attached to his body. Nevertheless, his mouth sometimes had a mind of its own.

"So who is he to you?"

"He's my son. And Valerie's. Valerie decided to let you go at the brothel, but we needed someone on you that you wouldn't suspect. You were bait. We had no idea you were going to go to Station Eight, but Poppy had a comms, so he was able to stay in touch and keep us updated."

"How…?"

"Shut the fuck up, Scallion. Let me tell you what you need to know and then don't ask again."

Scallion decided to be silent.

"I questioned Torgon myself, but he was a dead end. Then Valerie's sources started asking questions about a curio while supplying a girl to the lofts. We didn't expect any kind of response. Next thing, we were being escorted to the lofts by elites. Governor Frisk sent them. We were persuaded to tell them everything we knew. Then we were flown by shuttle to Station Eight. The rest you know."

Scallion wanted to ask more, to know more, but he was scared of Ninety-Six. He suddenly realised that he was scared of all of his current companions.

"So they knew we were coming," stated Demic. "I should have known it was too easy getting into the lofts and to the apartment. They cleared the way for us. A couple of token botdrones were all they put out for us. You still got the comms, Poppy?"

"No. They took it when they caught us."

"How'd you get a comms anyway? More than one I assume if you were keeping in touch," Demic asked Ninety-Six.

"Got lucky sometime back on a deal with a couple of elites. They gave me two comms for a time. I was supposed to return them after the deal, but they never showed up again. I've never seen them since."

"Probably got caught then. They'll be dead now."

Scallion leaned back in his chair, realising that there was so much going on behind everything, and he knew nothing about it all. He knew he was a lowlife, a petty criminal, in the eyes of the others. But now he also felt stupid. They all knew more about life in the stations than he did, and he had always thought that he was the smart one.

"There it is," said Demic.

Ahead of them was the fallen shuttle, a teardrop-shaped craft. It had ploughed a path churning up ground before finally impacting and felling a couple of large trees in a small copse. A charred area on the tail showed where the missile had struck it. In the main, though, it looked remarkably intact.

"I can't see any vehicles on the scanner," said Demic, "and there's nothing other than the shuttle ahead. This all looks wrong. Like they're letting us in again, just like the lofts."

"Maybe the cat did something to stop them from finding the shuttle?" said Poppy.

His comment wasn't as silly as it sounded, they realised.

"Would be useful if it could talk," remarked Scallion. "It can doing everything else, so why not a talking cat?"

"Right, I'm going to drive up to it, and then Sky and I will go inside the shuttle. The rest of you stay outside and keep watch," said Demic.

She parked the vehicle alongside, by the access door that was already open: a dropleaf with steps.

"Okay, so we know someone came out or went in. Stay ready."

Demic looked up over the smooth reflective surface of the shuttle. There were no windows, but other than the open doorway and the missile damage at the rear the exterior was smooth and flawless. The top curved over twenty feet above them, and from nose to tail, it was sixty-foot long.

"If your kids are in there and conscious, you need to get them quickly. I don't want them shooting me or me shooting them. Anyone else I'll deal with."

Inside, there was a cabin area. Eight plush highbacked seats around a central table. Beyond that was another door, which was closed. And on their left, as they entered was a further closed door.

Demic touched the panel for the nearest door and it opened. Inside were two pilot seats, empty, surrounded by control panels, all dark and inactive.

"That's normal. They don't require a pilot if the route can be programmed."

Moving through the cabin, they saw nowhere for anyone to hide.

"That's blood," stated Sky, serious concern edging her voice. "A lot of blood."

"Blood spread always looks worse than the bleed. There was no blood at the doorway, so whoever was injured, I'd say two people were treated before they were removed."

Opening the rear door revealed a series of lockers on both sides, all open. They searched for remnants of supplies, but everything was gone.

"Bring the cat inside," requested the bounty hunter.

Sky placed the cat in the left pilot seat as instructed by Demic.

"Ask it to fly the shuttle, turn it on."

"It can hear you."

The cat bounced off the seat and wandered casually back outside.

"It was worth a try."

"There are wheel tracks over there. I'm not sure they're related, but it's something," said Ninety-Six when Sky and Demic returned. Scallion was towards the rear of the shuttle looking into the distance, while Poppy remained in the carrier.

"It's all we've got." The pleading tone of Sky's voice was enough that following those markings was their next step.

"Okay, who wants to drive?" said Demic. "I'll walk in front following the tracks, and you can follow me."

"Not a good idea," replied Ninety-Six. "We can't learn all the console readings and drive as well as you in just a few minutes. We need to stick with our strengths. You drive, and I'll walk in front."

"So, we've got maybe a day left on our filters. Ninety-Six is using his up, and so, at some point, we aren't going to have enough filters for one each," said Scallion.

"Not now," suggested Demic.

They had been slowly following the tracks for less than thirty minutes.

"How long will the filters on the vehicle last?" said Scallion.

"The readings suggest five more days," replied Demic.

"And we're heading away from any place that is likely to hold replacements for us or the carrier. That's not good. We need a better plan," Scallion continued.

"Okay then, Scallion. What do you suggest?" Demic and Sky challenged simultaneously with apparent cynicism, causing Poppy to snigger out loud.

"Thought so," said Demic when there was no response from the back.

Ten minutes later, rain started. Five minutes after it started, the sky released a heavy deluge, forcing Ninety-Six to return to the vehicle. It passed in less than fifteen minutes, but it had been a significant downpour.

Ninety-Six went to find the tracks once again, but they were gone now. They had been patchy already and had grown more infrequent as they had followed them over ground that cycled between hard and soft.

Sky didn't want to give up, so she left the vehicle and searched a much wider arc than had already been combed, but she too found nothing.

As they sat in the stationary vehicle, the mood was dour and their prospects bleak.

"So what…" began Scallion.

"Shut up, Scallion. We don't need you pointing out the obvious bad news repeatedly," castigated Demic.

Scallion paused before trying to speak once again. "I was going to say…"

No one rebuked him.

"What I was about to say was that we've been going in a straight line constantly. Haven't we? So let's just go straight?"

No one replied or acknowledged him, but Demic engaged the vehicle's drive and they moved on, straight on.

Wasn't such a bad suggestion then, decided Scallion as he slouched back in his seat.

When nightfall came, they were once again out in the open. The ground had become an area of small rolling grassy knolls dotted with low trees. The uneven ground significantly restricted their ability to see clearly in any direction. Many of the dips between the small hummocks were deep enough to hide almost anything, and so they used this aspect of the land to stay off any horizon. However, being hidden in this way meant they were blind beyond a few yards in any direction and confined to the vehicle.

Scallion woke as dawn was just breaking. Demic was also awake, sitting on the bonnet of the carriage. He needed the toilet, so he put on his mask and left the vehicle. She watched him disappear around a curve of the land, out of sight for a little privacy.

The barrel of the weapon in the back of his neck dried up the flow of urine instantly. He hoped it was Demic being foolish, but when his blaster was taken from the holster, he knew it wasn't. Putting himself away, he turned slowly.

Three people, mutants, stood before him. Their loose-fitting clothing and assorted pieces of armour strapped over shoulders, arms, legs and chest were a mix of styles. Scavenged equipment, Scallion assumed. Their outfits were all coloured to blend with the greens, yellows and browns of the terrain and pockets of woodland. Their clothing, however, wasn't what held his attention. Their faces were gaunt and pale, their hair colour varied in length and colour, but their eyes were fiery red, other than the dark pupils. The skin on the necks and hands that was visible stretched tightly across the bones beneath. Then there were the sharp pointed teeth. Both upper and lower incisors were sharp and shaped for puncturing. The upper two fanged incisors of the mutant holding him at blaster point retracted as he watched.

The gun waved him back towards the vehicle, and he complied.

Ahead, surrounding the carriage, were ten mutants. On the brow of the small hills overlooking them were six other wheeled and non-wheeled vehicles and more mutants. Among those on the high ground was a human. A teenage boy was held forward, without a filter mask, by one of the mutants as an offering or warning.

Demic was holding Sky back, leading Scallion to believe the boy was probably Jeb, her son. Ninety-Six and Poppy also stood outside their carriage. Each wore a mask, but their weapons were gone. The towering bulk of Ninety-Six and the tall, muscular Demic dwarfed the mutants, the tallest being perhaps only five feet, and all of them slender like Poppy. Though Poppy was thin and small, the mutants were all gaunt and fierce-looking. When they reached the others, a push put Scallion with his companions.

"Move and he dies, and you die." A mutant standing beside the boy was addressing them, his voice coarse and rasping. "You will each be taken to a separate vehicle, and we will take you with us. We will not hesitate to kill you if required, so do not give us any reason to. You" – he pointed at Sky – "you are this child's mother?"

"Yes."

"Then you come with me."

Scallion was pushed back into their carriage on the middle seat, while the others were segregated and herded away. Four of the mutants boarded with him, two sitting behind him and two in front. The driver took control of the vehicle and they manoeuvred out of the gully to join the others. The mutants left the filters in the interior running, and so Scallion removed his mask. As they topped the hill, he counted eight other vehicles, some smaller and some larger than their own. The two larger ones had turret guns mounted on their tails. They had only been following the tracks of two carriages from the shuttle crash site, and so he assumed they had met up with the others only recently. The mutant in the front was discussing something about their prisoner with the two in the rear as they travelled. Scallion had no idea what they were saying as they spoke strangely. Some sounds were similar to familiar word pronunciations, but others were more like broken crackles and catcalls, all in course rough-edged voices. He had never heard another language spoken and had never assumed there was another. There was only one, the one every other person spoke. The new revelation intrigued and fascinated him so much as he listened that he forgot he was being held captive. The cat brushed his leg, out of sight of the others, and reminded him of his predicament.

An hour later and their convoy dropped to a gully that slowly became a valley. Four hundred yards into the valley they veered off into a large descending tunnel about forty feet in diameter. Only the lights of their vehicles shone here until they emerged into a massive underground lit chamber one hundred and fifty feet high at the centre and stretching out beyond Scallion's current line of vision. This subterranean burrow seemed to be home to the mutants, with buildings fabricated from the earth. Roadways divided the buildings, and it reminded him of towns in the stations, only with mud structures replacing metal containers.

Their vehicles stopped, and the five humans were reunited and escorted into a two-storey building.

"Did you see your children?" Demic asked Sky as they waited, assembled in an open floor space beyond the entrance. Eight mutants guarded them. There were no doors on the buildings, none that they had seen anyway. None internally either. A mound of earth, integral to the room, had been carved into a stairway to the next level. However, there was no furniture inside.

"Yes. Sara's injured. Badly by the look of her. I wasn't allowed near her, though. She was in the back of the vehicle. They wouldn't let Jeb and me speak, but he seems fine."

"What did they ask you?"

"Nothing. I could see my kids, but no one asked us anything. They spoke strangely to each other, though."

"Another language," interjected Scallion. "Did you know there was another language?"

None of the others did, and he was pleased by that. *At last, they don't know more than me.*

"There was another human in my vehicle – a man," said Poppy.

Their guards seemed not to mind them conversing.

"The governor maybe?" suggested Demic. "That would seem logical."

"He was injured too."

"We don't get many human guests." A mutant was walking down the stairs. He looked older than any they had seen so far, but how old Scallion had no idea. The gaunt stretched skin and unfamiliar features gave them no clues. He wore a loose red robe and at his waist was sheathed a shortsword.

"Yes, your daughter is injured, but we are dealing with that now. The injured man too, though I am told his injuries are not severe. We can offer you refreshments, food, water and a place to rest."

"Are we prisoners?" challenged Demic.

"You are free to leave, should you choose, but your equipment and vehicle will remain with us, as we have claimed it now."

"We can't leave without our equipment. But I suppose you know that?"

"I am aware of your limitations in our air. We have few filters here, as we do not need them, but we can offer an alternative."

The man was graceful, with a relaxed air of piety. He addressed them with no malice, nor did he show them any fear or prejudice.

"You are all from Station Eight?"

"No, Six," corrected Scallion.

"The injured man is possibly from Eight," added Demic. "If we aren't prisoners, can we have our weapons back?"

"As I have said, they are no longer yours, though you may earn the right to possess a weapon perhaps before you leave. There is accommodation waiting for you. You will be watched while you are here."

"Guarded?" queried Demic.

"Perhaps. We need to get to know each other before you may be allowed to wander without an escort. Your people have always meant us harm, but we do not judge humans collectively. We judge only those before us. These" – he waved at their escort – "will take you away now. But one at a time you will be brought back to me so that we can discuss matters."

"When can I see my children?" said Sky.

"Someone will take you to them now."

At that moment a mutant entered the room carrying the black cat by the scruff of its neck.

"She's mine," said Sky, not wanting any harm to come to the cat, and observing by the way it was being carried that the person holding it was not impressed with his find. "Well, it's my daughter's."

The mutant on the stairs waved a hand, and the cat was handed over to Sky.

"Do not let it wander freely. It may become a meal." Then he turned and walked back up the stairway.

As they walked through the settlement, they were viewed with curiosity by the inhabitants, but there was no hostility. Mutants went about their daily chores and tasks in tranquil peace and harmony that contradicted the impression given by the armed guards and assault they had witnessed on the train. Unlike the armoured soldiers, the locals dressed in loose brightly coloured fabrics. Each structure was unique in size and shape, though similar in construction, with earthen walls. There was no signage anywhere and nothing that looked like shops, bars, a brothel or a gambling house. Openings formed entrances and spaces to allow light into the interiors, but there were no physical doors or window frames. Everyone, even the children, carried weapons, and the general population wore swords, daggers, or carried spears or sported bows with quivers of arrows. Only their guards and other soldiers that they occasionally saw carried blasters.

They arrived at a two-storey building. The open-plan ground floor was large enough to accommodate them all comfortably. A wooden table and eight chairs were positioned at the centre and around the edges was cushioned seating. The colours of the upholstery were bright and bold. A flight of stairs carved from the earth led upwards, and one of their hosts told them that washing and toilet facilities were above, along with sleeping mats. Then their guards left them, and only one remained to stand outside the entrance.

"Doesn't feel like a prison," said Poppy.

"There might not be bars and lots of guards, but we can't exactly go anywhere else, can we," Demic reminded him. "My filter has maybe three hours left before I need a replacement and we don't have any. They have all our weapons, our vehicle, and I'm assuming they are better guarded than we are."

"My filter has less than an hour," added Scallion.

"I suggest we sit tight for now, though." Ninety-Six had spoken little since they had all encountered each other, but his demeanour and posture commanded attention. "They could have killed us, locked us up, tortured us or more. They want something from us, and until we know what that is, we have no plan. So we wait."

"What about filters?" asked Poppy.

"He said they have an alternative. So they will provide something soon, I imagine."

As Ninety-Six spoke, four young mutants entered carrying platters of food and drink. They laid these on the table, and three left immediately. The fourth stayed to explain their offering.

"We have brought you water, meats and bread, along with fruits. The four goblets on that platter contain a black fluid called chqaqaie. You should drink all of that, and then you will be able to remove your masks and breath normally."

"You drink this?" asked Demic, taking a goblet.

"No. This is our natural air. We do not need the chqaqaie, but you will need to drink it daily. However, each evening, before you sleep you will vomit up the crud from your lungs that the dark liquid had absorbed."

Scallion removed his mask and sniffed at one of the goblets of dark fluid. "Doesn't smell too bad." He sipped it, only to be told to drink it all at once for it to have maximum effect.

"It's not unpleasant, a bit like cheap watery whiskey."

"Remember that when it's coming back up later," said Demic, as she too drank from one of the goblets.

"You can then sleep without needing the drink until the following day," continued the mutant. "The being sick will be extremely uncomfortable as the vomit will be from your lungs and not your stomach."

"But if we're drinking it, how does it get into our lungs?" asked Poppy.

None of them could answer that, and the attending mutant didn't clarify the question.

A mutant soldier appeared at the doorway. "You come with me." He indicated Demic.

Two hours later Demic returned, and Ninety-Six was taken away.

"So what happened?" asked both Scallion and Poppy.

"We talked. The old mutant is called Fecting, though that's not his real name, it's one he used so that I could pronounce it. I couldn't even attempt his real name. He and four other mutants sat with me around a table, and they just wanted to know about me and life in the stations. It was all very relaxed. They offered me food and water and a type of wine, and we just talked."

"What did you tell them?" asked Poppy.

"Everything – I saw no harm, maybe even future benefits – how I was a former elite, how the social structure worked in the stations. How I met and came to be with all of you."

"What did they tell you about them?" asked Scallion.

"We, humans, seemingly refer to them as vampires as a race. I told them we know them as mutants, something left over from the Destruction. However, they told me that wasn't true, but they didn't elaborate. I've never heard of a vampire. Have you?"

They both shook their heads.

"It was a simple conversation about life in the stations, the work we do, the food we eat. Just life in general."

When Ninety-Six returned, his experience had been the same. He too had told them the truth about himself and his way of life. Next, it was Poppy and finally Scallion, and each of their encounters with the vampires were alike.

"Don't you think it's strange that we all, without any inhibitions, spilt our life stories to strangers?" Scallion raised something they had all been thinking.

"I'm now suspecting that there was something in the wine, or the water," offered Ninety-Six.

"Or the food maybe," added Poppy. "Either way, we told them everything. Now, what will they do with us?"

"Stop doing that," demanded Ninety-Six. Poppy was scratching the stump of his left arm through his shirt, where he had lost the limb just above the elbow. "You'll irritate the healing and it will become an annoying habit."

"But it's itchy."

Ninety-Six glared at him, the look a father uses to scold a child, and Poppy stopped.

"Anyone seen Sky?" asked Poppy, changing the subject.

On cue, Sky came into the room from the outside, accompanied by Jeb. Neither of them were wearing facemasks. The boy had the look of his mother, though his dark skin was slightly lighter and he was already taller than her, approaching six feet. He was lean, handsome and bright-eyed; full of the life youth grants.

Introductions followed and then questions about Sara.

Her daughter had been standing when the missile had hit them. She had been arguing with the governor, who had also been standing. The explosion had thrown them both. Jeb, who had been seated, was held by the automatic safety restraint of the chair. Sara had cracked her head badly, breaking the skin but not the bone, and until very recently had still been unconscious. Frisk had also landed badly and had broken his arm. The bone from the break ruptured the flesh and hence resulted in the blood they had found. Sky had used the last remaining splint-bandage from their medi-kit to repair the governor's arm. They had then taken him away to question him. Sky had been quizzed too, as had Jeb, in the same manner as the others.

Sara was awake now and seemed to be fine, other than having a nasty-looking bump and a future scar on her right temple. The mutants, vampires, had kept her with them for now. They knew that she was connected, and that seemed relevant. However, neither Sky nor Jeb knew why that was so interesting to their hosts. They had also kept the cat too, once they learned that it was an OD.

Two mutants entered the room carrying buckets, placing one by each of them.

What are these for?" asked Scallion.

"The sickness," was the simple reply, but they all felt well and had no uncomfortable abdominal feelings.

A little while later, though, they all had their heads in or over their buckets vomiting a gritty black phlegmy goo, and it wasn't a pleasant experience as they struggled to breathe while their lungs rejected the taint. It passed quickly, only a couple of minutes, but afterwards, they all sat with swollen moist eyes blinking at each other.

"I think I prefer a mask," said Scallion, breaking their

dazed and bewildered silence.

The following morning, though outside in the cavern the lighting levels had never varied as time had passed, the six sat at the table being served a morning meal and a fresh goblet of the black chqaqaie that Scallion had named 'Retch'. As they ate and idly discussed the possibilities of the coming day, a blood-sick adult entered the room.

He wore the loose colourful clothing that was common among the vampires. His eyes were pink around green irises and dark pupils. Two fangs protruded from his upper gum and sat prominently over his lower lip. He was skeletal in frame, as was reported to be the build of all blood-sick that made it past infancy. None of them had ever encountered any mature blood-sick, but they recognised him for what he was. Silence descended across the table; none of them moved, uncertain of what to do or expect. Demic gripped a cutlery knife and prepared to defend herself; Scallion and Sky did the same.

The blood-sick moved to the table and lifted an empty platter and then another as he circled the table. Collecting all the empty dishes, he then left as quietly as he had arrived.

"That was a…" said Poppy exhaling, not realising that he had been holding his breath.

"Blood-sick," said Scallion, finishing the sentence.

A soldier addressed them whom they recognised from the day before. She entered as the blood-sick left. "Fecting would like to speak with you all."

"That's a blood-sick," declared Scallion, pointing at the departing male.

"Blood-sick? Ah, you mean canine. He is called Cus.

He has been with us for more than ten years now."

"They are wild, feral, life-taking cannibals to us. They slaughter and kill indiscriminately," said Poppy. "They are a disease, a plague."

"Not so. They are a creation of humans. They have limited intelligence, but they serve loyally and are very clever and adaptable. By intelligence, I mean they do not speak, as we do, nor have the same faculties or mannerisms, but they are very smart and learn very quickly."

At that, the vampire dropped the subject as inconsequential. "When you have finished, Suarie" – she indicated the guard at the door – "will escort you to see Fecting and the council." Then she left.

"I'm guessing we are about to find out our worth," determined Ninety-Six. "Then, if we have any worth, we can start to negotiate."

Shortly after, they entered the building where they had first met Fecting. In the middle of the room was a large circular wooden table. One puzzling thought was that the table was far too large to have come through the doorway, an observation that was quickly neglected.

Already at the table were Governor Frisk, Sara holding the cat, and five vampires: Fecting and the four council members. Fecting asked them all to be seated before he continued.

"You were all very cooperative and truthful yesterday, all of you."

Scallion, and maybe the others, wanted to ask if they had been drugged in some way the day before but as no one else spoke out, he remained silent too.

"We were particularly glad to note that none of you knows what is meant by the term vampire. I will explain this shortly. Frisk was highly informative on the stations, and all of you equally on the way life exists there. We have not seen a human for over fifty years now. We see many of your vehicles on our lands and in our skies, but they are operated by botdrones. They are always doing one of two things. They are transporting goods or they are actively seeking us out to kill us. They fire upon us whenever they encounter us, and this has been the way for centuries. There has always been a war between our two species."

Fecting paused there, and, along with his council of two females and two males of varying ages, he studied their audience for any reaction. There was no recognition of the facts or circumstances to which he was referring.

"It would seem that little has changed in your understanding of what this world is since we last encountered humans from the stations. We have yet to meet a human from the Device, but we assume that they know the truth."

A further pregnant pause. The vampires were gauging the reaction of their guests before proceeding.

"We were hoping, after living below ground for so long now that it has become our normal way of life, that we might soon move to the surface again and build new homes. However, what you have brought to us has dashed that hope. I have sent word out to the other clans, and there will be a large gathering to decide what our people are to do now."

A further pause.

"Look," said Ninety-Six, "there's no need to keep studying us. We have no idea what you're talking about nor what history or past you're referencing. We didn't even know that you existed until yesterday. We thought that everything out in the Scorched Land was bleak, barren, and dead, with only mutants and beasts still roaming after the Destruction. So whatever it is you're building up to, just get to it."

"Humans first came to our world around seven hundred years ago, Fecting continued. "They came from the Device in great numbers. They build the stations to mine ore. They tried to slaughter our people from the very first days. They called us vampires. That is a creature from humanity's past or its dreamt horrors. This is because we drink blood to survive as you would drink water. We live three of your lifetimes. We are faster, stronger, maybe like your elites. But we are naturally this way and not…" He paused, looking for the word.

"Enhanced?" offered Demic.

"Yes, enhanced. The Destruction you talk of was a time when humans launched a massive onslaught across our world and drove us into hiding. That was five hundred years ago. We have lived beneath ground ever since. The weapons and the vehicles we have are taken from you and your botdrones. We cannot plant or grow enough to sustain our population, so we are forced to attack and rob your trains. We tried many decades ago to assault your stations, but we failed and took terrible losses. We, none of the clans, want war. We just want our planet back."

"Look. Everyone here knows I'm the dumb one who doesn't know half as much as these" – Scallion waved to his fellow humans – "but you're using words like planet and world. Like we humans are from another place entirely. This is our 'planet', we have always been here. This is Devil's Rock. The sky was once blue, before the Destruction, and there is only one place that survived the

Destruction, and that is Eden."

"This is what you are told. This is how you are educated in the stations. We know this, and you have all confirmed that nothing has changed in this regard since we last spoke with humans. Eden is another world accessed via the Device. For this, you need relics, what you call curios, like the one you have brought here. We had hoped that with stations becoming more inactive as the mines started to dry up you would maybe leave, but your arrival has changed that belief. We now fear that war will again intensify. This is why the clans will meet."

"So, if we humans are your enemies, what are you going to do with us?" asked Ninety-Six. "What value are we to you?"

"We wish the people of the stations no harm. We see you, them, as victims much like we are. It is the people of Eden that wage war on us. Others of our race have spoken with humans from Eden. We know much of your ways and nature. Humans are not a mystery to my people as we are to yours. We view Eden as your enemy as much as they are ours."

"You want our help? Our support?" suggested Ninety-Six. "You think we can be useful to you in some way?"

"Station Eight's mine dried up. The population was too large to be sustained eco-nomin-cally." Fecting struggled with the word. "So Eden culled the population. I would suggest that makes them your enemy too. What will they do when Station Six dries up?"

"How do you know Eden attacked Station Eight?" asked Demic, though she was staring directly at Governor Frisk.

"You are correct, Demic. Frisk told us what happened.

They were ordered to release canine among your population – wild, untamed canine developed in the Device. Once their work was done, they then destroyed the canines. This was Eden's way of controlling your human population."

"What are our options?" asked Ninety-Six. "What is our incentive. What stops you just killing us if we are of no use?"

"There are those in other clans that will want to kill you. If we can demonstrate that you have value, this might not happen. We will take you to the meeting of the clans, and there your fate and your worth will be decided."

"Until then we are prisoners?" challenged Ninety-Six. There was an aggressive edge to his tone now, but his body and expression remained relaxed.

"You are our guests, and we will treat you as such."

"Then return our weapons and belongings," suggested Demic.

"We would like to. But you yourselves do not trust each other. You are all different, from different backgrounds. Would you trust him… or him" – Fecting indicated Frisk and then Ninety-Six – "with a weapon at your back?"

There was doubt etched on all their faces. Demic conceded his point.

"We do not guard you to contain you but to look after you. This world, our ways, are something you do not know or understand. You might easily break one of our customs or laws without knowing you have. This would result in punishment, banishment or even death. You are free to wander our settlement, to get to know us, but our ways are old, strict and founded in the depth of our beliefs and religions. Any transgression, knowingly or not, will be met with justice. We cannot adapt our ways to shield you. You must learn them while you are with us if you wish to survive among us."

"Why not give each of us a chaperon?" This was the first time Sara had spoken. There was still swelling and bruising on the side of her face, but the family likeness was strong. She spoke confidently, unafraid. She was incredibly attractive, brown hair tied back, dark eyes, almost black. The colour of her skin was darker than her brother's, blacker than her mother's, and although still a teenager, her body was that of a woman.

"What is chap-eron?"

"A person of your race. A vampire who stays by our side, individually, to teach us and escort us at all times when we are among your people."

Fecting and the council debated the concept at the table in their language. After only a short time they settled on an agreement.

"This, Sara, is a good idea. We will select a cha-peron suitable for each of you today. Then you can move freely among our people. I suggest you learn our ways quickly, as when we go to Borsay you will be judged, and in front of the Great Council my words will not be enough to save you. You alone can do that."

chapter seven

Friends and Enemies

After the meeting, they were all escorted back to their accommodation. Sara, the cat and Frisk were now also to share the building with the others. The governor was quiet and subdued, concerned by his new entourage and feeling threatened as Sky was constantly glaring at him, her anger and rage towards the man that had stolen her children evident to everyone. He was a portly, balding man, who in his younger years had been fit and handsome, which showed a little through the additional plumpness he now carried. The rooms up the stairs slept two to four people on sleeping mats, and Ninety-Six offered to share with Frisk, as no one else would entertain the prospect.

Then they waited amid idle conversation and anxious fidgeting for the promised chaperons to appear. An hour later and the first arrived.

The vampire was named Cheter. She had offered her real name but deferred that to one more easily spoken by the humans. She wore a soldier's loose yellow, green and brown flowing camouflage fabric and carried a blaster rifle, pistol, shortsword and dagger. However, her armour wasn't a mismatch of styles, as worn by many, but all the same dark grey plate taken from a botdrone and adapted to her frame. She was the tallest vampire they had seen so far, close to five foot six and with a heavier, more muscular frame than the average mutant. She was also the first redhead they had seen, and her two fangs protruded a fraction more than the other pointed teeth, giving her a more menacing look than they had seen as the normal so far. She was to be Demic's companion, and they both left shortly after introductions.

The next escort was a young vampire; he wore a sword and carried a spear. His left leg, which he deliberately flaunted in the way he dressed, was that of a botdrone. The mechanical limb seemed fully functional. Such a device was entirely new for the humans, as none of them had seen the use of technology in this way. He was for Poppy, and once he'd been introduced as Pec, they left.

The process was repeated; an escort arrived, collected their ward and departed, until only Sara and the cat remained. The young female vampire that arrived, however, didn't follow the same protocol as previous chaperons. She introduced herself as Lonlin, but rather than leave straight away she sat at the table and invited Sara to join her. From a large pocket, she placed a small brown and white furry creature on top of the table.

"This is Iyne. She is like your cat. We call them gifts, and I am gifted; this is I think the best translation from our language to yours. You are connected. Is that how you say it?"

"Yes. This is a cat." Sara lifted the black OD onto the table.

"Cat? Is that her name or species? This mimics a tieve, but I have named it Iyne."

Sara studied the tieve. Its posture was upright, as the two hind legs were significantly shorter than the front two. The rear paws were huge in comparison to the eight-inch height and body size, while the front paws were smaller with sharp talons. It bore fangs, the two front incisor teeth at the end of a narrow long-whiskered snout and had long floppy ears that hung half the length of the animal.

"Tieves dig beneath the ground with their big back paws. They hunt and kill other animals twice their size."

"Cat is her species. There are none left in our world. I've not named her. She's young and I didn't get the chance."

"So do it now?"

Sara pondered, considering her options. "My ma says that she gets inside stuff. Scrunches up and wriggles inside, like water getting into cracks. I will call her Flow, like flowing water."

"Flow. I like that. Now I will take you to see some relics. You call them curios."

Scallion had trailed behind his guardian, trying to get the measure of the man. His clothing wasn't as loose and flowing as many others he had seen, but it was still of the same colourful style. He had wondered about his age and had asked. "One hundred and fifty years," was the answer. Other than his name, Ruseq, that was all the conversation they had.

They had walked through the settlement at a fair pace and eventually arrived at the outskirts of the buildings. A wide roadway surrounded the buildings, and across that was a tall dark tunnel. They entered the shaft and it wound downwards while curving to the left, and soon it was impossible to see anything in the darkness.

"Is there no light in here?"

"No, none."

The voice came from Scallion's left.

"Hey, where have you gone?"

"I'm still here."

The voice was now to the right.

"Okay, stop messing about." Scallion crouched and produced a cutlery knife in his right hand.

"That wouldn't stop me if I was messing about."

The sound was ahead of him now and a little distant.

"What won't stop you?"

"The knife."

"You can see that?"

"Yes. Now walk to my voice. The way is clear."

One hand took hold of Scallion's arm while the other gripped his hand to stop him from using the knife. "You are safe. Put the weapon away and I will lead you now."

They continued downwards until light appeared around the curve of the tunnel. Exiting the shaft, they entered a vast lit chamber full of vehicles. Here there was activity and the sounds of maintenance.

"So you can see in the dark, or do you have a device that does?"

"All vampires see in the dark. It's not exactly sight. We see heat. Glowing shadows, silhouettes and outlines."

"That must be useful."

"Only for hunting. As we all have the ability, it doesn't help us sneak about, as it can be more revealing than sneaking in the light where we see as you do."

"Never thought about that. What's this place?"

"Here we maintain, strip and investigate the use of vehicles, machines, botdrones, tools and weapons that we take from humans and botdrones, mainly botdrones. Everything we have ever stolen, acquired or found is here. We do not have the technology or ability to manufacture the majority of what we find, so we rely on places like this to keep your stuff useful to us."

"So you're an engineer?"

"Aaah, me no. I'm a thief."

"Does the council know that?"

"Yes. Unlike your people, it is a recognised and useful skill for us. How else do we obtain this?" He waved at the multitude of vehicles, workbenches, crates and cases that were strewn throughout the hollow. "These guys are the engineers. They keep everything working. Stripping one thing to fix another. It's useful that your devices haven't changed much in hundreds of years so we have lots of spare parts, but we've not many in full working order."

"So you're scavengers?"

"Not exactly. You don't leave much lying about, but we hijack trains, convoys, shoot down things when we can."

"Not much for a thief to do in that."

"We open things. We acquire things from our neighbours. We have our uses. We get into places where we are not meant to be. We spy, scout ahead and stuff."

"So I'm guessing this is why you are my chaperon?"

"Pretty much. I will learn from you, and you can learn from me."

They stopped in front of a wall of boxes and crates. "This is why you are here."

"What are these?"

"Stuff we cannot open. Or cannot open without using force and risk damaging what is inside. This is where thieves like me spend our spare time. I thought this might help?"

Ruseq held out Scallion's utility device. The palm-sized transparent tablet was a welcome sight. They were rare, and this was probably his most significant and most valuable asset.

"You know what that is?"

"I have an idea, but I don't know how to use it. Want to help me open some or all of these?"

"Let's get started."

"Good, but first a personal question."

"Sure," replied Scallion.

"Why is your hair two colours? The ends blond but the roots dark?"

Sara and Lonlin were in a long building one level below the surface. Flow and Iyne were following them, to a fashion, as they constantly disappeared only to reappear ahead of them or on a surface beside or above as they passed by. Or they were glimpsed briefly chasing one another crisscrossing their path.

"These are all curios, relics?"

"Most at least, we suspect."

Inside the room were tables, each separated from the next as far as was practically possible across the floor space. Sara counted ten tables, and on each surface was a curio. The majority were a simple cube, but others varied in size and shape.

"This collection has taken hundreds of years to find.

We are immensely proud of this collection as it is the largest outside Borsay. Some other clans have collections too, but not all of them."

"What do they do?"

"Now that's why you are here. What do you know of your gift, your connection?"

"Not much. I can fuse ore to objects and give them a purpose, like programming. The materials meld together to look real. That's how I made the cat."

"Do you know how you do this?"

"No. I just can. I just know."

"We are much the same. We just can. But some 'can' more than others, and some 'can' on a much bigger scale. Some relics have a purpose already designed into them. Others seem to need a specific environment or to be connected to something. Do you know any of this already?"

"No. Where I come from, if you are a connected you are taken from your family and never return. It is said we are taken to the Device, but I don't know for sure. I've never seen a curio or relic before. I've never been trained or told anything about what I can do. It's always been a secret. That is until someone found out and I was taken. Governor Frisk knew that I was a connected, and that's why he held me prisoner."

"Here, hold this," said Lonlin.

Sara took hold of the cube. All six surfaces were white, smooth and untarnished. It was noticeably light in weight and measured only a couple of inches on every side.

"What is it?"

"Turn it on."

"How?"

"Just see if you can."

Sara turned it over and switched it between her hands, examining it, looking for a way to operate it. There was nothing on any of the identical surfaces to give her any clues.

"It's not a switch that you're looking for, it's a thought. You think it to work and it does."

The cube became warm in the palm of her hand.

"Something's happening."

The person that appeared in the holograph before them was unfamiliar. Its appearance startled them both, and Sara nearly dropped the curio but quickly regained her composure when she realised it was an image and not a real person.

They couldn't determine if it was a man or a woman. It was neither vampire nor human. It wore an all-in-one white suit with nothing attached to it, no belt, no weapons, nothing, and a white helmet with a clear faceplate, behind which was a smooth grey face with two large circular blue eyes and a mouth, but nothing resembling a nose. The person had two legs and two arms and was visibly similar to them both, but it wasn't a race either of them recognised. It stood there looking at them, glancing between them.

"Say something," suggested Lonlin in a hushed tone.

"Hello," said Sara.

The image spoke, but neither of them understood the response.

"Do you think it's a comms? Is that someone on the other side, or is it just a hologram?"

"I don't know," replied Lonlin. "Ask it something else?"

"Who are you?"

Again the image voiced an unfamiliar response.

"I don't think it's a real person. It's too still, too unresponsive. Say something more."

"Do you understand me?" continued Sara.

There was a response, but the language was strange and unknown.

"You say something. In vampire."

Lonlin spoke and received a response but in the same language used to reply to Sara.

"What did you say?"

"I told it we are friends and asked it for its name."

"What is your name?" asked Sara.

The image replied.

"That sound, that word, Donkgroy, I think that must be its name. It was in your response too."

"I'm Sara. This is Lonlin." She gestured to each of them to identify with the names and finished by pointing at the image.

"Donkgroy," was the response.

"It understands us," declared Lonlin excitedly.

"Here, you try." Sara pushed the cube into Lonlin's hand, but as soon as she released it the image vanished.

At the end of the day, there was a buzz between the humans. Even the quiet Ninety-Six and isolated Frisk contributed to the enthused chatter around the living space of their building. Jeb had spent the day learning how to use a sword and to shoot a bow. His companion, Ectlor, was a teenage boy like himself, and he had hung out with him and his friends and had enjoyed his day. Sky, like Frisk, had a member of the council for a partner,

Arlet, a one-hundred-year-old female. She had wandered the settlement most of the day speaking with people, discussing issues, concerns and life as a vampire. Frisk had been with Avivas, a two-hundred-year-old male, still very fit and able despite the years, and they had discussed politics. The intricacies of manoeuvrings and scheming in such a field. Ninety-Six had first been amused and bemused by his escort; unlike all the others, his was of the opposite sex. She, Tryha, was also the smallest adult vampire that he had seen throughout the day, smaller even than many of the children, as she stood at only three and a half feet tall. Eighty years old and in charge of managing and maintaining supplies for the settlement, she decided what the patrols hunted, how many and who went out, and what were the scavenging priorities: where they should look, what risks they should take and when.

Their hosts had supplied plenty of wine for their end of day meal. Even the bout of vomiting didn't dampen their mood, as they talked across each other, nipping in and out of different conversations about their day, their experiences and the vampires.

Scallion's hair and clean-shaven face had attracted some passing interest. The blond tips were gone, and he had also changed clothes to match those of the vampires. He smelt clean and fresh and looked it, which made all the others a little self-conscious because although they could wash upstairs, they all wore the same clothes they had worn for several days now.

Slowly they began to retire for the night until only Sky and Demic remained.

"I think Ninety-Six may be right for once," said Demic. "I think the wine does have something in it that loosens the tongue. I would never have expected this group to chat so freely."

"I haven't seen any vampires drinking the wine, come to think of it."

"Oh, I have. I shared a goblet today with Cheter and a couple of others."

"Maybe it doesn't affect them in the same way?" said Sky.

"Have you seen any of them eat… or drink blood?"

"Yes. Not the blood, the eating. I saw what must be stolen rations and supplies from the trains or other places in the homes I visited."

"They've fed us well too. But I've not seen anything that looks like a farm. I'm curious how they feed so many, and the blood-drinking bit is a concern too."

"We've not been here long. Perhaps there's more to see?"

"Perhaps," considered Demic.

"What do you think of Ninety-Six and Frisk?" asked Sky.

"I can understand why Fecting doesn't want to give us weapons. Ninety-Six will only look out for himself and Poppy, though I'm not too sure yet how he views his son. Maybe he would sacrifice him too. I've heard a lot of bad things about him."

"Why do you think he's so distant and quiet? I would have thought he would be pushing us all around, trying to control us. Not only because he's so big but because of who he is."

"If it were anyone else I'd say he was mourning Valerie. If Poppy's their kid then they have been a couple for some time. Or maybe he's just sussing us all out. Who he can recruit, control, bully or who he might have to kill when necessary."

"You don't trust him?" said Sky.

"Not one bit. Why, do you?"

"No. But I don't trust Scallion either, but I think he's on our side?"

"Scallion has always looked out for himself," said Demic. "However, he does sometimes seem to care. Or maybe I just don't see his angle when he does."

"Are you two together?" asked Sky.

"No. We party sometimes but no. Why, you interested?"

"Oh, no, I was simply curious. What about Frisk?"

"Frisk. He's a governor. They're all snakes. We still don't know what he was going to do with your kids or the curio. Up in the lofts, they're the authority. The station masters control much of the day-to-day, but in so far as the hierarchy, the governors are top of the food chain there. We only saw the back corridors when we went up there, but there's a large living area, shop, bars, entertainment and whenever they go out and about they don't pay for anything. That's the kind of power they have at the stations," replied Demic.

"What do you think he'll do now he's with us?" continued Sky.

"Whatever his original plan was for your kids and that curio, I think that's still his plan. He just has to work out how to achieve it."

"What about Poppy?"

"I can't read him. He's not like his father or Valerie. He's not grown up in those circles. I'm guessing he's always been a secret of theirs. And tonight he was talking about religion and some of the vampires' beliefs, and I don't think either Valerie or Ninety-Six have, or had in Valerie's case, a religious bone in their bodies. I don't know about him at all. One to keep an eye on."

"And me?" asked Sky.

"You're all about your kids. That's easy. But we're all a distant second behind them, and I think you'd burn us all to save them. Not that that means I don't trust you. You're a good person. It just means I understand your priorities."

"And you?"

"I'm glad to be outside the stations. I was always watching my back in there. Much more than I need to out here, maybe?"

"You don't want to get back to the stations?"

"No. Do you?" asked Demic.

"I hadn't thought about it until now. But I guess I'm happy here too. So far anyway. I'm not sure about our hosts yet. Did you know that we're classed as property? We belong to Fecting, just like all our supplies do. He can decide our fate any way and any time he wants to, and his people won't challenge him."

"Cheter did say something similar today. How here we'll be treated fairly. Other clans might have already killed us or traded us… or worse."

"What could be worse?" said Sky.

"She didn't elaborate, and I didn't get the chance to find out."

The next morning everyone was collected by the same person they had been with the day before. Sara was last again, but this time Poppy was too, and they left the property as a four.

"We're going to the workshop today," said Lonlin.

"Is that where Scallion was yesterday? With all the broken vehicles and stuff," inquired Sara.

"That will be the place. Then later we will experiment with more of the relics."

"What are we doing later?" asked Poppy.

"That all depends on what happens after the workshop," replied Pec.

The functional vehicles formed the front rows that they needed to walk through. Then there were broken, partly disassembled carriages of all sizes and shapes. Beyond those were more workbenches, stacks and piles of parts arranged in some form of order that was evident, but how they were all categorised wasn't apparent to either Sara or Poppy. They moved through the workshop, passing workers; the place was a hive of activity. They saw Scallion over to one side, but he didn't see them.

"Here, pick one." Pec pointed at several piles and rows of broken and damaged botdrones. There were all shapes and sizes, but he was indicating the humanoid ones.

"Pick what?" asked Poppy. "A botdrone?"

"No, a new left arm. We are going to give you an arm today."

Poppy looked at Sara, who in turn looked back at him, equally perplexed.

Pec tapped his own prosthetic. "Like this one. You can have a new arm, but pick carefully, because once it's connected it will be permanent."

"How?"

"Don't concern yourself about that, Poppy. Just pick the one you like," encouraged Lonlin.

"Will it hurt?"

"No. It will feel strange, but it won't hurt. I think

mine's better than my real leg ever was."

He rummaged through the various arms with the help of the others. Some were attached to botdrones, others loose, until they found one that they all agreed was nice.

They left the workshop and took a route back through the settlement to where the relics were stored. This time, though, they stayed on the ground floor of the building. Here, like the floor below, were arranged spaced tables – eight tables, but six were empty, with only two supporting relics.

One table was covered by a blanket and removing it they could see a top imprinted with the shape of a body. The table itself was the relic. It had eight legs, and ten sections that allowed the moulded body to be stretched out or shortened both in width and length. Other than that, it looked like a regular table, currently six feet long and three feet wide.

"Get on then," said Pec excitedly. "I like this part."

The surface of the table was cold and smooth, and they had no idea what material it was constructed from, but it felt hard beneath Poppy.

"Right, Lonlin and I are going to adjust it. You just have to tell us when you're comfortable."

The sections slid effortlessly, adjusted so that Poppy lay within the moulded impression until he declared himself comfortable.

Then Pec placed the botdrone's left arm in the indent where Poppy's arm should have been.

"Now you turn it on." Lonlin was speaking to Sara.

"Me?"

"Yes. It's no different to what you were doing yesterday with those downstairs."

"But I know nothing about healing or medicines," said Sara.

"You don't have to. You just think of it. I put the leg on Pec. It was only my second time, but it was simple."

"Then you do the arm," she suggested.

"No. I know our physiology. I don't know yours, and I'm uncertain whether that is an important factor. You have to do this."

"When did you do his leg?"

"Twenty-one years ago," answered Pec.

"How old are you, Lonlin?"

"I'm fifty-seven."

Sara had thought that she was of an age similar to herself. Another teenager, like Jeb's chaperon.

"How old are you, Pec?"

"I'm thirty-three."

"Then you were smaller and younger when you got your leg. How often have you changed it?"

"You don't have to. It grows with you. Like I told you, it's permanent."

"Hey, are we doing this or not?" asked Poppy. "I would really like to try this if I can get my arm back. Even a botdrone arm would be really good. I miss my arm."

"What do I do?" asked Sara.

"Touch the table and imagine the arm attaching itself to Poppy. That's it."

Sara relaxed. She had activated four curios the day before and all with ease. She placed her hand on the table and closed her eyes to help her focus and imagine the outcome. The table's surface became warm.

"It's getting warm," stated Poppy, a tremor of concern in his voice.

"That's normal," replied Pec and Lonlin.

Sara felt the energy flow as she connected with the curio, and as she opened her eyes, the botdrone arm was transforming before her. Tentacle-like wires snaked out of the arm and linked with Poppy's stump. They penetrated his skin, but he showed no signs of pain. The left arm drew itself to join the stump. The fusion between skin and metal blurred where one stopped and the other began. It reminded her of when she had made Flow, but this time there was no ore involved. Then the visible metallic joints and plates started to melt into each other, becoming as smooth and seamless as an ore-drone's. The realisation that ODs must be made by other connected dawned on Sara. The energy passing from Sara to the curio stopped, and she withdrew her hand.

"Is it done?" asked Poppy with a mix of trepidation and excitement. As he spoke, he raised his left arm to look at it for himself.

"Wow. It feels real." He reached over with his right hand to stroke his left arm. "I can feel that; this is amazing. How long will it last?"

"It is part of your body now. It will last as long as you do." Lonlin was touching the left arm as she spoke. "This is excellent work, Sara. You are incredibly talented. The joints are perfect."

Sara looked at Pec's leg, and although the joints were almost invisible, they were still evident, unlike those on Poppy's new arm.

"Okay. I'll take Poppy away now," said Pec "I'm sure he wants to use his new arm and show it off. I'll leave you gifted to your experiments."

"It's Celebration Day tomorrow. Did anyone else know that?" asked Scallion when they were all once again assembled in their lodgings that evening.

"Yes," replied Ninety-Six. "And we are all invited, for those who didn't get a personal invite."

"So what's Celebration Day?" asked Sara. She and Lonlin had been too preoccupied with the curios, and Celebration Day hadn't arisen in their conversations. Their findings had been too engrossing. Lonlin had disclosed to her that she was the clan's most potent gifted of only three. The gifted were rare, and why her clan had so many was a mystery but considered a blessing. Other clans had never had a gifted, and of those that did, theirs were often taken to Borsay. All the relics in the lower level were those that she couldn't activate. Sara had managed to activate them all, but not all their functionality could be recognised immediately. They had decided that they would take each curio out into the settlement tomorrow to see if it revealed more of its purpose. They had spent time with the holographic image of the white cube trying to establish a language communication but had so far not achieved any meaningful dialogue.

"Celebration Day is a vampire feast," elaborated Ninety-Six.

"Does that mean blood?" asked Scallion nervously. "And if it does, it's not our blood, is it?"

"Yes, it means blood. And no, it's not our blood. This day occurs once every few weeks. Tryha told me all about it, but I'd rather not explain it. I think we should all just attend and stay calm."

"Stay calm!" There was definite unease in Scallion's voice.

"Scallion, it's nothing to worry about. Yes, they drink blood, but not ours. Don't get caught up in your own imagination. This is why humans persecuted them from the day they encountered them, because of silly superstitions and old legends. Just remain open-minded and observe. Now, I'm getting some rest." Ninety-Six rose and went to the stairs heading for sleep. "Oh, there is one thing, though. If they needed to drink human blood, they could do. They just choose not to."

Scallion's face went pale, and Ninety-Six chuckled with morbid humour as he knew the effect that remark would have on Scallion's imagination. "Have sweet dreams, Scallion," called the big man from the top of the stairs.

That evening it was Poppy and Sara that were the last to retire. The small man was still overawed by his new arm and unable to relax enough to sleep. Sara was self-absorbed with her own discoveries. A connected was more than just someone who could interact with ore. She had put a botdrone arm on a human. She had summoned what appeared to be another race in a hologram. She was more powerful, or potent as Lonlin described it, than any other gifted in the clan. She had no idea of her potential, or what she might be able to achieve with the curios. Were they all safe? Were any of them weapons? What if she hurt someone? She was also now a little warier of Frisk. Once he had seen what Sara had done with Poppy's arm, his attention to it and his subsequent questions had worried her. Sky too shared her daughter's concern, and she warned her to keep away from him.

The following morning they were delivered their meal and goblets of 'retch', but were also advised that they wouldn't be collected for a while as people were preparing for Celebration Day. A couple of hours later, they heard music and could sense an uplift in mood across the settlement. A little while after that, all their chaperons arrived together, dressed a little more colourfully than the normal day-to-day, and their clothes were more extravagant.

"For the dancing," disclosed Tryha, giving them all a twirl, and her garments billowed out as she did so.

They left their home and joined a procession of vampires and dispersed throughout them were also canines. Music played, rhythmically, with a steady beat. The pulse reverberated throughout the subterranean hollow like the heart of a living thing. The procession, everyone in the clan, moved along dancing, singing and rejoicing.

"You do this every few weeks?" Scallion confirmed with Ruseq.

"We do. We need to. It's essential to our wellbeing."

The parade left the line of the last buildings and crossed the roadway towards a dark opening. From there, in pitch darkness, they descended, music reverberating from every surface.

"The torches are for you. Stay between them. This is so you can see what is happening. We do not normally have light in here." This was communicated to each human as their guides left them.

Ahead were two long parallel lines of burning torches on tall poles. They had entered a vast cavern. They couldn't see the sides or the roof but the change in sound and air told them they had exited the tunnel. The vampires now stamped their feet and danced in time with the increasing beat of the music. The ground shook, trembling beneath them, and it was only when a giant worm broke the surface that they realised the ground had indeed been moving beneath them.

A massive scarlet-red worm breached the ground head first. As it rose, its eight jaws opened, splaying out like the long petals of a flower revealing row after row of spikey teeth. By the light of the torches, they could see an expanse of teeth stretching over a fifty-foot diameter mouth before it disappeared up into the darkness. The body of the worm kept ascending for hundreds of feet. Then it stopped, and in time with it coming to rest, the music ceased.

The vampires had formed a series of circles around the worm. A single voice cried out into the darkness and, in unison, every vampire responded. The front row moved towards the scarlet worm, and as they did so, the scales that covered its body folded in on themselves like thousands of fans, exposing soft pink flesh beneath. The two incisor fangs of the advancing vampires extended, and when they reached the flesh, they bit and drank; blood ran down the side of the worm as it was lapped it up.

The worm closed its lower scales and reduced its length by a couple of feet, exposing a fresh layer of pink flesh. The vampires engaged once again and drank. Once a vampire at the front had sated his or her thirst, they dropped back into the crowd behind them, creating an outer circle of people, and the next vampire took their place, and this continued until everyone had drunk enough blood.

At the base of the worm, the earth was slick and shiny in the torchlight where blood had pooled on the ground. Not one of the humans had spoken or moved throughout the spectacle. They had passed through all manner of emotional responses as they stood transfixed: horror, fear, astonishment, bewilderment, surprise and more. They had never seen or imagined such a scene in their craziest dreams or nightmares.

Once the last vampire had fed, and the circles were all reformed, a single voice once again cried out, and the vampires responded in a loud chorus. Before the echo of their voices had died, the music began again, but this time it was more lyrical, less of a pulsing beat, and a song broke out to accompany the melody. As the music played, the worm descended and vanished, and the parade reassembled and moved back towards the tunnel.

The humans were now ignored as the last vampire disappeared, and they realised that they needed to follow. Ninety-Six and Demic uprooted a torch each and led the way.

chapter eight

Curios and Connected

Two days after the celebration, Sara and Lonlin had made particularly good progress in identifying the unknown curios. Sara could unlock them, but Lonlin had the experience needed to test them and identify their purpose, or at least part of their functionality. Sara hadn't discussed her findings with the other humans, as she feared Frisk gaining any of the knowledge and what he might do with it.

Lonlin had begun Sara's education by demonstrating the two curios on the first floor for her. Both started as simple dull cubes, two inches square. When Lonlin activated the first, it transformed into a belt that she fastened around her waist. The second became a morning star, a weapon consisting of a spiked ball mounted on a shaft, with a long spike extending straight from the top and many smaller spikes around the sphere. While wielding the weapon, Lonlin activated the belt and it appeared to unfold itself, covering the vampire from head to toe in a flexible armour suit that was capable of absorbing the impact of a blaster or a ballistic handgun. The mace could release one or all of its spikes as lethal projectiles that returned to the ball on completion of their trajectory. It was also capable of a devastating strike that could demolish a wall or door with minimal physical effort from the wielder. She didn't demonstrate any of those capabilities as she didn't want to cause any damage or destruction inside the settlement. However, Sara donned the belt and wielded the morning star to understand them better before returning them to their tables.

Lonlin explained that Dimii, one of their gifted, now resided in Borsay. He was there to learn and represent their clan. Being gifted, he would be afforded respect by all vampires, and his presence there would also stand their clan well and afford them good representation over any of the Great Council's affairs. Iscrea, the other gifted, was out in the field undertaking whatever task the clan's council had set him. All three gifted were trained warriors, and due to their abilities were selected for missions that utilised their skills and the relics they could operate. Iscrea had taken five of the missing six relics from the first floor with him: an armour belt, a morning star, a shield worn as a bracelet, a ring that allowed a person to walk through solid walls and doors, and a communication device.

Lonlin carried another communication device with her at all times. It was a rectangular block that fitted in the palm of her hand. When triggered, it allowed direct communication to any other similar device provided that you also knew that device. It was remarkably similar in appearance to the comms used by humans, and meant that Iscrea, while out in the field, could communicate visually, vocally or by sending a text message securely with Lonlin at any time. However, as they didn't yet fully understand the device, it was only ever used when necessary.

The ten curios in the basement had taken time to understand, and even that knowledge was limited, but their time had provided some greater awareness of them. The holographic image had taken to pointing at objects and asking for its name. However, within the confines of the lower floor, there wasn't much for them to continually identify. There was another belt that, like the armour suit, covered Sara in a flexible outfit. It wasn't armoured as far as they were able to establish, and unlike the other suit, the visor inside had a display of readings, but the symbols and graphical representations weren't something they could understand. Although Lonlin couldn't activate the cube, they discovered she was able to wear the belt and activate the suit.

Another curio, stored as a cube, revealed a pair of goggles when transformed. When placed over the eyes, these adjusted themselves to fit the face perfectly. At first, there had been no apparent purpose other than as a protective covering. However, on experimentation, they allowed Sara to see in the dark, much like the vampires' natural ability.

One of the cubes became a headband, but other than that, they were unable to learn anything more about it. A further cube activated but didn't transform into anything. It emitted a soft vibrating hum, and it was only by accident that they discovered a potential for its use. Sara, while holding the device, had sat on one of the tables and the table had risen from the floor. They decided that it somehow defied gravity and took it to the workshop to test it. Mounting one of the heaviest derelict vehicles, Sara had activated the cube and the whole vehicle had risen from the floor, which had attracted the attention of the engineers nearby.

They had several small vehicles in the workshop, in working order, that hovered above the ground already. However, those vehicles utilised engineering for lifting and propelling them. The relic required no engineering to achieve its lifting. Sara and Lonlin decided to leave the cube inside the vehicle and dismounted. To their surprise, the curio remained active and the carriage remained in the air. After discussion with the engineers, they left the device with the vehicle for them to research.

Two small flat discs, six inches in diameter, offered another puzzle that they quickly solved, again, accidentally. Sara had activated a small spherical curio that was a little less than half an inch in diameter. On triggering the relic, an exact copy of her had appeared by her side. This had startled her, and she had dropped the sphere, which had landed on one of the discs while that too was active. Her doppelganger disappeared when she released the device, as did the sphere when it landed on the disc, but it instantly reappeared on top of the other disc on the other table. Lonlin had picked up the spherical relic, and a replica of her had materialised beside her. She touched her copy, and it was solid, not a hologram. She willed the twin to walk over to Sara, and it did so.

She returned the sphere to Sara by placing it on the disc adjacent to her, and it disappeared, again moving from one disc to the other. They paid another visit to the workshop and were greeted excitedly by the engineers who had begun working on the floating carriage and had fitted a working engine. They had been unsure how that would be able to transmit motion, but it had. When the wheels of the vehicle turned, the carriage had moved in proportion to the energy released from the engine. They had also loaded as much weight onto and inside the vehicle as was possible and it hadn't sunk any lower. On learning that the two women had brought them another functioning relic, they immediately offered any available assistance.

They placed one disc on the floor at one end of the workshop, and the other as far away as possible at the other end in an open space. An engineer volunteered to drive a small vehicle over one of the discs. No one stopped him, in their curiosity and excitement not considering the risk to the person, or if they did, they were willing to learn by any means.

Once the centre of the carriage was directly over the first disc the vehicle disappeared and reappeared over the second disc. Sara and Lonlin left the activated curios with the workshop for further experimentation.

The final two cubes transformed into unknown objects. The first was a narrow pin-like shaft of eight inches with a circular head that was flat on top but engraved on the underside where the pin extended. They couldn't derive any purpose for this. The other enlarged and sprouted spines from its upper surface, giving it the look of a pot of flowers with fourteen stems, but without the flowers at their heads. The purpose of this too couldn't be discovered.

Each curio that Sara activated she shared with Lonlin. The vampire hadn't been able to activate or deactivate any with her ability. However, she had been able to interact with and use all of them once Sara had turned them on. The last thing they discovered at the end of the day was that the holographic image could be activated and left active when Sara placed it down.

"Fecting and the council have declared that you can remove any of the relics from this storage area provided you do not leave the settlement with them and that you return them."

"I can? What will I do with them?" said Sara.

"That is up to you. You may discover more about them while you have them, and they may function differently in a different setting. The only way to know is to experiment with them."

"Fecting is okay with this?"

"It was his suggestion," confirmed Lonlin.

"I'm wary of Frisk though. I don't trust him, and he kidnapped me and my brother and stole the cylindrical curio with some plan in mind."

"The council are aware of that, and they say that you should not worry about Frisk. They are dealing with this on your behalf and are hoping to have a resolution soon."

"Dealing with what, and what resolution?" asked Sara.

"That I don't know. But I do know they want you to be safe more than anything. So I wouldn't worry about Frisk."

"All right then, I'll take some of the curios, relics, and see what else I can learn."

"We appreciate you, Sara. The relics and their use are an almost sacred thing to our people, and as you can activate more of them, we are beholden to you for that. This will give our clan more standing with the Great Council and win you more favour with them too."

"Do you know what the cylinder does?"

"I have not yet been allowed to handle it. Fecting has it now and is deciding what to do with it."

"Does that mean he knows what it is?"

"I am not sure, but normally I am the first to handle any relic to establish its purpose, if possible. This has not happened on this occasion."

That evening, along with their regular serving of food, there arrived fresh, clean clothing freshly made within the settlement and tailored to human styles. They hadn't been measured for their clothing, but later, as the evening progressed and each of them gradually washed and changed, they all commented on how well the clothes fit.

Scallion had gained significant attention early in the evening, as he had returned with a large ballistic gun holstered on his left hip with the grip forward. It was a heavy calibre weapon with a revolving chamber where seven bullets could be loaded. The design was new to the humans and Scallion referred to it as a revolver, as this is what Ruseq had called it when he had given it to him. He was the first among them to be trusted with a weapon. The belt, integral to the holster, bore sleeves that held more bullets. Ten of the pockets held additional shells while others were empty. Scallion boasted that the weapon was powerful enough to down an armoured botdrone with a single shot. He had nearly broken his wrist the first time he had fired it as the recoil was so severe. Demic and Ninety-Six had shown the most interest in the weapon, and Scallion had been concerned that they might try to take it from him, but they hadn't.

Sara had placed the cube of the holographic alien race to one side and activated it. The image interacted with everyone willing to try and converse with it as best it could. It had initially gained everyone's attention, but as the evening wound on, it was left observing as the humans discussed other matters. Sara also revealed other curio devices that she shared among them to examine and try out. The two belts were tried on and activated, and the morning star wielded, but no one attempted to use any of its functions. The goggles with night-vision were of great interest to Demic and Scallion, while the narrow pin-like shaft with a circular head and the cube that sprouted spines baffled everyone, but they all had a suggestion for what they might be.

The final device Sara revealed was the headband, declaring that this curio too was still a mystery.

"Sara, Sara." Poppy was trying to gain her attention.

"What is it, Poppy?"

"Look. The holographic alien seems to be extremely interested in the headband."

She walked over to the image and offered it the curio.

The hologram indicated that Sara should wear the device, gesturing for her to place it on her head. Cautiously she complied, and no sooner was it in place, and contracted to fit comfortably, than it began to tingle. The tingle increased to a throb that started to become painful, and Sara removed it quickly.

"What happened?" asked Poppy, noting that the hologram looked a little disappointed, or something similar to that emotion as it was difficult to read its features and expressions.

"It started to get painful."

"Maybe that's what it should do."

"Maybe, but I'll try it again tomorrow with Lonlin. If it does something I don't like, I'd rather have another connected with me to help."

The following morning Sara couldn't wait to raise the question of the headband with Lonlin. She in turn wanted to know how the humans had received the relics. Both were so excited that they spoke over each other for the first few moments. Finally, Sara conceded to her companion.

"So how were the relics received?"

"Great. Everyone tried them out. Demic thinks the other suit is some kind of survival or habitat suit. She thinks the readings are both representations of the wearer and the conditions outside the suit. Ninety-Six was very keen to operate the morning star, but we all agreed an open space should be where we first try that."

"So you could all use the devices?"

"Yes. Once I activated them, they were all free for anyone to use."

"That doesn't happen for us."

"What do you mean?" asked Sara.

"Only gifted can use the relics. When other vampires try to use them, even when activated, they do nothing."

"But we left the cube and discs in the workshop yesterday, and the engineers worked with them?"

"They weren't personal or user devices. They were some sort of general utility. In truth, this is the first time we have seen or heard of devices like that. Fecting has already sent word of all this to the Great Council."

"Maybe we should see if vampires can use them now I've activated them?"

"That was exactly what I was about to suggest. Oh, one small thing. If we are going to be going to Borsay, you should know that we do not like the term vampire. We, as people, are neway."

Sara was remorseful. She hadn't known this, and none of the other humans had mentioned it. She promised to let them know.

Lonlin took Sara to Fecting and the council, who were waiting with a small group of neway volunteers. As she had done the evening before, Sara activated the curios and then shared them among the group. Everyone was now able to interact with the relics. The excitement and chatter, in their language, was ecstatic. The atmosphere was palpable in the room and charged with potential, eagerness and exhilaration.

Fecting escalated the excitement when he ordered that all the relics were to be taken out of the settlement and experimented with, in an open space. Sara squealed with delight when she heard that she and Lonlin were to go with the group and work with them to identify their capabilities.

The world outside the burrow of the neway was a wonderous place to Sara. She had to correct her gawping on more than one occasion as she took in the beauty of the landscape. The others had already told her that it wasn't the bleached, scorched and dead lands they had always been told. That instead it was lush, fertile and full of diverse wildlife.

Sara instantly fell in love with the outside and never wanted to leave or return to any station again. Then a sadness came over her as she finally understood why the neway wanted to return to the surface and live in freedom without the persecution of the invading humans and their botdrones.

The group had taken three vehicles, the largest mounted with a turret gun. Six of them plus Sara and Lonlin would work with the relics to fathom more of their functionality. The other eight would watch their perimeter and the skies for any threats.

After a couple of hours of experimenting, both Sara and Lonlin sat on top of one of the carriers with the cat and the tieve beside them watching the others. Sara sucked in a deep breath of the clean air, deciding that the sickness each night was worth the compromise of not having to wear a mask outside. She didn't notice the taint anymore. Her throat no longer felt as though tiny insects clawed at it when she breathed without a mask. The natural smells were so much better and more varied to what she now realised was only stale air within the stations.

"I think I might know what this is for." Lonlin was holding the needle-like relic. "I had completely forgotten. It's been so long now, but there is a small hole with a circular groove on the table. The one you used to attached Poppy's arm. I never found a use for the hole, but this looks like it might fit, and the design on the head looks similar to the design inside the slot."

"We should try it when we get back."

"Yes."

"Oh, and we need to see why the hologram is so interested in the headband too."

One of the sentries called out urgently.

"What is it?" asked Sara, not understanding the words but noting everyone running for the cover of the vehicles.

"Something in the sky. Botdrones. We need to hide."

All three vehicles had netting over them: camouflage to help them blend into the terrain. No one entered a vehicle, but everyone ducked beneath the nets and waited.

A single craft flew over them. It was high in the sky but low enough to make out some of the details. It wasn't teardrop-shaped like the shuttle. It was longer, cylinder-shaped, with guns at the front, rear and underside.

"A hunter," remarked Lonlin. "These come from the Device. They scour the skies looking for my people, and any they find they open fire upon without fail. We do not see as many now as we once did, but they are to be avoided. Our turret gun would do little against one of these."

It passed by, and everyone returned to their previous tasks.

One of the other neway came over to Sara and Lonlin. "I'm going hunting, Lonlin. But you and Sara should remain here. I need to see what the morning star does to flesh, so it's an ideal opportunity to hunt."

"That's Oneiwa. He's the same age as me," explained Lonlin. "Acts like my big brother, but we're not related."

"Something more than a brother maybe," suggested Sara.

"No. We did kiss once when I was your age."

Sara still found that strange, and when she spoke with Lonlin she felt as though she was with another teenager, her age. Then she remembered that Lonlin was in her fifties.

"We didn't speak for several months after that kiss. But it's all forgotten now."

"Do neway get married?"

"Married?"

"It's when two people bond to each other as a couple, forsaking other relationships. It's a religious thing among humans. Not everyone does it, but some do. Others just partner up. Some stay together, but others just have sex and move on. I've never been with anyone like that."

"Yes. We call it ghiohly. That's when two people make a union. It's also a religious thing with us. We have three religions, but only one preaches ghiohly."

"What about the other two?"

"One states that parents should stay together until any born child is an adult. To us, that is fourteen years. The other has no requirements for what people do in this manner."

"Do you fall in love?"

"Yes, but as we can live close to or over three hundred years and remain active until we die, it can be a fickle and fleeting thing. Though I must add it's not for all. It is said that Fecting loved in his early years and still does. This is apparently why he has not taken another partner since he lost her. So, if that's true, then for some love must last."

Lainlof and Plirtgh returned having tried out the survival suit underwater at a nearby river. They spoke in human for Sara's benefit and declared that Demic's suggestion might well be correct. Both of them had dived beneath the surface of the water and still been able to breathe. The water had been cold too, but neither of them had felt the chill. The readings inside the helmet had changed while they had been testing the suit, but they still had no idea what they meant.

"I can see why Iscrea takes the other morning star out into the field with him." Oneiwa had returned from his hunt with a large buck of some dead animal slung over his shoulders, an eoa, a grazing herbivore that was particularly tasty when cooked and prepared. With everyone now back at the vehicles, they decided it was time to return.

They were out in the open on the return journey when the hunter in the sky found them. They had seen it before it had seen them and so the three vehicles were already splitting off from each other to take evasive manoeuvres. They couldn't lead it back to the burrow, so they needed to lose it and hide.

Before it was out of sight, the largest of the vehicles, with the turret gun, exploded as the hunter scored a hit, while the other guns trained on the remaining two vehicles fired. Sara held on tight as the driver zigzagged, taking anything but a predictable straight line.

"We have to go back and help them," called Sara.

"It's too late, they're gone," answered the driver.

"No, I saw the vehicle roll and people jumping. It wasn't a direct hit."

"Oneiwa was on that carriage. We have to try," added Lonlin.

"It will be suicide." But the driver, Lainlof, was already turning back. A gun blast missed them by inches, shaking the vehicle and tipping it to the point that it almost rolled, but to everyone's relief it dropped back, and they sped on.

Then the gunfire stopped.

"Look, the hunter's veering off." Plirtgh was pointing to the sky.

"What's it doing?" asked Lainlof.

"No idea. It's stopped firing and seems to be turning away to leave us."

"Not possible. They never do that."

Lonlin nudged Sara and indicated towards Flow. The cat was stationary, statue-like, and even with the vehicle still performing rapid and sharp evasive manoeuvres, it stayed in the same spot in the vehicle's rear storage space. Sara reached out to it, but Lonlin stopped her. "What's it doing?" she asked.

"I don't know," said Sara, and she put her hand on the cat.

"It's controlling the hunter. She's stopping the guns and sending it away."

"How do you know that?"

"I can sense it now. I'm connected to her, and I know what she's doing."

"Do you know how?"

"She has comms ore in her build, and that's allowing her to control the hunter. She's overriding the ship's systems."

The vehicle slid to a stop, and the three neway riding with Lonlin and Sara jumped out, calling to any survivors of the overturned and smashed vehicle. In a short time, they dragged and carried four survivors into their carriage. Everyone was alive. They had grazes, bruises and cuts but nothing serious.

"Get out of here now, quickly." Lonlin's voice was laced with urgency. "The hunter's gone, but it might come back."

They sped away, everyone but the driver watching the skies. When they reached the rolling hills, they dropped from any horizon and slowed. They needed to be sure the hunter wasn't observing them before they could return to the burrow.

Flow relaxed and returned to her normal, gentle cat mode.

"The hunter's lost us," stated Sara. "It's safe to return now."

Lainlof looked to Lonlin for guidance, who nodded in agreement with Sara.

"We lost a vehicle," said Fecting, "but if what you say

is true, it was worth the sacrifice."

Lonlin took Sara and Flow directly to the settlement leader, disembarking from the vehicle outside his home before the others returned it to the workshop.

"So the OD, Flow, took control of the hunter. Are you certain?"

"Yes," Sara replied to Fecting. "When I touched her, I was able to know what she was doing. Not how she was doing it exactly, but I knew what she was doing."

"Has Iyne, your tieve, ever done anything like this?"

"No, not that I know of," replied Lonlin.

"Has the cat done anything like this before?"

"I'm told it climbed inside a botdrone and operated it," replied Sara, "and the others suspect that she somehow stopped the elite from Station Eight locating the shuttle when it crashed. But this is the first time I've seen any of this."

"The cat doesn't speak?"

"No. I don't think I put that in her programming when I created her. I wanted a cat," replied Sara.

"So we don't know if it can do it again?"

"Ma said she spoke when she was inside the botdrone. That she used the botdrone's vocal unit. Maybe we can find a way for her to speak using another botdrone?"

"We do not have any functioning botdrones here," replied Fecting.

"But we do have broken ones," interjected Lonlin. "The broken ones will have vocal units. Maybe we can use one of them."

"That's a good suggestion. You can try this first thing tomorrow?" suggested Fecting.

"We could do it now," offered Sara.

"You've been through an ordeal today. Your first of that kind, I am assuming. Being fired upon by a hunter is a daunting thing. You should rest first. It's late, and you will no doubt vomit soon."

"You forget, I was shot down in a shuttle not too many days ago."

"Then I will leave it with you two to decide what needs doing. You are the gifted. Such things are beyond my understanding. But do let me know what you discover."

"What else can we do?"

They were walking towards the workshop when Sara asked Lonlin the question.

"What do you mean?"

"We can create an OD. We can activate curios. What else?"

"I don't know. All the gifted I know of have created an OD, as you call it. Why we do that, we don't know, but the urge to do so is overwhelmingly compelling. We can activate relics, some better than others, depending on how potent the gift is. I've never thought about whether we have other abilities."

"We should experiment on us too then. We might be able to do more?"

"We can start tomorrow. Let's see if we can get Flow to talk, and maybe Iyne too?"

Sara placed the cat among the broken botdrones and asked her to find a voice. They watched then as she moved among the broken and damaged parts, seemingly searching with Iyne close to her tail. Several times she disappeared, moving under, around or looking inside cavities. Finally, Flow returned with something held in her mouth.

They examined the mechanical device, a small cone only a quarter of an inch tall and wide with a couple of wires protruding from it. The tieve returned moments later with another cone.

"What do we do with these?" asked Sara. She was speaking to Lonlin, but Flow pawed at her legs to get her attention.

Sara picked the cat up and understood what she wanted.

"It's a receiver," she told Lonlin. "Flow wants me to fit it to myself using the table."

"What will it do?"

"I'll be able to hear her then. Sorry, not hear her… communicate with her. It's not a vocal unit but better."

"So she won't be speaking then?"

"It's outside her programming. Maybe you should spread the word that any new ODs your gifted create should be programmed to speak," said Sara.

"I don't know if they can. We all make an animal. It's what we do. Perhaps they aren't supposed to speak as botdrones do?"

"Do you want to go to the table now?"

"Yes, if you do."

"I'll go tell my ma where we are on the way, though. She'll be worried," said Sara.

Sara lay on the table while Lonlin adjusted the sections to make her comfortable.

"So how do we do this? Do you touch the table and perform the work on me, or do I touch it and do it myself?" said Sara.

"You are the more potent. I would suggest you do it.

And I'm not a human. I still think that may have some effect on the outcome."

Sara held the device behind her left ear and touched the table with the flat of her other hand. The whole surface became warm, and Lonlin watched as the cone and protruding wires sank beneath the skin.

She giggled. Then scratched and stroked the skin behind her left ear. "Nice to meet you too," she said aloud. "Ah, understood."

"So did it work?"

"Yes, I can communicate with Flow. It's like when I touched her in the vehicle and she was controlling the hunter. I know what she's doing or wants. It's not words, it's just I know."

"Can you speak to her?"

"Yes, but it's not a conversation. I convey meaning and I get a response. It's extraordinary. It will take some getting used to. And you're right that none of our familiars can speak in the way we do. That's why they call themselves familiars. They communicate with each other too. Oh! It seems that's it for now. She has nothing else to say. They want to play?"

Flow and Iyne pounced on each other, rolled around on the floor, and then ran off with the cat chasing the tieve.

"Seems they do have the characteristics and ways of the animal we create them to be. Flow is still young, and her moments of being an OD only intermittently override her desire to be a cat."

"Well, that's more than we knew before. Can she control a hunter again?" asked Lonlin.

"Her core programming is to protect my family and me. That's what I created her to do. So if it protects me, yes, but I don't think she can do it on command. I can't order her to do it. Maybe when I get a better understanding of all this I might be able to though?"

"Should I implant the cone too?"

"I don't see why not," said Sara.

"But I've never communicated with Iyne as you did in the carriage when the hunter was firing on us. Maybe I'm not able to?"

"Only one way to find out."

"Your work is better than mine, will you do it for me?" asked Lonlin.

"What about the fact I'm human and you're not?"

"I will risk it. It's not a major thing, so it might be all right. It might be all right anyway. There may not be limitations due to species?"

Sara adjusted the table for Lonlin and implanted the cone behind her left ear.

"Anything?"

"No, nothing, but they are playing at the moment so let's give it some time. While we are here, maybe we should see what this does?" Lonlin held up the pin-like relic.

The engraving on the underside of the head matched that in the recess of the table, and so they inserted the pin and it clicked into place.

"Now what?"

"I'll lie on the table and see what happens." Sara climbed onto the surface, and they adjusted it to be comfortable. Then she placed both of her hands palm down to energise the curio, and it became warm.

"Nothing's happening," said Sara.

"I'm not too sure of that. Your scar. The one on your head from the crash. It's fading away."

Sara reached up to feel the welt that had been there, and it was gone. "I think it must heal, or something like that. I have an idea, but we'll need to wait until morning."

"There's too much happening, and I'm not sleepy. Do you want to try the headband now before we retire for the night?"

"I need a bucket," said Sara, and Lonlin raced to find one and returned just in time for the vomit.

"I wonder if there's a curio to let me breathe the taint, so I don't need to vomit every day?" considered Sara as she stood from the bucket with eyes wide, wet and bloodshot from her ordeal. "Okay, let's try the headband."

With the holographic alien activated, Sara placed the headband on and waited for it to contract into place.

"If I collapse or anything bad, remove it," Sara requested of Lonlin.

It began to tingle, then to throb, and then it became painful. This time Sara endured the pain as it increased, and after only a few seconds it settled out at a plateau similar to a mild headache. The torment lasted for less than a minute, and then it stopped. The headband remained in place, but Sara knew it was now dormant.

"Well?" asked Lonlin, noting that Sara's screwed-up face had relaxed.

"I don't know."

"Hello, I am Donkgroy." The holograph was addressing them both.

"You speak our language? Is that the headband? Can you hear it, Lonlin?"

"Yes, I hear it."

"The headband allowed me access to your mind, where I was able to extract the necessary learning to understand your language. I am a chronicle and repository for learning and reference. How may I serve you?"

"What are you?"

"I chronicle your journal and serve as a repository for knowledge. Am I to serve you both or one of you?"

"You need to give a little bit more detail. We don't understand your function. And what exactly are you? Are you a person, an OD or something else?"

"I am intelligence, not sentient, but capable of cognitive choices. I keep track of your daily, important and historical events in calendar order so they can be analysed and referred back to as needed. I also store knowledge and learning for future references, such as your language. This has now been chronicled and can be utilised."

"Do I need to wear this headband all the time then?"

"No. That is a separate device. It allows the transference of knowledge at a significant speed that would otherwise take substantial time to learn and understand by more traditional methods."

"What are you?"

"I'm a chronicle and repository ..."

"No, I mean you are different. I am human. Lonlin is neway. What race are you?"

"I am a representation of an ohnsae. My image is the default. I can change my profile to be anything that you choose, human, neway, male or female."

"What is an ohnsae?"

"They are the race that created me and the headband that you wear."

"Where are they now?"

"I do not know. This is my initial activation. I have not been activated since my creation until now. I have only my basic but comprehensive programming and repository references at this time."

"Do you know what this is?" asked Lonlin, as she held out the cube with the fourteen stems sprouting from its surface.

"It is a rain-maker. It is used to gather atmospheric conditions suitable to create rain."

"And this?" Lonlin held out the suspected survival suit in cube form.

"That is a habitat suit. It allows the wearer to survive in any known climate, though it has limitations. The language I have from you does not give me the scales I need to translate the high- and low-temperature limits for you."

chapter NINE

The Journey to Borsay

Fecting himself arrived at the humans' residence the following morning as their food and the retch was delivered. He was accompanied by Lonlin and keen to see Sara, but the young woman was still sleeping, having been out late the night before. Sky offered to wake her, but the clan's leader declined the offer and said she should be allowed to continue her sleep. At the same time, he reminded Lonlin to ensure that her ward received her chqaqaie when she did rise.

Before departing, Fecting advised them all that they would be leaving for Borsay in a couple of days. That was a three-day journey by vehicle, and they should all discuss this with their chaperons as the journey wasn't without risks. He then left, asking Lonlin to come to see him with Sara once she was awake and ready.

"He could have demanded that you wake your daughter," offered Frisk.

Sky had no liking for the governor, and he had done nothing while they had been together to give her any reason to reconsider her opinion.

"Maybe he's just a nice person." The dig and implication that Frisk was not such a nice person were quite evident by her tone.

"You do know they hold the connected in high regard, don't you? Almost with religious reverence, and your daughter is the most powerful gifted they have ever encountered."

"I'm aware, yes. But you'd better keep your distance from her."

Demic stepped in to manoeuvre Sky away from Frisk. The brief interaction had raised the tension in the room quickly and dramatically.

Sky allowed herself to be led aside.

"I still don't trust him."

"I know, but for now we may need him. Cheter tells me that he has a part to play in their planning."

"Do you know what they're planning then?"

"No. Cheter only has an idea because she has been questioned by the council about us, me, everyone. Apparently, Fecting has a proposal for the Great Council and your daughter is key to that."

Sky tensed, becoming visibly wary and afraid.

"Oh, don't worry about Sara. There's no way they will harm her from what I've been told. That reverence Frisk was on about is real. Many of the vamp… neway would die to protect her, and they already have the measure of Frisk, so relax."

Lonlin was waiting alone when Sara came down the stairs. Her tieve was dozing on one of the upholstered chairs alongside Flow.

"Oh, I didn't expect to sleep for so long. Has everyone gone already?"

"Yes. I have already told Fecting what we have discovered, and he would like to see you as soon as you are ready."

"Okay, we can go now. I just need to drink my retch first. Did you arrange for Poppy to meet us at the table too?"

"He will be there shortly. Fecting and the council may want to be there too once you have spoken with them."

Fecting and the council were all waiting when they arrived. Lonlin had told Sara that Fecting had been to see her earlier and had left her to sleep. The neway greeted her politely and asked her to sit at the table across from them. Lonlin took a seat beside Sara.

"Have you spoken with your fellow humans about your recent discoveries?" Fecting addressed Sara.

"No. I got back late and, as you know, woke late."

"I would ask that you do not discuss any of it with your people. I am asking and not telling you to do this, and I will explain why. You are special. We have never known of anyone as potent as you. We have been in communication with the other clans and the Great Council, and no one has ever known such as you. Such a potent gifted. No one knows when the Device first arrived on our planet, but we do know that the humans arrived via the Device around seven hundred years ago. The Device that we called Hontex was a sacred place for us. We, my people, many of us thought it a temple. A place of worship, and some still do. We now know that it is a craft that flew through space and crashed on our planet. All the relics originate from Hontex, the Device. We know nothing of the people who arrived with the craft. But now, we know that they are, or were, ohnsae. Another craft, like the Device, crashed on Eden, and when it was discovered, humans found curios and then realised that connected existed too. They used a curio like this one" – Fecting lifted Scallion's cylinder of holes onto the table – "to travel to our world. Your species' home planet is a place called Earth."

"Earth as in dirt?" asked Sara.

"Yes, the name Eden is its given name in the false history that you have been taught. As we told you when you arrived here, we had hoped that the humans might leave us alone once the ore mines all dried up, but this relic changes that. Now humans know of it they will not stop until they have it."

"Why not give it to them?"

"With this, they might take the devastation they have brought to our planet to another, or more than one. We, all the clans, have decided that cannot happen. We will keep this, but humans will not stop searching for it, and we have already seen greater activity in the sky and patrols since you crashed in the shuttle. We do not know who wants this, but we do know that Earth's politics is fractious, and it could be one or many that hunt this and also you. We know that humans have very few connected, if any, equal to your abilities, therefore, they will want you too."

"How do you know all this?"

"We have a true historical account of your people on our planet. We have not been lied to as the people of the stations have. We also have another human who knows things. You will meet him at Borsay. Once you have spoken with him, we will ask you to help us defend our people and protect this relic. It cannot belong to humans."

"And if I don't help you?"

"Lonlin does not think that will be the case, and we trust her judgement on this."

"What makes you so sure I will side with the neway and not my people?" she asked Lonlin.

Fecting answered. "They are not your people, Sara. You are human, but the people of Earth do not consider you to be the same. What they did when they released the canine into Station Eight should give you an indication of this."

"Can I tell my ma any of this?"

"We would rather you didn't. Once you have been before the Great Council, you can discuss what you wish with whoever you wish, but I would advise that you wait until after that before discussing it with your own."

"Why?"

"We are one of, if not the most tolerant of the clans concerning humans. You are currently the most valuable possession that any clan might wish to own."

"So you do own me."

"This is our way, as I told you when you first arrived. Our ways are strong and set, with little change ever having been made to our laws and customs. I own you according to our laws. Therefore my clan and I can protect all of you. I cannot control your companions in the same manner as I can the clan, and should they learn of your worth and that many of our people would treat them cruelly, they might cause trouble that would not fare well for you all. The Great Council will decide what happens to all of you, but as I own you, it will be a negotiation with me, initially.

I would like to teach you how our politics works and the ways of the Great Council so that when we meet them we are ready. It would not be wise, in my view, that the others with you knew any of this – both for your safety and theirs. Frisk and Ninety-Six are capable of significant deceit and treachery. We hope to turn them to our cause, but it is not yet time or possible. While I can teach you of our ways, we also want you to let us learn from the ohnsae hologram as much as we possibly can. The more we" – and he indicated himself and Sara – "know of the ohnsae, relics, the Device, the better we can negotiate. Ultimately, we might buy you equal status alongside our own gifted."

"But what of my ma, my brother, the others?" said Sara.

"All will be decided by the Great Council."

"Then shouldn't they know that?"

"What would that achieve now? What harm might that cause to a situation that now only you have control of? If they influence you or betray you, what then?"

"Sara, we genuinely do have your, and your family's, best interests in mind," said Lonlin. "We want you to be free and to help us willingly. We will not keep secrets from you, but we ask that you work with us until we meet the Great Council. We think this is the best option."

"I have spent time with Governor Frisk," Avivas addressed Sara. "As you know, I have been his chaperon for days now, and he is already scheming against you. He has not said this, but we know that he is. It is important for everyone that you stay safe and well."

"And with the neway."

"Yes, with us. We have not hidden your value to us from you. But we cannot allow Frisk to have you either.

That might be the worst option by far."

"Then why don't you imprison Frisk. That will keep me safe."

"I suppose we could," offered Fecting. "We could also imprison Ninety-Six. Perhaps we should kill them, would that not be a more permanent solution? What of Demic and Scallion too? Maybe they are a threat. And Poppy, he is Ninety-Six's son. Did you know that it was Jeb, your brother, that told someone from the lofts that you were a connected? Maybe we should imprison him too. Then that would upset your mother. So imprison her too. Or kill them all and imprison you?"

Sara knew that Jeb had told someone that she was a connected. He hadn't meant to cause them any harm but thought it would get them all a better life. He had been stupid and naive and had admitted this to Sara while they had been held captive together. She had already forgiven him.

"So," continued Fecting, "given that your option includes imprisoning everyone and perhaps killing a few of your companions, would you not prefer to give our way a chance? Your companions are all free today. They will be given back their weapons for the journey to Borsay. They will have supplies and the tools to survive should anything separate us on the journey. You already know how dangerous being outside can be, and now there are increased patrols to contend with. I only ask that you learn, along with us, everything we can of the ohnsae, their relics, who the gifted, connected, are. What it is that links them all. And that you learn our ways."

Fecting switched to his language. "This can only befit you too, can it not, Sara? You already know our language.

Think about what else we all can learn before we meet the Great Council. The knowledge that no one else has is a valuable tool and dangerous in the wrong hands. If you can learn our language in seconds, with a headband and a hologram, what else can we achieve in the next few days before we stand before the Great Council? You will also meet the other human. He is from Earth. You will be as prepared as far as we can achieve when you stand before the Great Council. We only ask that you trust us until then."

Sara conceded.

Fecting accompanied both Sara and Lonlin to the relic table. Already waiting for them were Poppy and Pec.

"Why are we here? Is something wrong with my arm. It's great by the way, and I don't want to lose it."

"No, Poppy, there's nothing wrong with your arm," reassured Sara. "But we do want you to get on the table again."

He agreed, and they made him comfortable, adjusting the sections until he was happy.

"What are you doing this time?" he asked, not appearing nervous at all. "The arm's better than my real one. Like Pec says, I wouldn't want to swap back. Maybe you can do the other arm?"

"No, Poppy, we're doing something new." And Sara touched the table's surface.

"What happened?" asked Poppy when the table cooled. "I didn't feel anything new."

"Touch your right ear," suggested Sara.

"It's back. My ear's back."

"Yes, Poppy. It seems the table can heal and regenerate too."

Sara spent the rest of the day with Fecting, Lonlin and the hologram. They discussed a great deal. Unfortunately, Many, the name Sara had given the hologram, was only newly activated, and she, as they had decided on a female, could only offer facts from her database. She had no first-hand knowledge of the ohnsae and had no information on their history. However, she had extensive knowledge regarding the relics, and of the craft, the Device. She also listened to Fecting's explanations of the neway laws and customs and the ways of the Great Council, and offered insight and new perspectives, contributing significantly to the conversations and discussions.

Scallion and Ruseq had now succeeded in opening every locked container and crate in the workshop. They had watched with great interest as the engineers made vehicles disappear at one end of the cavern and reappear at the other.

"So, what can we expect in Borsay?"

"In the main, you will be accepted. You will not be able to go anywhere without an accompanying neway. You are property, and although your presence will be okay, you will not be able to purchase anything, nor sit out alone in public, and there will be those who will regard you with distrust, though I do not think anyone will mean you harm. Humans are an exceedingly rare sight, and you will attract curiosity more than anything else. I've been asking, and it seems that any humans held by any clans are all being brought to the Borsay at the same time as you."

"How many will that be?"

"I don't know, but I doubt it will be a significant

number. From what I'm told, the eight of you are the biggest group ever found at one time. The others out there, I know nothing about."

"And you say the history I have about Eden is a lie?"

"Yes, but you can't share that with anyone. I will get in trouble if you do. I don't think they will banish me, but I don't want to find out. They will tell you everything when they think it's the right time."

"And today I can have all my stuff back."

"Not all. You won't be getting the relic back that you brought. Fecting himself still has that, and he has not let any gifted near it yet."

"Why? What does he think it is, or does?"

"No idea."

"Okay. You said you would teach me to drive today. Let's do it."

That evening Sara explained to Sky that she would be moving out of their shared domicile and staying with Lonlin. She reassured her ma that she would be safe and that she was learning a lot from her neway chaperon. Sky welcomed the move. She wanted her daughter as far away from Frisk as possible. The other humans barely noticed her departure as they focused on their newly acquired weapons and equipment. They had been able to select any weapon they had wanted from swords, knives, spears and bows to blaster pistols and rifles to ballistic weapons. They had even been allowed their grenades and to select any armour they had wanted. On top of this, Poppy had revealed his new ear, another subject of great speculation about what the curios were capable of.

"Does this mean they trust us?" Sky asked Demic.

"They are at least giving that illusion. But we still can't go anywhere. We have nowhere to go other than here. Frisk, on the other hand, might want to get back to a station, so we should keep an eye on him."

"I've never stopped watching him."

The convoy of vehicles to Borsay was substantial: twelve carriages. The four largest were each mounted with turret guns, and the remainder a mix of those with wrap-around windows or enclosed with only a front windscreen. All were wheel-based, with no hover capabilities. Their occupancy varied between six and ten passengers. They were all well loaded with bags, cases and crates on all the available storage decks and roof racks. The eight humans were divided among the vehicles, with no two travelling together, for their security.

They were leaving at night, using the darkness outside to hide their place of origin. The order came to board their vehicles, and the engines started. They left the tunnel at speed, not excessive, but neither was it slow and sedate. They exited the small valley and stayed close together, one behind the other, as they raced into the night. It was only when dawn began its approach that the vehicles split into four groups of three. The humans hadn't known of this manoeuvre, nor that they wouldn't be together again until they reached Borsay.

Around midday, the vehicles stopped under the cover of some trees, and Sara disembarked to see who, human, was travelling with her. She found Scallion. He was glad to see her, but Sara had hoped to find her mother or brother.

"They'll be fine," assured Scallion. "It's a good tactic to split up the vehicles. Harder to see from the sky and less of a target."

"We will watch out for you," added Ruseq.

There were twenty neway in their troop but Fecting wasn't one of them. The man in charge was Vious, a veteran soldier. He introduced himself to Sara and promised he would do everything he could to get her safely to Borsay. He allocated a soldier, Eanea, to be her bodyguard for the trip. Eanea was an amiable person, and her confident and relaxed manner did put Sara at some ease. Twenty minutes later they were on the move again.

They made it through the first day without incident. Sara had enjoyed the majority of the journey as she had been able to view the landscape through her window and observe the great variety of wildlife and vegetation. She was amazed at how lush and beautiful this world was, happy that it wasn't the bleak, barren Scorched Land she had always believed.

That first night when they stopped, Eanea suggested that Sara and Lonlin bedded down inside the vehicle, but they both declined. Everyone else was dropping mats on the grass, and they had spent enough time in the vehicle already. The chance to sleep out in the open beneath the real sky was a first for Sara, and she wasn't going to miss the opportunity.

No one saw the hunter until it was too late. It was early morning, and they hadn't long been on the move. The first two successive shots of the barrage of blasts that the craft rained down on them struck the larger vehicle with the turret gun direct. The carriage disintegrated and exploded behind them, Sara's vehicle being in the lead.

She looked to Flow to see if she could take control of the hunter.

"Well?" asked Lonlin, following Sara's gaze.

"She's trying. Something or someone is countering her attempts. She'll keep trying."

They were thrown around the interior as one sharp evasive manoeuvre after another tried to lose the hunter above them and avoid being hit by their guns.

Two rockets took to the sky from their rear vehicle, fired from shoulder-mounted launchers. Both hit the hunter, but it didn't veer away or cease its gunfire. There was a forest ahead, and they raced for the cover of the trees.

It was slow progress under the leafy canopy. The terrain wasn't ideal for vehicles, but they continued to make progress as best they could. The hunter was firing indiscriminately into the trees, and by the spread of their blasts, it was clear they didn't know the exact location of their targets.

"How long will they keep looking for us?" asked Sara.

"Indefinitely, or until they destroy us," replied Eanea.

The blasting of the forest around them ceased.

"Flow has control of their guns. She doesn't control the craft yet, but she can tell me that they are heading away from us. They've lost us."

The forest would conceal them for many miles, Sara was informed. It had already been along their planned route, and so the two vehicles would proceed as planned.

Sara had expected a sombre mood when they stopped for the night. The neway had lost six of their own. She had expected that to dominate the mood and conversation, but it didn't, and so she asked Lonlin and Eanea about that. There would be no mourning of the fallen; the soldiers were used to taking casualties, but that wasn't why. The neway that would grieve over their losses would do so privately and with no outward display of sorrow. Once the journey was completed, they would celebrate the lives of those that had perished along the way; this was the way of all neway and not just the soldiers.

Scallion checked on Sara, but he didn't impose his company on her. Sara noted that he seemed particularly friendly with Ruseq and that they remained together for the majority of the time.

"Do you know how to use that?"

Eanea was pointing to the blaster pistol holstered on Sara's hip.

"Not really. Point it at the bad guy and pull the trigger, right?"

"That's the quick lesson I suppose. So you've never fired a blaster? Any weapon?"

"No, never."

"Can you use a bow, spear, sword?"

"No. We don't train with any of those like you do. We go to school then work. Fighting isn't part of our education."

"I'm told that your cat stopped the guns of the hunter." Vious stood over them where they had sat down on their sleeping mats.

"Yes, but she couldn't send it away."

"They would have fired on us for hours if they needed to. However, I suspect there will now be consequences too."

"What do you mean?"

"The botdrones aren't the smartest, but their systems and their commanders might have noted your interference. You diverted another hunter recently and now this one. They may just think we have a new device or relic that does this, but if it were me up there, I'd be thinking that you are involved. I would be bringing more air cover to this section now on the chance of finding you," said Vious.

"They weren't trying to find me; they were firing on us all."

"True. But if they make the connection or suspect that it's you, they might not fire on us again, but they will send ground troops."

"What else was I supposed to do?"

"Nothing. You did what you could and probably saved some of our lives. I am not ungrateful. I am just letting you know."

Vious left the three women to resume their conversation.

"He's a little sharp isn't he," commented Sara.

"A little maybe, but he's one of the best we have. You're in capable hands with him," said Eanea.

They stopped at the edge of the forest. The going had been slow at times due to obstructions, ditches and embankments. Going around and finding a better route had been the norm for most of the day. Darkness was falling, and Vious planned to take advantage of that. They would drive without vehicle lighting, relying on their dark-sight ability. The land ahead of them was relatively flat and open for the next three hours. Then they would reach a vast area of hills that gradually grew in height and breadth until much farther north when they rolled into mountains. Once they were among the hills, it would be easier to avoid any search from the skies.

They waited, watching the land before them for any sign of threat. The blanket of darkness crept over them, and then Vious announced it was time to go.

The two vehicles stayed well apart. Lonlin assured Sara they could still see each other, though. Everyone was tense and alert. The hunter knew that they had to leave the forest somewhere, but it had a vast perimeter to patrol.

Sara saw the shadow of the hills outlined against the night sky. They grew taller and more defined as the final minutes of the open ground passed slowly by. They were almost there; surely they were going to make it. She watched the sky, watched Flow, for any indication anything was out there.

They moved into the hills, one vehicle behind the other, and the tension eased. From here they had good cover in the shade of the well-vegetated hillsides for the rest of the journey. The downside: anyone hunting them on the ground had the same advantage. The brush, trees, valleys and gullies they would use to remain out of sight were also ideally suited to ambush.

They found a suitable spot under the cover at the edge of some trees and, after netting the vehicles, they settled for a well-earned rest.

"Have you stood before the Great Council before?" Sara asked Lonlin.

"Once. I accompanied Dimii when it was decided he would reside in Borsay."

"Is it intimidating?"

"Yes. So far, you've seen a relaxed side of our lives. Fecting is a realist, he knows the laws and customs, but he doesn't overly police them. He doesn't ignore them either. If any infringement is reported, he will investigate and penalise. More often than not, he will banish rather than harm anyone. I think he's fair, but I don't think all our laws and customs are."

This was the first time Sara had heard any form of dissent from Lonlin, and she was surprised. Back at the settlement, everyone seemed to be happy and content. She hadn't heard of any trouble while she had been there, no infringements of any kind, but now that she thought about it there probably was. It was impossible, she acknowledged, for everyone to agree on everything all the time.

"How do you get blood while you're out here?"

"At the settlement, we tend to gorge on Celebration Day, and that sates our hunger for a few weeks. Out here we feed off any animal we can capture. We drink more often but lesser amounts when we are out here. Though we don't have to feed every day. We are all still satisfied after Celebration Day so that we will be fine until Borsay."

"Do you kill every animal that you feed on?"

"No. We farm them for their blood. We only kill to eat, as you would."

"Is it true you can feed off humans?"

"Yes, we can feed off humans. We can feed off each other too. Blood is blood. Why the sudden interest?"

"It's something I've always wanted to ask, but I thought it might be rude to do so. But after spending so much time with Fecting, discussing your ways, I figured it would be all right to ask you. What happens if you don't drink blood?"

"We die. Think about it like you not drinking water."

"But if we have no water, that's because there is none. A neway is never without blood if they have someone else with them?"

"That's something you don't need to worry about."

Sara thought that something in Lonlin's voice hinted to the contrary on that, but she decided not to push the matter. She still wanted to know but decided that now was maybe not the best time to pursue the subject.

Sara woke with a hand clasped over her mouth. Eanea held her still until she recognised her. "Botdrones, patrols, close. Stay with me and keep quiet."

Sara looked around her, and she counted four neway, plus Scallion, Lonlin, Eanea and herself. The others were gone, with the remaining hidden beneath the netting that camouflaged the vehicles, all with weapons in hand. Sara put her hand on her blaster, then decided to leave it where it was. She had reasoned that her best option was to stay with her protector and not to engage in any fighting herself.

Blaster shots shattered the fragile calm and silence. Behind them, in the trees, a fight had begun. A single shot stood out from all the others, and it was when Sara realised the target that she understood why it was so significant to her. Eanea was dead. The shot had clipped the top of her head. A shot that hadn't come from the trees but the other side of the vehicles; they were surrounded. The neway and Scallion positioned themselves and began firing over the vehicles. The trees behind them filled with the sounds of fighting. A vehicle window exploded and sprayed glass, and a salvo of other blaster shots peppered the far side of both vehicles. There were too many shots to count, and Sara kept low. She wanted to look, to see what they were up against, but she dared not.

Scallion made a quick dash, shots narrowly missing him as he reached Sara.

"You all right? You hit?"

Sara followed his gaze and saw that she was covered in

blood. "No. It's Eanea's."

"Keep low. I promised your ma I'd look out for you."

Vious emerged from the trees, alone. He was wounded but still returning fire at whatever was pursuing him.

"Get in the vehicles and get away," he ordered. "We are surrounded and outnumbered. Get Sara away from here now."

Scallion opened the carriage door and pushed Sara inside. "Keep your head down." He climbed in beside her and took the driver's seat. Blaster shots still peppered the vehicle, all the windows were gone, and there were glass fragments everywhere inside the vehicle.

Scallion started the engine, and as he did so Lonlin and Vious clambered inside the vehicle. With them came Flow and Iyne.

"Go!" ordered Vious, pressing in beside Sara as he fired out of the vehicle's window openings.

A blast rocked their carriage, lifting the front wheels from the ground before it bounced back, jarring everyone violently.

Sara didn't need to have her head above the defensive line of the vehicle's interior to know that their other vehicle had been blown up. The ball of flame rose high enough that it was visible from her crouched position, and a wave of heat washed over her.

Scallion crashed into the burning vehicle as he accelerated past it. They were moving.

Another explosion and they stopped; their carriage lurched to a halt at a strange slant.

"They got us," hollered Scallion at Vious.

Sara saw Scallion's large ballistic revolver suddenly aim towards her. She screamed as she heard the shot and felt its impact. But there was no pain. She wasn't hit. She looked to her left to see Vious dead. Scallion had shot him.

"He was about to shoot you," offered Scallion in defence of his action.

Sara went numb; she lost her focus. She recalled Fecting more than once saying, "It cannot belong to humans". She had assumed that he meant the relic, but now she realised that he had also meant her too. Vious was about to assassinate her rather than let her be taken. She wondered if Eanea, her alleged protector, had the same orders. Did Lonlin know about this? Did any of it matter now? They were as good as dead or captured. Her mind fought back through the fog of realisation to her current situation. It was quiet. There was no longer the sound of fighting outside.

"Lonlin, you alive?" someone called from outside in the neway language.

"Yes."

Scallion pointed his weapon at the neway. Lonlin threw her blaster out of the window to show that she meant no harm.

"Who's outside?" demanded Scallion, the threatening tone of his voice implying that if he didn't like the answer, Lonlin would quickly follow Vious.

"They are the banished."

"The outcast neway?"

"Yes."

"Why—?"

Scallion didn't get to finish his sentence as half a dozen weapons appeared over the vehicle's edges pointing inside at them. Behind the weapons were the faces of neway.

"Put your gun down," suggested Sara to Scallion.

He looked at her, then Lonlin, then the others.

For a moment Sara thought he might still shoot Lonlin, but he holstered his weapon. Sara was momentarily impressed at his bravery… or stupidity. He hadn't dropped his weapon in surrender but merely submitted, something that might well have cost him his life, but it didn't.

Beyond the vehicles, bodies were everywhere. Dead neway lay among botdrones. Sara couldn't count the numbers, but she estimated thirty botdrones but far less neway, maybe six. Those standing all around them, including along the treeline, were all neway, maybe sixty men and women.

"We need to get moving," stated the neway whose voice had called out for Lonlin; he had switched to the human language. Lonlin embraced him. He was bald, the first hairless vampire Sara had seen. His skin was tightly stretched over his bones, and he was much gaunter and paler than any in Fecting's clan. All those that surrounded them had similar drawn and pale characteristics. The taut skin sharpened his features, giving him a very menacing and threatening appearance.

"We have vehicles nearby," he told Lonlin, in human language, and then they set off. Scallion and Sara were encouraged under blaster point to follow them.

"We saw the patrols closing in on your position," the man was telling Lonlin. "We had hoped they would pass and not find you, but they did. We had stayed back, and so they had already attacked you before we could get close enough to engage them. This is a lot of activity. They must be looking for your human."

"Stay close to me, don't let them separate us," Scallion

whispered to Sara as they moved. "If they try to separate us, argue or get your cat to save us."

After eight hundred yards they reached three small vehicles, far too few for all the neway that accompanied them. Sara looked behind her; most of the neway had gone. She nudged Scallion and alerted him about their reduced escort.

"I know. But where else can we go? Lonlin had better have a good story for all this."

Each vehicle was open-top with two seats in the front and two in the back. Sara and Scallion were put in the back of one behind Lonlin and her new companion.

The sound of hooves caught their attention, and a dozen neway riders came into view around the corner of the basin that hid the vehicles. Their mounts were sleek long-necked animals with four legs and built for speed. Sara had seen a few herds of them out in the Scorched Land as they had travelled. Their muscular haunches and shoulders implied great strength, and the curve of their back seemed designed for the saddles they wore. She knew they were grazing animals called wandae, but she hadn't known they could be ridden.

"What about the botdrone vehicles?" asked one of the mounted riders in neway.

"Leave them. They might have tracking, and we don't want them following us," replied the man in the driving seat of Sara's and Scallion's vehicle. Again he used the human language for the benefit of his captives.

chapter ten

The Banished

They drove into a tunnel, not unlike the one used to access Fecting's clan settlement. However, inside there was no overhead lighting, there were no buildings, nor ordered roadways. In places, pools of light had been created from a multitude of sources, including vehicle lighting, portable lighting stands, campfires and burning torches. The remainder of the chamber was in total darkness. They drove to one of the most substantial puddles of light, to a large, pitched tent, where Lonlin asked them to disembark and enter the shelter.

Once they entered the tent, the sound from outside was immediately dampened.

"This will give us some privacy," stated Lonlin. "I'm sure you have questions?"

"Damn, fuc— right," stormed Scallion, showing no signs of being a captive. "Your story had better be a good one, Lonlin. Lots of your people died out there." He coughed hard at the end of his outburst.

"Chqaqaie is coming," said the bald neway.

"And who are you?" demanded Scallion.

"I am Retisen. I am Lonlin's older brother."

A female neway entered the tent carrying a heavy canteen.

"And this is Lonlin's mother, Eopleen."

The woman passed the canteen to Sara, advising her to drink. It contained chqaqaie, and once she had taken her fill, she passed it to Scallion.

They sat on boxes and crates arranged for seating.

"Lonlin?" Sara indicated that she should tell them what was happening.

"No one was meant to die. The banished were going to ambush us and overwhelm us with numbers, and that should have avoided any deaths. We did not expect the botdrones to find us, and that is why there were deaths."

"So you knew about this?" asked Sara.

"Yes. I planned it, along with my brother."

"I trusted you, Lonlin."

"You still can. Let me explain."

"It had better be good," interjected Scallion.

"When I was born, I was born into a clan that did not offer the same freedom as Fecting's clan. It was soon known that I was gifted. The clan I was born into paired off gifted children from an early age with prominent clan members for breeding. They hoped to produce more gifted with their family ties."

"Did that ever work?" asked Scallion.

"Not that I know of. Eopleen and Retisen were not willing to allow this to happen, and so they stole me away along with a relic and sought a new clan. They found Fecting's and handed me over to them. They used the relic to pay my way into the clan, as befitted our customs.

However, as they had stolen the relic, they became banished."

"So let me get this right. If you steal a relic, you are banished, but if you receive the stolen goods you're not?" asked Scallion.

"Yes."

"That's unbalanced but workable."

"Scallion, let her finish."

"As I was saying, Fecting took me in both because I was gifted and the relic paid the due. That was over fifty years ago, and my brother and mother have been with the banished ever since."

"I rose through the ranks," began Retisen, "not without my mother's and Lonlin's help though. We found ways to keep in touch over the years and finally acquired a pair of human comms devices. That helped significantly."

"So are you in charge here?" Again Scallion interrupted.

"Yes. There are bands of banished, but I lead this one. We are constantly on the move, and we do interact with the other banished, but we are forbidden from interaction with any clans."

"How many are you?"

"Scallion, let them finish," restated Sara.

"There are two hundred and forty-six men and women here. I do not count the children, and I have not included today's losses."

"When you arrived I had an idea," continued Lonlin. "A way for the banished to rejoin the clans. However, we needed you to side with us to stand any chance of achieving that."

"So we are your property now?" asked Sara.

"No, banished cannot own any property. And after today, I may now also be banished, and so I do not own you either."

"So are we free, or do we still belong to Fecting? From what I've learned, we are now free?"

"Yes, technically you are free, but the first clan to capture you will then own you. You humans are not allowed freedom. You are considered beneath even the banished in our social structure."

"So what was all that talk about me gaining gifted status with the Great Council?"

"That is still possible. Then you can be free. You can own property, own your other humans, your mother and your brother."

"So what's this plan of yours?"

"If you side with us there is an ancient law that permits the banished to return to the clans. You could invoke that law."

"Why don't you just sneak back into the clans, spread out and infiltrate?" asked Scallion. "If you are all scattered then who would know?"

"We do that very occasionally with our children. There is a market for the young." Eopleen joined the dialogue. "However, those banished cannot."

"Why? You all look the same. No offence, but many of you do," said Scallion.

Eopleen bared her teeth, protruding her sharp upper canines.

Scallion's hand went to the revolver on his hip.

"No need," exclaimed Lonlin quickly, noting him reach for the weapon.

"She is demonstrating what they do to the banished.

They cut the tendons that extend the fangs. Banished cannot extend their fangs; this separates us from all other neway."

"Can you still feed on blood?" asked Sara.

"Yes, but it is more difficult and a bit messier," answered Eopleen.

There was a sound at the entrance of the tent, someone requesting entry.

Retisen permitted the person to enter, and they reported in the neway language.

"Is Ruseq one of the prisoners?" asked Sara in neway; this surprised everyone, except Lonlin.

The messenger looked to Retisen for permission before he would reply.

"Yes. One of them is named Ruseq."

"Ruseq's alive," Sara told Scallion.

"Any others?"

"He said there were three prisoners. So, what is this plan?"

"It all depends on your worth and how well you negotiate with the Great Council. They know what they are doing, and you not so much," said Retisen.

"She knows more than you think, brother. Fecting himself has been teaching her, and we have these."

Lonlin took five curios from her large pocket where Iyne regularly travelled.

"We too have three relics. We found them, and we haven't offered them to Borsay as we are supposed to do."

"So your whole plan is based on me getting a good deal with the Great Council?" said Sara.

"Yes."

"And how does that include the banished?"

"We still have to work that out, but with Many" – she indicated one of the cubes – "we might be able to devise a way."

"You have the hologram? Wasn't that supposed to be with Fecting?"

"All these relics were supposed to be with him. I stole them. So that will make me a banished too if you do not succeed," said Lonlin.

The neway of the large camp watched both Scallion and Sara with wary anticipation. Their hopes and aspirations varied widely, knowing what they expected from her. She was, however, the first real prospect that anyone could recall for their potential salvation.

Scallion had insisted on seeing Ruseq. They found the neway restrained along with the other two captives. Sara recalled both of the faces of the two prisoners, but she'd had little contact with them. One of them was wounded, but the arm had been treated and bandaged, and would fully recover in time. Scallion assured Ruseq that he would come to no harm and that he should relax as best he could. He also told him that they would all soon be going to Borsay, and he would be set free, and so he shouldn't do anything stupid and just wait.

They walked the camp, Lonlin and Retisen keen to show them the differences between banished life compared to the clan. The humans were encouraged to ask questions, and they did.

They learned that only the clan leaders knew the secret of raising a worm to drink blood, and so the banished couldn't call the worms for them to feed. The banished were also not protected from the worms who created the subterranean chambers where the clans resided; another secret held only by clan leaders. Therefore, the area they currently occupied could be disturbed at any time by one or more worms who had no regard for the people there. They rose for a variety of reasons – one was to mate – and as they thrashed and roamed the cavern, they were easily capable of destroying and crushing vehicles and squashing people. Therefore they needed to remain alert at all times and be ready to leave at a moment's notice. The banished lived a nomadic lifestyle, moving from one underground cavern to another, as resources dictated.

The worms were an integral part of the neway life. More so now that the race had lived below ground for centuries. The worms made the tunnels and burrows that the neway occupied. They secreted a fluid along their length when they chose to that hardened the earth they displaced, which gave strength to the underground structures without the need for any additional supports. The same fluid was scraped from the worms and used to harden the earth-built walls of the buildings the clans made.

The worms weren't tame, they were wild creatures, but the clan leaders held enough secrets to both summon them and keep them away from their settlements. They usually lived deep below ground and rarely surfaced other than to rise to the shallower ground to mate and give birth.

Scallion recalled the creatures attacking the train and asked about that. The neway believed that the vibrations the train created as it travelled agitated worms within the range of the tremors and this caused them to attack. This was useful at times if neway were in the vicinity as their assault dislodged containers and cargo and provided the banished and clans with easy pickings, but when and where they would rise was not a predictable thing and was an opportunistic moment.

A corral contained the wandae, the primary transport for the banished. They had some vehicles but maintaining them and obtaining parts was difficult as they changed locations so often. They also relied more on their traditional weapons to hunt, as maintaining blasters was also difficult without parts; blasters were reserved for defence against any botdrones they encountered.

The banished still held close to the three religions of their people, but they had discarded some of the laws and customs that they deemed cruel or immoral. Both Lonlin and Retisen admitted that this would be a problem should they once again be accepted back into the clans, but that was something to deal with at a later date; they needed to be accepted first.

Scallion asked them why they wanted back into the clans. They seemed to thrive and exist quite well outside those circles. The answer was a simple one. Collectively the neway had a better chance of survival against the humans and botdrones than they did divided. The Great Council knew this too, but their ways and laws functioned in such a way as to divide not only the banished but often the clans too. Their race needed to be unified if they were to regain their planet and once again live on the surface. There were thousands of banished roaming the Scorched Lands and all believed the same.

Sara took the opportunity to speak with some of the banished as they wandered through the encampment. They all seemed nervous near her and looked to Retisen before they would engage in conversation with her. He told her this wasn't fear or reluctance, but because they hadn't seen a human in a long time; some had never seen a human and this, coupled with the fact that she was the most potent gifted that had ever lived, daunted them. The other factor was that she was inherently their enemy, but she was the one supposed to save them.

Evening fell, and both Scallion and Sara were given the tent as accommodation. Scallion believed this was because it was easily guarded, but both welcomed the opportunity for the privacy, food and hospitality that they received.

The following morning they were separated. Not because of any malice, but Lonlin, Sara, Retisen and Many needed to start discussing possible solutions and options to Lonlin's plan. Sara had decided to help the banished if she could.

Scallion was left to his own devices and went to see Ruseq. The prisoners were being treated fairly and after sitting with them for a while, Scallion asked a guard if Ruseq might be freed to walk the camp with him. Initially, this was declined, but Scallion managed to persuade them to ask Retisen and went along with the guard to give his reasoning. He believed that if Ruseq saw what he had seen the day before, and understood why the banished had taken Sara, he might side with them, or at least be sympathetic.

Retisen had been reluctant. He knew Ruseq was a thief and would more than likely try to escape, and he had the skills to have a reasonable chance of success. They couldn't afford him getting to Borsay before they did and exposing their plan. Scallion argued that if they couldn't win one clan member over to their cause, what chance did they expect with the Great Council and the clans? Sara conceded that he had a point, and with Scallion assuring them that he would take responsibility for Ruseq, it was finally agreed.

"You know you have put your life on the line for me, don't you?" Ruseq asked Scallion.

"I guessed as much, but you won't try and escape, will you?"

"We could escape together?"

"No, my place is with Sara. I promised her ma, and truth is, I think she's not only my best chance of surviving all this, but yours, the banished and all the clans too. She's only a young woman, a girl really, but she has something about her that I trust."

"Then I will not try and escape, so long as it is true that we will be returning to Borsay."

"Oh, that bit is true. Me, part of me, thinks that's a bad idea, but again I'll stick close to Sara. Now let's explore the camp."

The next day, the other two prisoners asked for the same privileges as Ruseq, but it was Ruseq himself that advised Scallion and Retisen that that wasn't a good idea. He had come to respect Scallion and Sara somewhat and was considering Lonlin's plan, but the other two would try and escape. Therefore they weren't given any greater freedom.

Another day passed, and both Scallion and Ruseq were summoned late on to the tent. There they were engaged in a conversation with Sara, Lonlin, Retisen and Many.

"So, Ruseq, it's time for you to make a decision," said Sara.

Before his arrival, they had agreed for Sara to lead the discussion; if she were to stand before the Great Council and plead her case, she could test herself against Ruseq first.

"I'm listening."

"I am assuming that Scallion has confided in you what our plans are?"

He looked to Scallion for support, and he was permitted to speak freely.

"Yes, he's told me what he knows. You are going to go before the Great Council and ask that the banished be allowed to rejoin the clans. To be truthful, I don't think you have much chance."

"Did you know that Fecting was also going to put me before the Great Council too?"

"It seemed quite obvious with us all heading to Borsay."

"Do you know why Fecting was doing that?"

"Probably to win favour for the clan, get us more rights and privileges. Maybe he wanted the clan to be given a permanent location in Borsay."

"He wants more than that. He wants to challenge the humans. He wants to seek a return to the surface for the neway and push back the human occupation and control of your planet."

"That's a big ask. We've dreamt of such things for lifetimes, but it's not possible."

"What if I told you that it was possible, and you could be an integral part of making history."

"Then you would have my attention, but also a whole bucket full of scepticism."

"Then I will tell you broadly, only broadly, what we are proposing. I cannot give you all the details as it isn't my place to do so. I am, after all, only property and a human."

"You're maybe a little more than that I think."

Sara outlined what she wanted Ruseq to do, and how he could help them, help them all. He listened quite intently, asked a few questions, and then took only a few moments to agree to what Sara proposed. When he and Scallion left the tent, Retisen asked if they could trust him.

"Our whole plan is based on gaining the trust of others. We have to start somewhere," replied Sara.

chapter eleven

Answers and More Questions

Riding the wandae was a delight for Sara. They had left the banished by vehicle, but a day later had met up with a small group who had gone ahead of them. There they had swapped their carriage for the neway mounts. Sara's was unusually docile and unlikely to bolt or panic, with the mount chosen explicitly for the rider. After a short lesson, Sara had adapted quickly to the nuances of riding a living animal. Her initial discomfort quickly disappeared, lost amidst the pleasure she gained. Beside her rode Lonlin and Retisen.

Retisen had dressed in bright colours, as was the way of the neway, but he wore no armour and carried no blasters. He was armed, though, with a sword and dagger. It had taken a while, but Sara had finally noticed his family resemblance to Lonlin. It was mainly around the eyes, their shape, and his cheekbones. He did look older than his sister, and he was by fifty years. His body frame was broader across the shoulders than most neway and being five foot six tall he was among the tallest of his race. Sara had already decided that she liked him, even though his gaunt, ashen features still struck her as menacing. Lonlin carried her blaster, her tieve in her large pocket and showed no indication that she was concerned over the fact she could soon become banished.

Sara was also now dressed in the manner of the neway. Her clothing style matched that of Lonlin: bright, overlapping skirts and a billowing top. Around her neck, suspended from a cord, were small net pouches, two, and in each was a relic cube. On her waist, she carried a mace, a blunt weapon, a type of club with a massive head on the end of the handle to deliver powerful strikes. The mace was also a relic, featuring a head and shaft made from an unknown material. It added to her image, as any neway would immediately recognise it as a relic and treat it with caution. The mace weapon was the first of its type seen by the neway, who had inspected it and tested it the day before. Over her shoulder, she wore a slouch purse, and inside was Flow, his head peeping over the rim. Alongside the cat were the other curios they possessed.

They were escorted almost to the main entrance of Borsay by well-armed and vigilant banished, though they retreated and remained out of sight when the three began their final approach. Sara was nervous, but she wasn't showing it. She took strength from the casual but unassuming manner of both her companions. Scallion had told her that the con was mainly attitude: if you believe it, then your mark will too. Now she needed a forte that she never knew she possessed. It was also crucial that the people of Borsay already knew who she was. Scallion and Ruseq had gone ahead, along with the two other prisoners, to ensure that.

The tunnel opening was large but invisible due to the outcrops that surrounded it, hiding it from view until it was directly in front of any approach. They were aware that sentries had already seen them from their hidden posts along the valley and on the overlooking hillsides, but no one had challenged them as they rode calmly towards Borsay's entrance.

They stopped in the daylight just before entering the tunnel, and Sara put on the curio-goggles so she would be able to see as they manoeuvred into the dark interior.

It was immediately apparent that they were expected. Every twenty feet, on both sides, stood an armed guard; this was not normal.

"You look impressive," said Lonlin quietly. "The goggles add to the image. Whatever Ruseq and Scallion told them, we have everyone's attention. I bet the whole city knows you are here already."

It was a long winding path in total darkness, going down deep beneath the ground, but they rode slowly and without haste.

When the light appeared ahead, Sara removed the googles. She had known what to expect, so she didn't become overawed and show a human reaction, a weakness.

Emerging into the city's artificial light, she saw large buildings ahead, some fifteen storeys high, stretching into the distance. The road before them was awash with bright colours, flags and banners declaring clans who resided within Borsay. A massive open metal gate protected the tunnel. On either side ran a long building comprising three levels. The many slit-window openings each had a blaster protruding out and pointed at them. She knew she had nothing to fear, not yet at least.

As they had hoped and expected, Fecting and an entourage were waiting for them a short distance inside, standing in the middle of the road. Fecting was the only person Sara recognised. They pulled up their wandae with several yards to spare. Any conversation at this distance would need to be loud and clear with their greeting party.

"Who are you?" asked the neway dressed in the camouflage colours of a soldier. His armour was gold in colour and he was the first Sara had seen wearing a hat. Both the hat and armour marked him as the commander of the guard. It was his responsibility to protect Borsay.

Sara spoke, as addressed, in the neway language.

"I am Sara, human, the property of Fecting. I am gifted, and the most potent gifted that has ever been known. I am here at both my master's bequest and that of the Great Council. I am to speak before the council on important and urgent matters that will affect every neway that lives and will live."

Now it remained to see if the commander would follow protocol or if he had other orders.

There was a hushed muttering among the waiting entourage. A stern look from the commander silenced that.

"Who is with you, Sara, property of Fecting?"

"This is Lonlin, my keeper, also of Fecting's clan. This is Retisen, my saviour from a recent botdrone ambush."

"You two must both bare fangs," ordered the commander.

Lonlin did so. Retisen protruded his upper canines, but the fangs remained short.

"No banished is permitted inside Borsay on penalty of their death."

The greeting protocol remained the precedent; under

any normal circumstances, a horde of guards would have rushed forward and seized the banished and dragged him from his saddle without any respect or concern for his welfare.

"He saved the life of not one but two gifted. My master requires him when we address the Great Council. He will disarm and submit to Fecting's authority, and my master will be responsible for him until the council decides his fate."

On cue, Retisen dropped his belt holding the sheathed sword and dagger to the ground beside his mount.

"Fecting," the commander addressed the clan leader, "is this all in order?"

"It is, Commander."

"Then you and your whole clan are now responsible for any transgression that either your human or the banished commit. Any infringement of law or custom will be dealt with swiftly and severely. You may take your property."

Fecting approached the three and told them to dismount. He turned from them and walked into the city. The three followed, leaving their mounts behind, and walked through the small neway corridor that the greeting party created.

"That was impressive," said Fecting once they were beyond the entrance. "I will admit I had my doubts, but it seems Ruseq was quite convincing with his persuasion. I hope you are up to the task at hand, Sara."

A cart waited for them; no vehicles or mounts were allowed inside the city. Instead, the open carriage was pulled by four tethered canines. The open carriage was a deliberate choice, as throngs of neway watched their arrival, occupying every window and doorway. They progressed deeper into the city limits on a clear roadway. The route had been ordered clear by the council, and no one was to address Sara or her companions before they appeared in front of the Great Council.

"As you can see, your proclamation has created quite a stir. Once it was read out to the council, word spread fast; this is a far more elaborate plan than we had discussed, Sara. And I understand that it is your plan?" Fecting looked at Lonlin as he finished.

"Yes, it is entirely my plan. Mine alone," replied Sara.

They had a whole building to themselves. Eight large floors each divided into several rooms. The humans were on the third and fourth floor along with their chaperons. The neway from Fecting's clan were spread across the other floors. Fecting himself, and a select few, had the top floor. Before Sara could see her ma and brother, she was escorted to the highest floor along with Lonlin and Retisen. Waiting for them were Scallion, Ruseq and Avivas, the only other member of the clan's council to have made the journey.

"You have outlined an impressive proposal and scheme, Sara. What makes you think you can deliver it?" Fecting, once they were out of public view, wasn't too pleased with the events that he had been pressured to become involved with. "You are a human, after all. It will be hard for the council to take you seriously no matter that you are a potent gifted. They may simply choose to eliminate you and your other humans as a pest, a nuisance. And you have dragged my whole clan into your scheme."

Sara didn't shrink one fraction before Fecting's scolding tone. She knew she had to hold her position now even more than along the roadways they had just travelled. Convincing Fecting was another critical step along the voyage of her journey of discovery. She was the core, the crucial and vital component, to everything in motion. That included the safety of her family and friends.

They were all seated at a single table, but Sara rose and paced the floor, something Lonlin had told her not to do as it was known to annoy Fecting.

"It's not my plan, Fecting, it is yours. True, I've added a few things, but you said we would need to adapt, improvise and make changes along the way. You told me to learn your ways, to find a way to weave through the laws, customs and traditions that the Great Council would not only throw at me but rely upon when they made any decisions. You told me that when that moment came, it would be me, and me alone, that stood before them and delivered my case. If I failed, you said it might cost my life, or worse, and that of my family, and would mar your clan for centuries. So I have done exactly what you asked of me. I have taken your plan and reinforced it, laced it with traits and hooks that align with your laws, customs and traditions. And so far it has done what you proposed it should."

Sara stopped pacing and faced everyone squarely. Inside she was trembling. Had she taken her role, her façade of confidence, too far? She looked at every face before her and held their stare confidently before moving on and finally looking at Fecting. She was before all her peers, and a moment before she started to crumble, Fecting spoke.

"I suppose that is exactly what you have done."

Sara looked at Scallion, the only other human in the

room, and she smiled. He was beaming. The grin on his face was so full it was pushing up his ears. He was proud of her. She liked that feeling.

"So how did you derive this plan?" Fecting gave Lonlin another cursory look.

"I took some of the relics with me when we left the settlement. I know you said that I shouldn't, but I needed Many to help me decipher your ways and come up with a solution. Together, Many and I analysed every detail we had learned, and that is how the plan came to be."

"So, what next?"

Sara almost faltered, as the clan leader was asking her; he was beginning to take her lead. A girl, still in her teenage years, standing before centuries of life and knowledge. She looked once again to Scallion. He was still grinning, and he nodded. He had told her that once you have them captivated you should capitalise on it. If the masquerade slips then you risk a catastrophic failure.

"Next, I need to talk with you alone."

No one argued as Fecting ushered everyone from the room.

This conversation was going to be another crucial moment of trust. While still maintaining assumed authority, and not once letting the performance slip, Sara told the clan leader every detail of the plan that she now nearly had all the facts to complete. As she spoke, she realised how significant was both the risk and the gamble, but her confidence convinced even herself that everything was possible; Scallion's advice was now appreciated.

"So, you expect me to tell you the secrets of the worms? Something that is only shared between clan leaders. Not even my council knows those secrets. This is how we hold together the entire structure of our lives."

"I won't succeed without that knowledge."

"You also have a lot of variables in your plan. Too many if you ask me."

"I would say that the variables remain the same as when you first proposed this."

Sara expected a rebuke, but once again Fecting conceded to her point.

"My people have suffered for centuries, denied the surface life that is our birthright. Our laws and ways have stagnated because of this, and like Lonlin I agree that many are now no longer practical or fair. Yes, I know of her views. We have discussed them often, but she has never, perhaps until now, given me a reason to doubt her."

Sara remained silent, unsure if Fecting was luring her into a disclosure that would sentence Lonlin to banishment.

"My plan risked the welfare of the clan. And my goals were not so far-reaching as yours. I suppose if the clan is to be relegated in its standing due to my actions, it is better to reach for the highest glory than to shrink before a lesser challenge. I would ask one thing in return, Sara."

He looked her in the eyes; the fiery red surrounding the dark pupils had once made Sara uneasy, but not now. She saw that he genuinely cared for his people, not only his clan but all neway. He wanted their freedom, and now that there was a real chance for that, and he could influence the outcome, he couldn't let it slip through his fingers.

Whatever he saw in return, deep inside Sara, he committed to his course.

"When I tell you these secrets, you must never share them with anyone other than a clan leader. To do so might bring greater harm than if our current course fails."

Sara simply nodded.

"You will hold one of the greatest powers of my people. You do know that?"

Again Sara nodded. She was too frightened to speak. Scared that her voice might fail her, reveal that she was just a girl making it up as she went along, performing a charade. A child playing with the fate of two, maybe more, races.

Fecting didn't call everyone back to the room. He released Sara to see her ma and brother and then found some privacy to strengthen himself for what was to come. He knew, more than Sara, that the risk was high, but the ultimate reward was priceless.

The hug from Sky nearly broke her back, but everyone was glad to see her safe and well. After the initial fuss, she was introduced to Anco and Yonage. Anco was Frisk's new chaperon: a soldier, old and experienced, menacing, and quiet. The first thought that occurred to her was that this was a man who wouldn't hesitate to kill the governor if he became a threat, triggered by her memory of Vious and Eanea and what their secret orders had been. Her ma's chaperon, Yonage, was a pleasant woman, always smiling and attentive. Sara had now become so accustomed to the expression of the neway that had been shrouded at first by their taut, bone-stretched pale skin and flaming eyes, along with their sharp teeth and fangs, that she had no trouble seeing the kindness in Yonage.

Lonlin had already introduced Retisen, who would be sharing the same floor as the chaperons and their wards. He wasn't guarded or chaperoned, but Lonlin told her that he wouldn't be allowed to leave the building without Fecting himself being alongside him.

When they had a private moment, Lonlin asked Sara if she had got what she had wanted.

"I did. But you must never ask me about it. Promise me that? And you cannot tell anyone what I know."

Two hours later Sara was summoned, alone, to see Fecting.

When she entered the room this time, there were two strangers before her. One was a human male, old, appearing late in his years and quite frail, and already seated at the table. The other was a cruel-looking neway standing over the fragile human. Sara didn't assume he was a cruel man based on the characteristics of his vampiric racial features. The man had a real demeanour of cruelty; this wasn't a nice man, she decided instantly.

"Sara, this is Aris, he is the clan leader that owns this human. This is the human you asked to speak with when you wrote your letter to the Great Council."

Aris ignored Sara when she greeted him, his contempt for her obvious.

"I would not be here if the council did not demand it, Fecting. Keep your human on a leash. I do not care if she is gifted." Aris spoke to Fecting as though Sara wasn't present in the room.

There was a brief, very brief moment where Sara was frightened of the clan leader before her. That moment passed quickly as her anger at his racism and discrimination fuelled her determination and bolstered her courage. Now she had to trust that Fecting would protect her should anything go awry. She needed the knowledge that the human had. He was from Earth, a place of which she knew nothing. He alone could answer many of the questions that she needed to reduce the gaps in her plan before she stood before the council; at that time, she would only get one chance. If the whole council was to be similar to Aris, she was determined not to falter before one bully now.

"Fecting, master," began Sara in the neway language, pleased to see that Aris was surprised by this. "Would you ask Aris, clan leader, to grant his property permission to speak freely?"

"Aris, would—"

"I heard what she said. Yes, it can speak freely."

Sara understood that their protocol had irritated him, but it also visibly knocked him down a peg or two as he shifted from dominant to wary.

"Fecting, master, would you ask Aris to tell it that in the human tongue, as it will not listen to me otherwise."

"Peter, this human girl will ask you things. You tell her what she wants to know, or you will suffer." At that, he dragged his chair from beneath the table and sat down.

Sara waited for Fecting to offer her a seat at the table. She knew that it was important she remained his property in all appearances.

"Hello, Peter, I am Sara."

The feeble man looked up for the first time; his eyes were a stark contrast to his physique, with a strong, determined and unyielding gaze.

"You are the gifted that will save everyone, I assume." He spoke confidently, his elderly years not evident in his tone.

"Tell me about yourself."

"My master is not a patient man, so I will keep my answers short."

Sara saw what the two neway, sat on either side of the

human, could not see. He winked, a twinkle of mischief evident in his eyes. He might be weak of body, but he was still full of fight, decided Sara; she liked him and was already working through options where she might save him, or, as the neway would have it, acquire him.

"I am from Earth, but you know that. There is a prison on Devil's Rock, this planet. We call this planet PTX12000Z. Your name better suits it though. The prison is for Earth's political prisoners. A place you are never supposed to return from, but I never got there. My transport crashed, shot down I'm guessing, but I don't know for sure as I woke up later in the possession of Aris and his clan. By my count that was ten years ago, but I may be out by a year or two on that."

There he stopped.

"Why were you imprisoned?"

"My politics disagreed with the then governing bodies over the Device. Politics is an awkward playing field at the best of times."

"The history I have of the humans here is a lie. What is the true history?"

"Earth archaeologists discovered the Device around nine hundred years ago. They found it on the edge of a desert in a continent called Africa. The team that discovered it was a multinational one, which was good as it brought in multiple governments to manage the discovery from the beginning. There was a massive dig to expose the structure. We didn't know what it was for a long time, but we knew it was from off-world. Then a young scientist on his first time working on the Device touched a section and a door opened. It was as easy as that, but it took nearly two hundred years to make even that little amount of progress. He was the first connected that we became aware of. We could then confirm that it was a craft of sorts, a spacecraft. There were no remains inside, and we also discovered that it had already been looted. All evidence points to the ancient Egyptians having found access and robbed the interior. That fits in with a few of Earth's other mysteries too, so it is a very plausible theory. A few years after that, a cylindrical curio was found, and the scientists worked out that it was linked to an interface inside the Device. It was put in place and a powerful connected triggered it. That opened a portal to this world.

"That was the start of our occupation and a dramatic shift in Earth politics. The ore and plant life discovered here became the source of true global power. Whoever controlled the ore, in particular, could control just about everything else.

"The original conglomerate of businesses that led the start of the occupation decided that the indigenous people were civilised but not developed, and a legal ruling was passed that they could be enslaved. The fact that they had been identified as vampires probably went a long way to help that law get passed. However, it proved too difficult to control the neway as they fought back. And given they had abilities beyond the average human, such as super strength, a new law was passed that permitted their extermination. Botdrones were programmed to hunt and kill them on sight.

"Earth built the stations and mined the ore and grew the local plants all to be shipped off-planet. People were brought here, humans, with the promise of a new life. But some wanted to return home and. initially, that was permitted, but they took back a new disease that hit Earth hard. The resulting pandemic killed one-third of the world's population, and so return travel was banned and made illegal. That was when it was decided to manufacture a new history for the settlers forced to remain. Oh, and just to top things off, Earth emptied all its prisons here as a final influx. Everything here that related to Earth was banned, even the name Earth could not be spoken. This was enforced by governors, many of whom had been selected from particularly cruel and domineering former prisoners. Their life was to be so much more privileged than the subjugated humans if they succeeded in eradicating any history of Earth. They did an incredibly good job. Even they no longer know the truth. The fabrications even went so far as to create new religions, introduce old measuring systems, imperial I recall, banning all languages apart from English. Ah, by the way, I am French by origin. That is another country on Earth with its own language.

"This planet was then quarantined indefinitely. That quarantine has never been lifted. The supply chain for ore, plants and other resources operates now without Earth humans having to risk any kind of contamination. There is still two-way travel to and from Earth to the Device, but it is strictly controlled."

"Master, did you know this?"

"Yes, Sara."

Now Sara made her plea, knowing that neither Fecting nor Aris would be in favour of it.

"Master, can I have this human for longer? Could you acquire him?"

The slight frown on Peter's face provided Sara with a hint that he understood what she was asking in the neway language.

"No! That was not part of the deal." Aris rose angrily, scraping his chair across the floor.

Fecting said nothing initially. He remained calm and assessed the situation, studying Sara, Peter and Aris. When he was sure the other clan leader couldn't see his gesture, he nodded to Sara. Then. "No, Sara, I do not want such an old creature. What would I do with it? It cannot work, and other than tell old stories that we already know, it has no real value. It is not something I would agree to."

The bait was there. Not even being polite enough to offer a menial sum for the human was an insult to Aris. Even if Fecting didn't want the property he should have made an offer to be refused. Would Aris take the bait?

He bit!

"You call my property worthless. No other clan has a human from their origin planet. No one. Not even Borsay itself has such an object."

"I meant no insult," said Fecting defensively.

"I will have words with the council about this. Not only do you demand my presence, but then you insult me, claiming my property to be worthless. This will damage your standing with the council, and I believe you are to stand before them the day after tomorrow. This will not go well for you, Fecting."

The clan leader seemed genuinely angry, but Sara learned quickly. Aris wasn't as annoyed as he appeared but playing his own game. He was looking to force Fecting into making an offer; whether he had intended to sell Peter or not there was now a negotiation in play. Sara decided to play the fool and hope that Fecting would go along with her.

"Master, I am remorseful. Maybe this would pay for

the human?" She placed the curio-mace on the table.

"Sara, put that away. That is a valuable relic."

She started to remove the weapon.

"You cannot control your human? Are you telling me that the human made the offer without your permission? You have no authority over such as that?" He pointed towards Sara.

"She is an object. I have total control over her."

"So the offer remains?"

"No, the—"

"So she made the offer without authority?"

"No, she—"

"Does she now lead your clan? A human!"

"No—"

"You are not the neway you once were, Fecting."

"The offer stands," declared Fecting reluctantly.

"Then I accept. The human is yours and the relic is mine." He held out his hand for the mace.

Sara deactivated the relic back to its cube form. Then, feigning disappointment and showing fear towards Fecting to imply her anxiety for the coming punishment that would follow, she handed the cube to Aris.

"Ah! A better day than I expected." Aris strode from the room in triumph, ignoring any protocol to excuse himself.

"Bravo, you two are good," said Peter. "He'll realise eventually that he can't open the curio and that you manipulated him."

"He will not reveal that, though. He would lose face. He will brag that he has a new relic and that you are worthless. You may be worthless. Why do we need him, Sara?"

"You know more than you've said, don't you?"

"I know lots of things, but I've never seen a human work with a clan leader like you just did. What's this really all about?"

"Is there any way for a human or neway to find a way back to Earth or to live inside the Device?" asked Sara.

"No. Not legally anyway, and I doubt anyone would want to take a human or anything living back to Earth or inside the Device. The hatred and fear that developed regarding neway and mutants since the pandemic is rife everywhere. You are what Earth humans now call mutants; did you know that Sara?"

"Then that fact alone is worth the trade. That also means that you're stuck here too?"

"Yes."

"How would you like to have a better life than you've had so far on Devil's Rock?"

"What do you have in mind?"

Peter was assigned a chaperon, Temart, a young male neway and an engineer. They would stay with the other humans on their floor, and Peter was provided with clean clothing and the opportunity to clean himself up before meeting everyone else.

It turned out that he was around sixty years old, as far as he could calculate. The Aris clan hadn't treated him well. He had been their only human, and they had left him to wander alone throughout their settlement. He had begged for food, but he had always received chqaqaie. They would parade him at occasional meetings as a symbol of their wealth, but the truth was they considered him worthless, other than being used as an occasional status symbol.

Sara spent the time leading up to the audience before

the Great Council with Lonlin, Retisen, Many and Fecting, working and scheming together. Peter had provided information that helped them knit together greater detail and possible solutions. The plan still had holes, and crucial gambles to play, but it was developing a greater chance of success, but with that were higher risks too.

chapter twelve

The Great Council

Sara wore make-up, something she had never done before. Her ebony skin was matted to prevent it from shining, and her upper and lower eyelids had been painted red along with her lips. Her brown hair was plaited so tightly down the back of her head that it had been a painful experience to achieve the result. Laced between the plaits were red ribbons that trailed down to her waist beyond the hair. The dress she wore was unadorned and very tight, and also crimson red. It flared at the hem over red shoes. Her breasts had been lifted, bound beneath with wrapping around her back and torso so that they heaved out of the open cleavage cut that fronted the garment. The fabric had been adhered to her skin with tape to prevent her nipples from being exposed; this was what the neway crowd wanted to see. Sara felt uncomfortable. The garment was restrictive, and she thought the make-up was gaudy. Everyone had reassured her that she looked beautiful, commanding, alluring, and used other similar remarks to calm her. However, it was

Scallion that finally put her at ease. He reminded her that this was all a charade, a very elaborate one, and every little detail needed to be right if it were to succeed. The outfit and make-up should be putting her into character and not detracting from the delivery of the scam. She needed to own it. It was a means to an end.

The audience would be a packed gathering; hundreds would be in attendance. To the neway, these events not only served a function but provided entertainment. Bets had already been placed on the possible outcomes. Fecting had told her that the majority of the betting was not in her favour. He wasn't trying to dishearten her but to prepare her. She also knew that while she waited, as there were two minor audiences before hers, agents of the council and the gamblers would make attempts to weaken her resolve. They wouldn't employ any physical attacks, but a barrage of carefully selected comments, derision and insults; this was one of the reasons for the preceding minor hearings.

The open-topped carriage arrived, drawn by two canines, designed to display Sara. Only Fecting would accompany her. Everyone else was already at the stadium. The route to the council was lined with spectators who jeered her.

"This is not the most direct route," Fecting informed her. "The council is making every effort to shake you. I have learned too that you are the first human ever to have been allowed to speak directly with the council. You have most definitely created a spectacle that will be remembered."

Finally, they began the approach down the wide promenade to the stadium. The flags of the clans lined this route, fluttering over the crowd below.

"I think no matter how this goes there will be a big celebration across Borsay tonight; this has too much of a festival feel for it to subdue quickly. I hope we are included among those festivities."

"We will be," assured Sara. Her defences were in place. The persistent scorn hurled at her over the last twenty minutes had hardened her resolve; this was the only way to save her family.

"Scallion, keep still," demanded Ruseq, kicking the crate where the human was confined.

"I can't breathe and can't move. And I've got a fucking itch," complained the muffled voice from the box.

"Quiet, we're here."

The canine-drawn cart stopped outside a twelve-storey building, and unlike most of the city's structures this one had doors and framed windows on all levels; the windows weren't glazed but latticed to prevent anyone from passing through them. These measures protected the chambers of the Great Council. Here they were officed and performed their official duties.

The guards halted Ruseq and his companion, Ossebe, demanding to know the purpose of their visit.

"We have Clan Leader Fecting's offering for leniency. As is the custom, we are delivering this before the case is decided. We all know his stupid human is going to lose." The scorn in Ruseq's voice sounded real.

"Okay, take it to the clerk on the first floor. Follow the signs."

"Wait," demanded another guard as he rounded the cart. He laid his spear to one side and then started to examine the box. "What's in it?"

"You know we can't tell you that."

"Then maybe I will take a look."

"You're not permitted."

"Oh, and you would tell on me, would you?"

"No," replied Ruseq.

The guard grabbed the crate and pulled it towards him with ease; the weight was negligible to the neway's strength. Scallion felt it slide along the bed of the cart and wished he had his ballistic revolver with him, but he was unarmed. They all were. If caught, they were to surrender and not resist.

The guard lifted it at one end, testing the weight. "Seems light to me."

"We don't have that many relics to offer," Ruseq let slip.

"Ah, so that's your bribe, is it. Won't work, you know. The council has hundreds of relics already."

"It's Fecting's best offer. Maybe we have one they don't."

"Okay, take it inside."

The clerk wasn't surprised by their arrival.

"Good, you just won me free drinks all night," she said. "I told Vide that Fecting's clan was expecting to lose. Why would they let a human speak for them anyway? It will be the end of their clan."

She led them to a locked room. Once the door was open, she told them where to place the crate. Before leaving, she checked that the create was securely closed, the lid nailed in place.

"Good," she said. "I wouldn't want the other clerks taking a peek. Now you two can go."

Ruseq and Ossebe returned to the cart outside, and then to the building where the clan was housed. Their part was done.

As expected, Sara stood unaccompanied in a tunnel looking out to the open ground of the arena. Tiers of seats rose around the arena; it was a full house and already very vocal. The Great Council, comprising ten members, sat on a raised dais at the far end of the arena: men and women robed in elaborate outfits, with every detail designed to inspire awe and to intimidate. Beneath them at the centre of the stadium was a small podium. There the petitioner stood.

She watched the cases that preceded her. While she did so, neway approached her to offer her refreshments. The stream of offerings was continuous, and with each one, as she declined them all, came an insult, a disparaging comment, a slander, slur and taunt after taunt. Nothing knocked her resolve; she was ready.

The first case was lost. The claimant was seeking a reversal of the banishment of her son. The second also lost. He was seeking retribution for an insult made upon his clan. Then Fecting took to the podium. He was booed and catcalled. Sara knew this wasn't a good sign. As a clan leader, he should have received greater respect, but the crowd had been goaded to the point that they thought it right to ignore custom and procedure; after all, it was only a human that was going to be speaking.

Above the noise of the crowd, slowly being quietened by the gestures of the council's reader, she heard Fecting introduce her. The acoustics were transmitting his voice around the entire stadium.

"…Therefore, I have permitted my human property

to bring this before the Great Council. I, Fecting, clan leader, believe this is the right thing to do."

His final statement sealed his fate. No matter what, his fortune and that of his whole clan would now depend on Sara's performance.

She was made to wait as low-fenced pens were quickly set out around the arena floor, just below the tiers of seats. Then she watched, as what she estimated to be one hundred and fifty humans, men, women and children, were herded into those pens. Among them were Fecting's property, and she saw her mother and brother as they were closed into one of the pens. The only person missing was Scallion, who was already working on something else with Ruseq outside the stadium: they had left their building early that morning. The pens were unexpected, but she knew things like this might happen.

"Go." The guard at the tunnel opening directed Sara to the podium.

The roar of noise as she entered was deafening. She swore that some of the council smirked, but at this distance, she dismissed it as her imagination. It was a cacophony of noise, but some insults sang out clearly.

It was a long walk, mentally, to reach the podium, and once she stood upon it, the heavy burden of what she was about to do weighed on her.

"Scallion don't cry out. It's Iscrea."

Cautiously, keeping noise to a minimum, the neway prised open the lid of the crate.

"I never want to do that again," said Scallion, almost collapsing as he lay out at full stretch on the floor. "That was the worst ordeal ever. Why you have to present your bribes in a wooden crate is stupid. You people have too many unnecessary customs."

Iscrea stood over the human. He was slender, with an almost feminine look to his features. "We need to move, Scallion. You need to get up, and we need to get out of here."

Slowly stretching out his cramped limbs, Scallion stood. Iscrea was already standing by the wall. "Stay very close behind me," he advised as he reached out and touched the wall. The ring on his hand pulsed and they both stepped through the wall into the room beyond.

"This is Dimii, and he has permission to be in this building and free access to most areas without question. We don't have that, so we need to keep out of sight as much as possible."

"We need to be as quick as possible," said Scallion. "Sara will be at the stadium, and we have to find what we are looking for or let her know that we failed before she speaks out."

"Dimii has keys to most of the locked doors. Much of the building is empty because the council is in the arena, but there are still a few people here. He will go ahead and check each room; we will follow, passing through walls. We have to get to the top floor, all without being seen."

"Let's move then."

They went from room to room by passing through walls, but when a corridor was clear, they ran its length, ducking through an open door to an empty room where Dimii waited. They sprinted up the stairs as there was nowhere to hide on them. When they reached the landing of the top floor, they had no key to unlock the wooden door before them.

"There should be no one on this floor. Only the council can be up here. What you need must be here somewhere. I will wait here for you," said Dimii.

Iscrea and Scallion stepped through the closed door and emerged on a long corridor beyond. Doors lined either side of the passage, and unlike all the other floors, this one was carpeted along its full length.

"Why do rich, powerful people always have carpets?" Scallion said.

"Because they can. Each door will be locked, but we can walk through them. There should be no one here, but if there is, we cannot get caught."

"So what do we do if we are seen?"

"Whatever is necessary."

They entered the first room, a large office; many of the rooms on this floor were offices, fourteen of them. Each was extravagantly furnished and adorned with expensive bric-a-brac.

"Don't steal anything," warned Iscrea. "They will notice, and if we can get out of here without anyone knowing we were here that would be the preference. Now do your thing. Ruseq says you're good, so prove it."

The doors and furniture might all have been antique and quaintly designed, but the safes in each office were not. Each was hidden and secured in a different place. Scallion's task was to find each and open it. They were too small for the relic-ring to be used, to simply pass through and step inside. So while Scallion searched for safes and attempted to open them with his utility device, Iscrea searched shelves, drawers and other areas for any information that might be useful.

On finding the first safe, the thief smiled. It wasn't

going to be difficult to open; he had seen this design before, and the utility device made quick work of it. Inside, there were pieces of ore, two relic cubes, a blaster and some papers. Iscrea examined the papers as they were written in neway. There was also a data-pad that Scallion unlocked and handed to Iscrea to decipher. They found nothing, so returning everything to how they had found it, they went on to the next room.

Sara stood silent as she waited for the council to decide to silence the crowd. They allowed the chorus of voices to deride her for several minutes before demanding silence. When everyone was finally hushed, the reader rose at the foot of the council's raised platform. He wore black robes, and the make-up lining his eyes and across his lips was also black. To Sara, he resembled a corpse.

He introduced Sara by name, hoping it would be infamous before the proceedings finished. He performed the correct opening phrases for everything to commence and his elaborate tones and gestures enthralled the crowd. Then he announced that he was to read the human's original letter aloud for the audience to hear.

"*Great Council, the ruling body for all the clans,*

I, a mere human, have been blessed with being the most potent gifted to have ever lived. It is due to this blessing that I have been able to discover matters that would have been previously hidden from you, as they would have been locked inside the relics that cannot yet be activated. I do not know why such a gift was given to me, but as I serve the neway, I can only assume it is to benefit my master and all of his race. I have sought Fecting's, clan leader's, permission to make this bequest to you. I am now at your mercy to grant me an audience."

This wasn't the letter she had written, but much of the real content wouldn't have been read aloud anyway. This wasn't unexpected.

The reader finished and made a flourish of folding and pocketing the letter. The crowd rose once again to a cascade of insults and jeering.

"Is this the petition you sent to the council, Sara?"

The reader would dictate the proceeding unless a council member spoke out directly.

"Yes, reader." This was a lie. If she didn't play the reader's game, she would be closed down before she had a chance to deliver her performance. If she lost, all of her lies would be exposed to show without any doubt that she had always been false.

"So I understand you have a plea prepared. That you intend to offer something to the council so that your clan can be granted the elevated status of residence within Borsay?"

"There is more that I would ask too."

"Really. Then let all hear what you wish to ask the council to grant you."

The reader's tone and gestures continued to be overly dramatic as he sucked the crowd into his performance.

"In addition, I would ask that I am granted the same status as any other gifted."

The crowd remained silent. Then a mutter ran around the stadium as they asked their neighbours and friends if they had heard her correctly.

The reader wasn't prepared for the silence and quickly

intervened by repeating Sara's words with added pomp and grandeur. He finished with raucous laughter to mock the demand and raised his arms to encourage the crowd to join him, and they did. When he was happy that he once again controlled the crowd, he brought them to a quieter state and continued.

"Do you have anything else to demand of the council?"

"Yes, that the banished are once again permitted to rejoin the clans."

This time there was no muttering among the silent crowd. It was a known, but an unspoken thing, that much of the population didn't support banishment when trivial laws could separate them from their loved ones forever.

The reader once again resorted to repeating her request and concluding with laughter, but his support from the crowd was now significantly less. The encouraged laughter was erratic, with only short outbursts in small pockets of the gathering.

"And anything else?"

"I would like permission to present a plan that would free all the neway from the threats that emanate from the Device, their botdrones and their human stations. To rid this world of that invasion."

The reader hadn't expected this, and he faltered. He looked to the council for guidance, and the crowd waited.

One of the council, all of whom had remained stoic so far and unresponsive to the proceedings, gestured to the reader that he should continue.

He regained his composure quickly, and although some of the drama had disappeared, both from his voice and gestures, he went on with his performance.

"And so, Sara, we come to your offering. What do you offer that would win the council's favour on these matters."

Now the stage was hers. She had completed the first and possibly the most significant challenge. She had got to the point where the council were permitting her to present her performance. At any time they could have shut down the proceeding under any pretence, but now the audience wanted to see the show. Now even the council risked turning the crowd against them.

Sara waited. And waited. *Scallion would be proud of me.* The suspense in the crowd built up slowly. She remained as still as a statue. Muttering began, questioning what she was doing. Was she going to do anything? Then, just at the moment she believed any heckling would have begun, she spoke. Now she mimicked the reader's pomp and drama. Her voice carried throughout the stadium, and she accompanied her words with gestures and bodily movements, rotating as she did so to face every section of the tiered seating.

"I have asked for four things, and so in return, I will present four wonders never before seen by anyone, neither neway nor human. Each act can be verified now, in this arena, by the reader himself. Would he be willing?"

She turned to him to seek his acknowledgement, and this time the crowd was with her, and they called upon him to comply.

The dark figure looked once again to the council. There was no precedent for this; this was new. The same council member waved him on.

"Gladly," he called, rising to his feet, and bowing to the crowd.

That was their cue. Fecting himself led out the two

neway carrying the table. The relic that had given Poppy his new left arm and had regenerated the part of his missing ear. Behind them followed half a dozen more with musical instruments, dancing and singing in time with the measured pace set by their clan leader.

The crowd clapped and joined in with the well-known tune. The reader descended to the arena and walked to meet Fecting.

Sara raised her voice above the song.

"Some of you may know this relic. It is not a secret. Many of you may have had limbs attached by one similar to this one. I know that Borsay boasts of having no less than three of these tables. Some clans may have more. But it can do more. It can do much more."

Fecting halted a short distance from Sara, who remained on the small plinth allocated to her. Her position still made her the centre of attention, and from that spot, she also commanded the best location acoustically to be heard in every seat.

Sara raised her hands to focus the crowd on her. Then, just as the reader had done, she slowly lowered then to bring the crowd to a hush.

"Reader, would you ever raise a weapon to harm a clan leader?" She didn't wait for his reply. "Would you put hard, cold metal into the flesh of another neway with a sword like this?"

Fecting raised a polished blade above his head, flourishing it to catch the lighting. There were gasps from the crowd, astonishment, as no one was permitted, other than the guards, to bring a weapon inside the stadium. The attention of more than a thousand eyes moved from the blade to the reader, to the council, all wanting to know what was going to be done against the breach of law. However, they also wanted to see the show, to know what came next. Sara didn't need to see the council; she watched the reader and knew when he had received the signal to continue. She let him speak, his voice now quieter because he wasn't in the position designed to amplify his words.

"No. We have a law that says we cannot harm another without just cause or reason."

"What if I told you that no harm would come to Fecting. Would you do it then?" Again, she didn't let him respond.

"Fecting, hand the weapon to the reader. Reader, give the clan leader a non-fatal wound."

Fecting offered the man the blade, and the rest of the clan began to chant one word. "Reader. Reader. Reader. Reader." The crowd followed.

Sara raised her voice over the chant coming from every spectator.

"You have my permission," said Fecting softly, so that only the reader could hear him.

"Come now, reader, it's not a difficult task," called Sara. "You have the weapon; you have the council's permission. You have Fecting's permission – take the blade."

The reader accepted the blade, and with the flurry of a drumbeat, the chant was changed to: "Cut. Cut. Cut."

Fecting took the point of the sword and held it to his left shoulder. The penetration would miss any vital organs, but the pain would be real, and he was prepared for that; it had to be real!

Fecting leaned onto the blade, taking hold of it with both of his hands. He needed the reader to thrust, for the crowd to see him do so, and he goaded him on. The reader lunged; it was a half-hearted attack, but Fecting used his grip to pull the blade deep into his flesh. Then he withdrew the blade and blood flowed.

The crowd gasped and fell silent. The reader dropped the weapon. Fecting stood, head bowed, blood quickly staining his clothes and descending to the arena floor.

"Reader. Reader," repeated Sara to get his attention. "Can you confirm that the wound is real?"

"It's real."

"The crowd cannot hear you, reader. Is the wound real?"

"Yes, the wound is real," he called out.

Sara stepped down from her dais. The two neway who had carried the table quickly grabbed Fecting and carried him to the table, which was already adjusted for him. As they laid their leader out, they tore off his garments to expose his naked torso and the wound that was bleeding profusely.

Sara didn't run, though she wanted to. She casually approached the table and laid her hand upon it. A moment later Fecting rose, dismounted the table, and using the torn remnants of his clothing wiped away any blood from the area of the wound. As he did that, Sara returned to the dais.

"Reader, can you confirm that the wound has gone? That Fecting is unharmed?"

The dark-robed figure approached the clan leader. Then he prodded the shoulder in disbelief.

"Reader, is the clan leader unharmed?"

"Yes."

"Louder, reader. The crowd is waiting."

"Yes, he is unharmed."

The musicians began a merry tune and cheered. The crowd went with them, and as the song intro finished, they broke into another well-known song and the crowd accompanied them. Fecting used the interlude to leave the arena and return in fresh clothing.

Following Fecting back into the arena walked Lonlin, and on a long leash and collar, she led Retisen. The music stopped.

"Behold a banished," Sara called out. "The first to walk inside Borsay for centuries. I asked that these banished neway be allowed to return to the clans. But how can that be achieved? It is forbidden."

Sara was pulling on long-suppressed emotions now. Many in the crowd would have lost someone they cared for to an ancient law or custom that had banished their lover, family or child. The rules of the neway hadn't changed from the time they walked and lived on the surface, and many of the old ways hadn't adapted to the new way of life.

Lonlin had always looked for a way to be reunited with her mother and brother. She had studied their laws and customs, and asked Dimii while he stayed in Borsay to search through the archives and libraries for possible solutions to the problem. Several years ago, she had found something, but even though there was then a possibility, she had no way of executing the solution, and it wasn't a guaranteed outcome either.

"The banished thrive outside the clans. They live closer to the old ways now, and some have discovered how to call the worms."

Silence descended. Calling worms was one of the

greatest secrets and powers that only clan leaders and Great Council members possessed. The banished, considered outcast and unworthy, held supposedly in a disdain close to that felt for humans, could not have learned that secret.

Sara turned a full circle on the small dais, arms raised as she made her announcement. Although the move was part of her theatrics, it served a purpose. She watched the ten members of the Great Council as she rotated and a few broke their stoicism. They were turning to their neighbour whispering something. Sara had an idea of what that might be. If the banished could call worms, if they possessed a relic table that could heal their torn fangs, then they were in a position to set up a new civilisation, a new way.

"There is an old, ancient law of the neway." Sara had completed her turn and drew the focus of the audience back to her. "It says, in its simplest form, that should any neway commit themselves to an act that saves their people from disaster, then that neway shall be exalted. The banished are still neway, and they are willing to lead the forces that can remove the humans from your planet. Surely that would be a great act worthy of being exalted? Surely, if they can remove humans from your planet, and you can once again live on the surface, that would be enough for them to return?"

The crowd buzzed with whispers. Sara rotated again and saw the council members engaging with each other.

"The banished have also learned a few tricks while they have been outside. Reader, take the leash that holds the banished man and keep him by your side."

Lonlin handed the lead over and drew Retisen to the side of the reader.

"Touch him, reader. He is there, isn't he? He is real?"

As directed, the dark-robed man prodded the banished man before him.

"Well, reader? Is he there?"

"Of course he is," he replied, turning to face Sara.

"Are you sure?"

The audience gasped. The reader turned back as the collar dropped to the floor and the man it had bound simply vanished.

"Seems the banished have a new skill. I wonder to what use that might be put."

The band struck up a low, ominous beat.

"If the banished can simply disappear, what use would that be?"

Sara needed to hold them until Retisen was in position. One of the relics he had possessed was a ring that on activation turned the wearer invisible. Now she had to give him enough time to move.

"Aaargh!" The cry echoed around the stadium, as there, standing high on the raised platform of the Great Council, stood the banished man. He was mere feet away from the nearest council member and brandishing two swords above his head.

Some of the crowd screamed; guards converged on the council. The nearest members of the council moved quickly, scrambling away from the would-be assailant.

The drum in the band boomed, and the singers wailed a high-pitched tone that caused everyone to look towards them. It was only a fraction of a moment, but when they looked back to the banished man, he was gone again.

"What indeed could be done with such a skill." Sara hoped that Retisen was fleet of foot. The commotion they had just created brought more guards into the arena, and they were not only closing on the raised platform but her small dais too.

As the armed soldiers surrounded her, she raised her arms and proclaimed loudly, "But there is no need to worry, as the banished man is still on his leash."

There stood Retisen, head bowed, the collar on and no weapons in sight. Orders were barked and the banished man was seized and brought to his knees by the guards.

"Council, may I proceed?"

Sara didn't address the reader. This time she spoke directly to the ten ornately dressed leaders, who were gradually returning to their seats and regaining their composure. Such a spectacle had never been seen before and the crowd applauded. The fact that she, a mere human, was speaking directly to the council, was overlooked as the crowd called for more.

The lone council member that had signalled for the reader to proceed earlier performed the same motion, but now it was to Sara.

"Guards, release the banished. He has more to show us all."

Hesitantly, as they had never taken an order from a human, the soldiers complied, and they all withdrew slowly. Orders were issued among the guards and soldiers, and now many of them formed a protective rank around the platform of the council.

Lonlin had retreated to the entrance tunnel, out of sight and tucked away in the shadows. In her hand, she held a comms device and waited.

Retisen raised his right arm and then dropped it sharply. As he did so, Lonlin gave the order, and there in the open arena appeared a large vehicle moving at speed.

On its rear was mounted a turret gun and holding on tightly screaming challenges were armed neway. Retisen raised and dropped his arm again, and a second vehicle, a lighter open-topped buggy, raced in from nowhere, appearing from nothing, following the first carriage.

Many of the audience panicked, rising from their seats to escape the stadium. Others screamed with delight at the spectacle. Chaos and turmoil swept around the stadium.

The two vehicles turned sharply, performing a one-eighty turn almost on the spot, and then they raced back to their point of origin and vanished.

Sara waited. It took time for the crowd to return to their seats, for composure to return to the stadium, and when it did, the hush that fell felt like a physical curtain weighing her down. Now Sara prepared to lift that and reveal her final act, but Scallion hadn't yet succeeded, and she had a dilemma to solve first and only seconds to decide on her next course of action.

They had opened six safes and found all manner of treasures, but not yet what they wanted. The seventh office, though, was grander than the others, and Scallion believed this one had promise. They had heard the roar of sound from the stadium and knew that Sara was speaking. How long remained before they failed her, they couldn't know, so they pressed on with increased haste.

This safe had something new, something that hadn't been in any other, a comms device.

"You know how to use this?" Scallion asked Iscrea as he handed him the comms.

"Of course." The neway studied it a moment before handing it back. "There are messages, but they are in human writing. I'm good at speaking your tongue, but my reading needs improvement. You look."

"This is it. This is what we want. There has to be something here for Sara."

The comms device held by Lonlin became active when Iscrea sent her a text phrase. She had no idea what it meant, but if he had sent it, then it could only be for Sara.

There was a hush outside now, and Sara faced the council. Lonlin couldn't simply run out to her though. Flow might have helped, but both she and Iyne had been left back at their building for their safe keeping should this all go wrong. Lonlin struggled with what to do. The fear of letting Sara, her clan, her family and everyone else down washed over her and the despair triggered a response.

'Lonlin? What? How are you in my head?'

'I don't know. Scallion sent you a message.'

'What is it?'

Lonlin passed on the message and Sara addressed the crowd once again.

"As promised, I have asked for four things, and I have now presented three wonders that I am sure have entertained you all."

The audience cheered.

"The fourth request was for permission to present a plan. A plan that involves the banished, a plan to free the neway from the human occupation of this beautiful world. However, I think that plan should be presented to the Great Council and not here in this stadium."

The crowd booed, but it wasn't with real disappointment. Everyone knew that only the council could hear such a thing; this was the whole purpose of the performance: for the human, Sara, to gain a private audience. If she had failed, then she would no doubt have suffered publicly, but so far as the crowd had decided, she had succeeded. But what of the council's opinion.

"Great Council, would you grant me a private audience to discuss this plan? Perhaps we could name it Operation Magpie?"

The phrase 'Operation Magpie' was what Scallion had sent. Sara wondered if perhaps she had already done enough to succeed, but if Scallion's phrase was linked to what he had been searching for, then those two words alone might both help her or condemn her. It was her gamble, and she had taken it.

The crowd had begun to chant: "Yes. Yes. Yes."

Sara knew that winning the crowd was a great achievement but still not necessarily enough to sway the council.

Full pomp, ceremony and procedure had returned to the arena. The council once again sat impassively, hard-faced and emotionless. The reader stood with his back to Sara; he had moved to a position where he could speak quietly with the council. It was the reader that would proclaim the outcome.

The dark-robed figure returned to his original position. He moved slowly, building the suspense, and as he took his place, silence fell once again around the entire arena.

He waited a moment before slowly raising his arms and then he waited again.

Sara had kept her composure throughout. She had wrapped herself so profoundly in her performance that she had forgotten what depended on her. Now, in these last few seconds, she could feel the sweat running down her back. Her heart pulsed so quickly and intensely that it echoed in her eardrums.

"The Great Council will meet with the human Sara."

She had done it. The entire neway audience rose to their feet, cheering. The humans penned around the arena joined the celebration. Sara's legs wobbled, and she nearly collapsed as the relief washed over her. Then she reset her resolve. It wasn't all over yet. Now she had to face the council without a public witness.

chapter thirteen

An Audience

Sara woke next to Retisen; she was naked and so was he. When they had left the stadium, the roadways had been lined with people cheering Sara. The fact that she was human was seemingly forgotten as word of her spectacular performance spread. As Fecting had predicted, the mood of Borsay stayed buoyant and quickly shifted into a festival, with dancing, singing and parties breaking out across the city. Fecting, his clan members and his human property stayed close to their building, but as more and more neway turned up to see the human Sara, it wasn't long before the wine, spirit alcohol and food was free-flowing.

They had danced late into the evening. In the city, the lighting dimmed as the day progressed, giving the illusion of nightfall. Sara had hugged Scallion, glad to see him well, and appreciated what he had achieved. She was introduced to Dimii and Iscrea too, and she hugged them, the drinking and relief over her recent success fuelling her growing fondness for the neway people.

She remembered kissing Retisen. She had kissed boys before but had never taken anything beyond that. Now though she'd felt ready, and the neway, although over one hundred years old, aroused her. He, in turn, did not shrink away from her because she was human. They had sneaked away from the roadway party back into their building to Retisen's room, where he currently slept alone. Sara was the one who instigated everything, but the neway was the one who guided her and treated her well. They had closed the curtain over their doorway, a signal that they were not to be disturbed. The fact that there was no solid door and their noise would carry beyond the veiled opening never occurred to them. Sara lost her virginity, and when she woke beside her lover she had no regrets. She rolled into him and hugged him. His arm lifted and then brought her closer. She lay there for a little while and then decided to get up. Her head was foggy, and she needed water and chqaqaie.

Closing the curtain behind her as she left the room, she turned, and there was Sky. Her ma too was leaving a room that wasn't the one they shared. Before that curtain closed, Sara saw Scallion pulling on his pants. The two women looked at each other for a moment, both unsure what to say or do next.

Demic entered the hallway. "Morning, you two," she greeted them. "Now that was a party. Oh! I know that look," she said, noting the expressions on both their faces. "If you don't regret it then own it, that's what I say. Who were the lucky men... women maybe?"

"Let's find something to drink," said Sky, breaking the awkwardness.

"Wine so early?" queried Demic humorously.

"No, water, retch. We need to shake off the morning-after effect because there's still a lot to do."

They entered the common room, to find Fecting sat at the table with Dimii.

"I'm glad you are up. The council has set a time to meet with you. It's today. We have three hours to get you ready. Dimii has been here in Borsay for several years. He will tell you what he knows of each of the council members. Everything all right?"

Fecting had noted the sheepish looks on both the faces of Sara and Sky.

"They're fine," replied Demic. "Probably more than fine. They had a good night. Both of them." Demic smiled broadly, amused by the situation.

Scallion was next into the common area, followed by Ruseq and Ninety-Six. Fecting suggested that Dimii take Sara to the top floor, where they could have some privacy.

Later, when Sara was getting ready to leave with Fecting, Sky helped her to prepare. There was no formality or theatrics required for the meeting, and so it had been decided that Sara should dress casually, as a neway would. She was seeking elevation to a high standing among these people, equal with other gifted. Therefore emulating them was seen as prudent.

"I understand that you spent the night with Retisen?" said Sky.

"You were with Scallion."

"I'm not judging. You're nearly eighteen. We aren't in any station, and out here everything is strange. But he is a neway. You are property."

"Ma, if it was a one-off I'm okay with that. If it's not,

then we will need to see. I'm about to challenge the whole way that the neway have lived for centuries, and who I slept with last night is not that important now. Is it?"

"No, I suppose not."

"I might not return from this meeting, Ma. Let me enjoy the memory."

Sky hugged her daughter and held her long enough that Sara needed to prise her away.

"So, Scallion, eh? One-off or…?"

"I don't know. We were drunk, and it seemed a good idea at the time."

"Have you spoken with him since?"

"Yes, but neither of us mentioned it."

"Well, just bear in mind if I don't come back from the council meeting, I'm guessing things might get unpleasant for everyone. Talk to him, talk with Demic too. You need to plan for the worse and get Jeb and you out of here if it all goes wrong. You'll need Scallion and Demic for that. While I'm away, go find them and sort it. Retisen and Lonlin too. I'll leave all the curios active with Lonlin. You might need them."

The roadway wasn't lined with people now. The timing of the council meeting with Sara hadn't been publicly announced. However, when she was observed travelling with Fecting towards the council's offices, people stopped and stared. Some called out encouragement to her. No one threw an insult.

"The possible return of the banished to the clans has won you great favour," acknowledged Fecting. "The risk they have posed to our current way of life has been considered a threat for some time, one the Great Council could not find a way to deal with. I must admit that being taken by Retisen and his outcasts was a thing of fortune. How you managed to do that I will not ask. In truth, as our laws currently stand, I never want to know."

"Will they all see me or just one? Will you be with me?"

"I don't know. Dimii has told me, as he has probably you, that there is a hierarchy to the council. No one outside the council knows what that is, but I am sure Dimii is right. I suspect you and I will meet two, maybe three of the council. But I really don't know."

"Any final advice?"

"You've got this far by being bold. I would recommend more of the same. And Sara, so far as I am concerned you are not property. You are one of the clan, and if we are allowed to leave, but without gaining any support, you will not be considered property by me or any of the clan. Neither will Sky or Jeb."

"That means a lot, Fecting."

A clerk met them at the main door of the building and escorted them to the upper floor. There, he left them at the door on the landing. He wasn't permitted to enter the offices beyond. He told them to knock and wait.

The door opened almost immediately, and before them stood a council member in a plain red robe. Sara recognised him as the member that had signalled for the events in the stadium to continue. He was very tall, five foot eight, at an equal height with Sara. His gaunt features weren't as pale as Fecting's; there was a hue to the skin that indicated he had not long since gorged on blood. He smiled at them warmly and with the genuine appearance of being glad to see them.

"I am Vereign. It is a pleasure to meet you finally,

Sara." He addressed her in the neway language.

"It's an honour, Councillor Vereign."

"Firstly, today, there is no formality. We have a lot to get through. Follow me to my office."

They moved down the carpeted hall and entered a luxuriously furnished room. A circular table was central to the space, with three chairs placed at it. Against the far wall was a large wooden antique desk.

"Carpets and wooden furniture are new to you I see," said Vereign as he caught Sara staring around the room. "That's actually a good thing for me. It lets me know that you are more than likely genuine and not an agent of the Device."

They each took a seat at the table.

"No one else will be joining us?" asked Fecting.

"The others will meet us shortly in a larger room further down the corridor. I wanted a private conversation with you first."

Sara was wary now; she hadn't expected such a warm welcome. Vereign seemed genuinely pleased that they were there. She suspected this was some form of a ruse to put her off her guard.

"A few direct questions to start I think," began the councillor. "First, do you know what a magpie is?"

"It's an Earth bird," replied Sara. "It's black and white and likes to steal shiny objects."

"How do the clan leaders call the worms?"

She had expected this question, and she answered correctly.

"How do you know this?"

"A relic told me."

"I will accept that for now, but I will need evidence

shortly. Can you heal the wounding that is done to the banished, to their fangs?"

"Yes, with the relic table."

"And you have the cylinder here in Borsay."

Sara looked at Fecting. "Yes, it's here," answered the clan leader.

"Last immediate question. Do you believe your plan has any chance of success? Your plan to rid us of the humans, of Earth?"

"Yes."

"I read your letter with great interest. Did you write it?"

"Yes." Sara still didn't know where the conversation was leading, and so chose to keep her answers short to avoid any traps that may be getting laid for her.

"How did you learn our language? I know they do not know it in the stations, and you have not long been outside of one."

"A relic taught me."

"In such a short time?"

"Yes."

"I can see that you are both suspicious of me. I assume you expected a mean authoritarian, keen to disprove you and find a way to discredit you, kill you, banish you maybe? Your expressions are enough to confirm that. Little is known of how the Great Council works outside the council itself. The Great Council existed long before the Device was discovered, long before it was known as the Temple of Hontex. It has always been central to how we govern. Fecting knows this. So I will tell you one of our secrets. The council is always an even-numbered body. There is one elected to be senior to all the others. That person carries two votes to the single vote each of the others holds. This does not give the senior councillor total authority, but when a decision is closely divided among the council, it prevents a deadlock. The vote as to whether we give any credence to your plan, whether we hear you out, was such a vote. My two votes broke the deadlock. You will get a hearing before the whole council, and then there will be another vote. That will be today before you leave."

"I assume if we lose the vote we won't leave?" stated Sara.

"It is apparent already that you are well taught in our ways. So you already know that answer."

"So why are we here now, with you?"

"I would like you to win your vote. I would like to think that it is possible to both free the banished and remove Earth's threat to us."

"Why?"

"Now, you will hear my truth. If you win, then it will no longer have to be secret. If you lose, then you won't be telling anyone else. I have a comms device that allows me to communicate with the Device. The others in the council know this. I work with the Device to ensure the ongoing survival of our race. Humans, Earth, has weapons that can destroy our city and any clan settlement. They know the locations of them all, and they remain only because we, the council, give them what they want. This is politics, and not anything any member of the council likes, but it is or has been so far, necessary; this, as you know, is Operation Magpie. But how did you know that?"

"Peter. The human once held by Aris. Now the property of Fecting. He was originally from Earth. He told us."

"We questioned him a long time ago and decided that he was irrelevant, no threat."

"He only recently decided to be helpful."

"He supports your plan then?"

"Yes, and he may even be an important part of it."

"Interesting. I will need to see this relic that told you of the worms."

Sara placed the cube on the floor and activated Many. She explained who the holograph was, and then Vereign questioned her. Many couldn't lie but was able only to give details that supported her owner's statements. She could recount a tale in such a way as not to expose all the facts. She knew what to say to protect both Sara and Fecting.

"That's an extremely useful relic. Where is this headband that you have referred to?"

"Safe, with the clan."

"Now tell me all the details of your plan and all the risks and issues. I need to know everything if I am to persuade the whole council to follow it. Time to decide whether you now trust me or not, Sara."

Seeing no other option, she told Vereign everything he needed to know. Fecting, too, learned details he hadn't previously known. There were, as with all great plans, risks and possible flaws and failings, but Vereign accepted those and also implied that he might be able to help reduce some of those risks.

They finished discussing everything as a knock rapped on the office door.

"That will be the council ready to hear your plan."

Sara and Fecting started to rise.

"No. You are not permitted to speak before the assembly; I must deliver it for you. You must wait here. I will also need to take Many with me."

"Sara, you need to sit down."

"But it's been ages."

"Pacing a path through the carpet will not make it happen any quicker."

"But they might already be at the building arresting my ma and brother. Your clan might already be suffering."

"We knew the risks. All those we have left knew the risks. They are prepared, and I've not heard any sounds of fighting out there, and I'm sure we would have if things had gone wrong. Retisen has all his forces on standby to appear fully armed with vehicles inside the city. Demic will not go peacefully. The silence, the wait, is all a good sign. Now sit."

The office door opened, and Vereign stood there. "Come with me, and from this moment, follow protocol and watch what you say carefully."

"What happened?"

"Say that again…" Vereign glared at Sara.

"Councillor Vereign, can you tell me what has happened?"

"That is better, human." Vereign's friendly tone and manner had evaporated entirely.

They walked down the corridor, and outside the room they were about to enter stood a dozen guards. Vereign left them outside as he went on and the guards searched both Sara and Fecting thoroughly, with no regard for their dignity. Then they were allowed to enter.

The room was larger than the previous office, but bare of furniture other than a single bench along the far wall. On the bench sat the council. To the left and right were more guards. A circle was marked on the floor and a guard placed them inside its circumference.

"We will now vote," said Vereign.

The guards raised their blasters towards both Sara and Fecting.

"All those who agree with the human's demands, and agree to execute her plan, raise your hand when I call on you." As he spoke, Vereign raised his right hand.

This was not what Sara nor Fecting had expected. They were not going to be given a chance to speak. Sara had prepared an excellent speech that she hadn't yet used. They had no idea what Vereign had told the Great Council. They had trusted him blindly, a man that worked with the humans of the Device, worked to aid Earth. This vote might now end everything, and they would die.

"Vote now."

Every hand was raised, and the guards lowered their weapons.

"Remove them," ordered Vereign.

Both Sara and Fecting were escorted back to the office they had just left, and the door closed behind them.

"Have we won?" asked Sara. She felt like crying. She had thought she was about to die, but now she had no idea what she felt.

"I would say yes, but what we have won I don't know. It all depends on what Vereign told them."

This time they didn't have to wait long for Vereign to return.

He entered and closed the door. The previous glow of his face had gone and he appeared paler and weary. He leaned with his back to the door and looked hard at both Sara and Fecting.

"That was not what I expected. They did not all indicate their support until the actual vote. It was unanimous. Now they want me to set things in motion and quickly. There may be spies among our people, and so we have to move with haste and secrecy. That will not be easy."

chapter fourteen

Preparation

"So, let me get this right," said Frisk. "You are going to take control of Station Six?"

"Yes," replied Sara. She stood before all of the humans and their chaperons brought to Borsay by Fecting. With them were also Fecting, Peter, Dimii, Iscrea and Retisen.

Everyone had been collected by guards and delivered to a bunker beneath the city. It was a large bunker with many rooms, and so as not to alarm them, Fecting had gone with the guards to let them know that both he and Sara were fine. Sara had been taken directly to the bunker by Vereign from his office.

"And you want all of us to help you?"

"The council has agreed to what I have asked. We will all no longer be property, and the banished can return to the clans. However, they will not announce this. The whole plan is bigger than that. We are going to disconnect Earth from Devil's Rock."

"It can't be done," stated Frisk.

"It can." Peter spoke up, standing as he did so from the earthen table that sprouted directly from the ground beneath it. The oval table had seats to spare, beyond the numbers in the room.

"Sara's plan is possible, but we all will have a part to play."

The metal door slid open and Vereign entered. Several of the neway started to rise in respect to his authority, but he told them to be seated and then took a place at the table.

"Carry on. I'm here to prove that Sara has the support of the Great Council."

"And you think this can be done without taking any lives?" continued Frisk.

"No. It can be done with minimal losses and hopefully without taking any lives."

"And the neway's Great Council supports this?" Frisk directed his question to Vereign.

"We do. But as I'm sure Sara has already told you; we cannot do this openly. A man like yourself must know that. We, the council, must stay out of this. Earth will ask us to get involved if you are successful. And while they still have the ability to destroy all life on this planet, we cannot risk our involvement being known. This is the biggest political game that has ever been played. Surely a man like you will want to partake?"

Frisk fell silent. His plans of living inside the Device and visiting Eden, which he now knew to be Earth, had been dashed. Peter had spent a good deal of time with him, at Sara's request, detailing why he would never be allowed inside the Device and why they would never allow him to go to Earth. He was a mutant; he was considered unclean, a carrier of any number of diseases. However, he could still hold authority on Devil's Rock if he worked with Sara and the neway.

"Is there anyone here that doesn't want to be involved in this?" asked Demic.

No one spoke.

"So by the silence, I am assuming you are all in?"

Some said, "Yes," others nodded, but everyone was willing.

"Okay. Demic, Frisk, Peter and Ninety-Six, you will accompany all the neway, except Lonlin, to Retisen's banished." Sara had walked around the table to the door as she spoke. There, in front of the door, she dropped the curio-disc.

Retisen was already on his feet and walking to join Sara at the door. He walked over the disc and disappeared. Demic was the next to follow him, and one after the other all the neway and the assigned humans followed.

"What are we going to do?" asked Scallion.

"If you would all come this way," said Vereign.

They were led down a long corridor, and after passing a few doors, the councillor stopped and opened one to his left. Beyond was a vast room lined with chest-high plinths.

"We are going to activate and identify all these," stated Sara.

"These are all relics?" asked Lonlin.

"Yes," replied Vereign. "There are two hundred and three, and none have ever been activated. No gifted has ever been potent enough. Sara, however, might just be able to activate them all, and you will all help her to identify them.

"And Earth doesn't know you have all these?"

"No, Lonlin. We are supposed to hand over all our relics. We are then permitted to keep some so that they are seen amidst the general population. How else would we hide the truth if people did not see relics occasionally?

"Let's get to it then," said Sara. "These and the banished will be of use when Frisk gets us back into Station Six." And then she entered the long room.

Word spread throughout Borsay that the human Sara had met with the council and had been sent back to the banished as their envoy. The public announcement detailed that she needed to establish the loyalty of the banished if they were to be afforded a chance of a return. If they did want to return, what act could they possibly achieve that would raise them to an exalted position? The neway people rejoiced at this, and the opinion that the banished should be accepted, and that many of the laws and customs were unfair, began to be spoken aloud.

"You know that this could start a revolution?" The assembled Great Council were meeting, and the question was directed to Vereign.

"We all agreed to this. If this human fails, we can blame the banished. The Device will then destroy all the banished settlements and wipe them out."

After the meeting, Vereign returned to his office and opened his safe. He removed the comms device and, as expected, a message waited for his attention.

'Confirm that the human girl is now safe and that you will soon have the cylinder.'

Vereign replied.

'The girl is safe. The council released her, and she is now retrieving the cylinder and will bring that to me soon. Once she has returned with the cylinder, I will have them both sent to the Device.'

chapter fifteen

Execution

"'m Governor Frisk, now let me in." He was shouting at the comms in his hand.

The turret round exploded close to their speeding vehicle.

"That was close," said Scallion.

Demic steadied the vehicle and set a straight course for the distant Station Six.

"We have mutants out here shooting at us. Now open the gates and let us in."

Ninety-Six leaned out of the window and fired a flurry of blaster shots at the pursuing vehicles.

Sara's mask had started to clog, and so she swapped in a clean filter. It was the last one they had. If the gates didn't open, at least a couple of them would be breathing tainted air by morning.

"We thought you were dead, Governor," the voice repeated over the comms device.

"Well, I'm not. Now get either the station master or Governor Jerim to authorise the gates."

"Governor Frisk, this is Station Master Rime. Can you confirm the colour of the hair on my head?"

"You don't have any hair. You're bald. But your beard's grey."

"The gates are opening, Governor. Once inside, stay inside your vehicle, as the botdrones still have authority to shoot anyone who exits your vehicle."

One of the cannons on top of the wall fired, and the glowing globe projectile sailed over them and exploded just in front of the mutants behind them. The six pursuing vehicles veered off. They weren't willing to risk the station's defences, but Demic didn't slow down as they were still in the range of their turret gun.

The gap in the outer gate was barely wide enough as Demic passed through. Then she raced through the second gate and came to a halt.

"We're inside, Rime. Close the gates," ordered Frisk.

Twenty botdrones stood in the loading area against the backdrop of stacked containers. Their weapons were raised as they positioned themselves to surround the carriage.

"Stay in the vehicle, Governor. Someone is on their way to verify your identity."

After ten minutes, six elite came into view and approached them. The men and women approached cautiously, weapons ready. They used the circling botdrones as cover while they surveyed the interior of the vehicle. Finally, content that the occupants were human, their officer approached.

"Never expected to see you again, Governor. Welcome back," said the officer through the open window. "Can you vouch for your companions?"

"Yes, they're with me."

"Understood, Governor, but we will still need to ask that you all surrender your weapons. Routine, Governor, you understand."

They all disembarked the carriage and were relieved of any weapons.

"What's this?"

One of the elite was holding Flow. The cat was inside an airtight bag with a facemask attached to it so the animal could breathe.

"It's a cat," stated Frisk. "Be careful with her. She's probably the last of her kind, and that makes her valuable. She's mine."

"This way, Governor."

The soldiers followed the new arrivals as the officer and Frisk walked ahead.

They passed the containers and passed through a security door to a walkway wide enough for two people abreast. The elite remained at the rear, still with weapons ready.

"As you know, Governor, these lifts can only take two at a time. You and I will go up first."

Sara and her companions had expected this. Demic had advised them that the officer would ascend first, and only with the governor; this was a method used to separate their primary concern from any others trying to enter the station. While they travelled up to the lofts, the officer would check with the governor that he wasn't being held or coerced by anyone among the new arrivals that might have bad intentions for the station's safety.

What none of them knew for sure though was whether Frisk would turn on them and expose them immediately;

alternatively, whether he would warn the officer of their plan and then lead them into a trap. With the elite still positioned behind them, and nowhere to take cover, the wait was a nervous one.

Ninety-Six and Sara, were ushered into the lift on its return and accompanied by two of the soldiers. Next were Scallion and Demic with another pair of elite.

In the room at the top waited more elite, and with them was a tall, gangly man. Here no one wore masks. The tall man was bald, and his face sported a bushy grey beard. When Sara and Ninety-Six arrived, the man and Frisk were having a subdued conversation adjacent to the exit door. There was no way of knowing what they were discussing.

None of the soldiers had yet to take their aim from the new arrivals. The only person not being covered and threatened was Frisk. The quiet conversation between Rime and Frisk concluded, and the station master left after briefly speaking with the officer that had escorted them to the lofts.

"A lot of whispering," muttered Scallion, loud enough to be heard by those close to him.

"We're committed now, so suck it up, Scallion," whispered Demic.

The door to the room opened, and in rushed a well-dressed young man in a white shirt, blue trousers, and a matching jacket. On the left of his coat was the insignia of a gold-coloured eagle. Following the man were eight fresh elite, and they too bore the same insignia.

"Governor Frisk, so glad to see you well and alive."

"Governor's envoy," Demic told the others, not lowering her voice now. "Looks like we cleared security."

"These people are with me, Grig. Now I want a

shower, clean clothes and a good meal. Arrange the same for them too." And he indicated those that had arrived with him.

They left the room with Frisk's elite escorting them, but they were no longer covered by any weapons nor threatened. Their weapons were not returned though.

They walked along a clean corridor, where all the surfaces were backlit in white. Grig was alongside Frisk at the lead, and much of what he was saying could be heard by everyone. It seemed that the governor had returned just in time. Six others had put themselves forward to replace him, and their campaigns had already begun. Grig told Frisk who they were, but the information meant nothing to any of them except perhaps Demic. The envoy also updated the governor on how his trade had fared and finished with a review of the other stations. Station Twenty-Eight was close to failing, and discussions had already begun on how they might reduce the population.

Sara listened with interest, but when they passed through a door off the corridor, she stopped in awe, needing Scallion to move her on. They had walked onto a platform above the concourse below. From here she could see scores of people moving about below them. The large square was well lit and a buzz of activity. Voices rose to them, all sounding happy and satisfied. Sara leaned over the balcony, and below were glass-fronted shops, bars, restaurants and cafes all facing into the square. Other wide walkways led from the square, and they too were lined with shops and food outlets.

"Welcome to Wonderland," said Demic as she returned to collect Sara, who had fallen behind the others. "I told you it was nothing like the town. No containers here. The lofters have access to real food, fashionable clothing, entertainment and more." They were walking to catch up now, with Sara still gazing over the balustrade. "It's not perfect here, but crime is minimal. They all know what it's like below where the grounders live, and that this is all a secret to them below. The only punishment here is death. We don't have prisons. So you can imagine that not very many risk anything too nefarious."

They took a lift down to the square, and from there they walked in procession past the shops and bars. People moved out of their way as they passed. A few pointed, and several comments they overheard were in surprise at seeing the governor alive.

They left the bright shopping and entertainment area through another door at the end of one of the long corridors that spanned out from the square. As the door opened, they stepped through a second open door into a tube lined with seats. There had been a small queue of people waiting at the door, but the governor and his whole entourage went directly to the front. Before they sat down inside the awaiting tube, the other passengers inside disembarked, all of them. Those who might have been going further were told to leave by the elite.

With only the governor's party inside, the tube set off. The motion was smooth, and Sara had no idea how fast they might be travelling. The carriage stopped at six more doors, but with the elite standing at the tube's doors, no one who was waiting entered the tube. They reached their destination and left to another backlit corridor, but this exit door had required a code before it would open.

"I know where I'm going, Grig, so take my guests to the Blue Rooms and make sure they have all they need."

Frisk turned left with his elite escort while the envoy led the others to the right.

Sara, Scallion, Ninety-Six and Demic were shown to their chambers off a central shared common area. Here the furniture was all of exceptional quality, soft chairs and sofas, wall hangings, shelves with ornate bric-a-brac. The walls and ceiling were backlit in a soft blue, whereas the floors were all carpeted in a thick pile. Each of the personal chambers had a large soft bed and a private bathroom.

While they all showered, a selection of clean clothing was delivered to their rooms. The men and women delivering it treated them all as though they were important guests to be served. After they had cleaned up, they were served a meal in the common area at a large dining table. The food was freshly prepared, and there was no sign of any ration packs or preserved cuisine.

"And everyone lives like this?" asked Sara.

"Not exactly like this, but yes, everyone in the lofts has access to real food, clean clothing and all the amenities that we saw on the way here," answered Demic.

"They all work though, right?"

"Yes. Here they are paid wages too, but unlike grounders, the wages vary. The more prestigious the job, the higher they are paid. That creates a class structure, so some serve, like those that brought our food and clothing, and others don't."

"Can we get weapons?" asked Scallion. "I know only the elite are armed up here, but surely there's illegal stuff?"

"No illegal weapons up here. If you are found with any sort of weapon, the sentence is death. That proves a highly effective deterrent."

"Do you think we can trust Frisk?" asked Sara.

"We don't have a choice," replied Ninety-Six.

"He knows the truth of this world now. It's whether he believes it or not that's the real question. If he still thinks he can get to Eden or the Device, he might still sell us out. He needs both you and the curio for that, and at the moment he only has you."

"Are you really with us?" Sara asked the huge man that had always frightened her until recently. Ever since Borsay, Ninety-Six had seemed different, more relaxed and open.

"What Valerie and I did in the town was to get a better life for us and Poppy. We only did what was necessary, but as you know, that was not always considered… Well, let's say we did everything that we thought necessary. Now we have a chance to make everything better for everyone. I'm on board with that."

They finished their meal, and as their table was being cleared by serving staff, Frisk arrived in their quarters. He was alone and sat at the table with them and waited until all the servers had left.

"Governor Jerim is off station at the moment. He is at Station Eight, my station. Word has been sent to all the stations that I'm still alive. My suggestion is that we act sooner rather than later. With Jerim away, few would challenge my authority here. So I've asked Rime if I can show you all the main control centre and he's agreed."

"Who does he think we are?" asked Demic.

"As we discussed. You are Razer, a disgraced elite officer believed to be dead. Rime believes you are responsible for saving me when my own elite could not find my shuttle that crashed in the Scorched Land, and for that, I am looking to reinstate you. Ninety-Six is Ninety-Six. He's already known here because of the deals he and

Valerie had with some key authorities in the lofts. Rime also saw him before he was flown to Station Eight on my orders. So Ninety-Six is working with me to apprehend Sara. They know now that you are connected. That secret was not well kept after they thought I was dead. Scallion, well I've told them you work for Ninety-Six. It was the easiest story."

"Do they know about the cylinder?" asked Scallion.

"They know I have a particularly important curio that I was going to send to the Device, along with Sara. Other than that they don't know anything more."

"Are we safe here?" asked Demic.

"Not really. There were six candidates for my position. Now that I'm back, some of those might still want my position and so accidents happen. Now they know Sara is connected others will want her too. We can't trust anyone. I think for now we are okay, as many will want to know what and where the curio is too before they make any moves, but that's not for certain. We need to be cautious and get this done quickly. I only have twelve of my own elite on Station Six, and I can't be one hundred per cent certain they are still loyal."

"Do you still have the humanoid OD?" asked Sara.

"What OD? I've never had an OD."

"The one you sent after Scallion when he first stole the cylinder at the flight dock."

"That wasn't me."

"But it knew Scallion by name and that he had the curio."

"This is the first time any of you has mentioned an OD. I've not seen one of them for years. The last one was sent here from the Device to collect the last connected that was discovered, but he had nothing like your potential."

"So we need to be quick then is the bottom line?" interjected Demic. "When are we going to see the main control room?"

"We can go anytime. Rime is there for the next few hours, and so long as he's there, we will get access."

"Do you still have the comms device?"

"Of course," replied Frisk.

"Then tell the banished to be ready. We are starting now."

As they prepared to leave their quarters with Frisk, Sara handed the curio-disc to Scallion that had been hidden inside the lining of her slouch bag. "You know what to do, Scallion. Don't lose this, no matter the cost." Then she picked up Flow and placed her inside the bag.

They travelled by the cylinder transport to another area of the lofts, with Frisk leading them past any elite patrolling along their path.

"Past this next door is the control room. Once we act, there will be no return for any of us," said Frisk.

"Remember, we don't want to kill anyone if it can be avoided. We want all these people to support us when this is over." Sara knew that the chances of success without any injuries were slim, but she felt it was important to try. It was no one's fault here at the station that their world was the way it was.

"Welcome, Governor Frisk," called Rime as he left his central chair to walk down and meet the guests. "Razer, you will have seen this room many times, but I understand that it is the first time for your friends. Let me tell you what happens here."

The room was circular. From the central raised seated

podium it cascaded down onto four more levels. On each level were controllers, twenty people in total, sitting at an array of control desks. Not all the desks were occupied, but all displayed holographic readings. Around the outer perimeter of the room were four elite soldiers, each armed with a rifle and a holstered blaster.

"As you know, there are other control centres spread throughout the lower level manned by grounders. Those apply direct operational changes to the systems for lighting, air, factories, the mine and just about everything else. Those systems also feed some of the services up here, and some of our services feed those down there, and that is why there are conduits between the two levels. Here" – and he waved around the entire room – "we can monitor everything in the whole station. We don't necessarily have full control of the systems, but we can see everything and tell the lower control stations when to make changes."

The four guests attempted to spread out, moving away from Rime and Frisk as they took an interest in different areas.

"No, let's stay together, shall we." Rime brought them all closer as he moved from the outer ring towards the central control chair.

"But I doubt that excites any of you. You all know that services have control rooms, and many of the grounders are engineers who work on the services or in those control rooms." Rime stopped and checked his party. "Where's Scallion?"

They were passing the third tier in, and one of the group was missing.

"Here. I dropped something. Coming now." Scallion was crouched down to the left of the entrance door, but he sprinted up now to join the others.

"We can seat a hundred controllers in here if necessary and monitor all the grounder stations, but that's not necessary, so we operate with a smaller crew just to keep an eye on things."

They had reached the central chair.

"This is the only place where the botdrones can be redirected." Rime indicated the chair. "The majority of the botdrones act autonomously, most in fact, under normal circumstances, and follow their primary programming. But from this chair, I can change some of that programming and assign them new tasks. I can, for example, order them, or a number of them, to hunt a single person or every grounder. I can tell them to block access to the mines, the factories and more. And only the people authorised to sit in this chair can do that."

The station master was immensely proud of that authority.

"I can deputise others for when I'm not available, but I only ever allow them access to the level one functions. Only I, not even the governors, have access to the full range of commands that can be issued to the botdrones of this station."

"No, you don't have access to all their commands or all the functions of this station."

Peter was standing by the entrance doorway, and beside him, with his back to the room, was Ruseq, locking the door with Scallion's utility device.

"Who are you? Guards..."

The four elite were nowhere to be seen.

"Where are the guards?" Rime reached quickly for the chair to raise the alarm.

The sound of the heavy calibre ballistic gun and the impact of the round penetrating the back of the chair stopped the station master still.

"I wouldn't touch that alarm," warned Scallion.

"Damn, there was no need to fire, Scallion," said Demic. "That could have been heard outside this room."

The twenty controllers had stopped what they were doing. They looked on the scene with confusion, uncertain of what they should do. A loud high scream broke the silence as Ruseq turned and the nearest controller saw him. The pale skin stretched over his skeletal frame, his blood-red eyes, and sharp teeth were most definitely not human. "A mutant!" shrilled the woman as she backed away in fear.

"Now!" ordered Sara, and the perimeter of the room was filled with thirty neway that appeared from nowhere, many outfitted in new curio-armour, though none carried any curio-weapons, instead trusting blasters as they weren't gifted.

Demic had grabbed hold of the controller, restraining him before he made another attempt to raise the alarm.

The room was in turmoil as the controllers panicked. Some screamed, others fainted, a few ran for the doorway to escape. As those that fled were confronted by an armed neway, they recoiled and ran the other way.

"Everyone calm down," shouted Frisk for the sixth time before finally the human controllers huddled into small groups, stopped trying to escape, and stayed still. "These people are with me. Don't do anything stupid, and no one needs to get hurt."

"I won't give you control of the station," said Rime defiantly.

"You don't really have control of the station," said

Peter, who was heard above everything else. He was walking the perimeter of the room examining the wall. Everyone focused on him as he completed a full circuit and arrived back at the door.

"Peter," said Sara, "we need you to focus, find the panel."

"It's designed to be hidden." And he started to walk the room's perimeter again until he was once again back at the door.

Someone banged on the door from the outside. "Is everything okay in there? The door's locked."

"Elite," stated Demic. Rime made to call out, and the former elite hit him hard and he dropped to the floor unconscious. "Governor..." Demic indicated that he should respond to the inquiry at the door.

Before the governor could frame a response, a controller screamed, "Mutant! There are mutants in here!" Then others too screamed, "Mutant!"

It took several seconds for the neway to silence the humans by threatening them with their weapons.

"Peter, we have less than ten minutes before they get through that door," stated Demic.

"Turn all the lights out." Sara had noted Retisen among the neway, but his team had so far operated without any instruction from him.

"You." Frisk pointed at one of the controllers. "Do as he says. And before any of you do anything stupid, these mutants can see you in the dark, so stay still."

"Governor, is everything okay in there?" A fresh voice outside was calling out. He sounded muffled through the door, but he could be heard clearly.

"Buy us as much time as you can," pleaded Sara as she

turned to the controller. "Turn all the lights out now," she ordered.

The woman broke away from her colleagues and moved over to a control panel. The room went dark, but it was not absolute darkness as the various holographic information displays set an eerie glow across the room.

"Who is that outside?" called Frisk as he moved towards the door.

"Officer Ovrom, Governor, you know me."

"Ovrom, everything is fine here. There's a problem with the door is all."

"Is the station master with you? We heard a sound like a ballistic being discharged and people screaming 'mutant'. Are you sure everything is okay?"

"Is this dark enough?" Sara asked Retisen.

"Can it get darker?"

"Only the station master can turn the panels on or off," said the controller who had turned out the lights.

"This is it then," Sara told Retisen, looking at the fallen Rime.

"Everyone look for any anomaly in the wall. Use anything, use your dark-sight as best you can, get up close if you have to."

The neway began examining the perimeter wall, while others kept close to the frightened humans.

There was a thud on the outside of the door.

"That's a cutter," stated Demic. "Whatever you've said, Frisk, they don't believe you. They'll be inside now in minutes."

"Here," called one of the neway, and Peter rushed over to his location to examine the wall.

"This is it," he said after a moment examining the

surface. Peter produced a long six-inch fine pin and pushed the end to the wall, where it penetrated the small hole that was hidden there. He felt a soft click through the pin, and beside him, a hidden door opened. Beyond was a small room and a single console and chair.

"Be quick, Peter," demanded Demic. The sound of cutting had commenced on the outside of the door.

"Defensive positions," ordered Retisen, and the banished spread throughout the room using the consoles for cover.

"Get down," Sara told the controllers. "Stay down. We won't hurt you intentionally, but if there's going to be a fight, you need to stay low." The controllers, all frightened, complied.

Sara joined Peter in the smaller room, barely large enough for the two of them. The old man was sitting at the panel and the keyboard typing in instructions.

"No good," he said. "My authority has either lapsed or been removed. Not surprising really."

The inside of the door to the control centre started to glow hot. "They're almost through," warned Demic as the outline of a large circle took shape on the door's interior side.

"Back to the original plan then," said Sara as she placed Flow on the panel.

"They're through," hollered Demic, informing everyone to take cover.

The circular plug was pushed in and fell heavily to the floor on the inside of the door. Immediately behind it came half a dozen stun grenades that flashed and banged loudly, filling the room with smoke.

The neway fired at the doorway; they were partially

blind to anyone trying to enter but hoped to suppress anyone or anything trying to come through the hole.

Flow dropped to the floor beneath the panel. The smoke reached the small room, but not with sufficient density to entirely obscure Sara's or Peter's vision.

"Is she quick at this stuff?" asked Peter.

"No idea. She knows what I want but…"

Blaster fire picked up in the room, and screams could be heard.

"Botdrones, flying, six of them." Sara recognised Retisen's voice calling out the warning.

As Demic had predicted, the elite had sent in botdrones to clear the room of hostiles. A stray blaster shot scorched the back wall of the small room, and both Peter and Sara took cover as best they could. She looked for Flow, but the cat was nowhere to be seen.

There were two small explosions, one after the other. The smoke was starting to clear, and the neway had brought down two of the flying botdrones. They didn't celebrate, though, as four remained and the elite beyond the door had commenced firing through the hole they'd made, forcing the neway to stay low as the botdrones took the high position and targeted the intruders.

A botdrone fourteen inches in diameter flew inside the small room where Sara and Peter were taking cover, its guns trained on both of them. Neither of them was armed.

The characteristic boom of Scallion's large ballistic pistol rang out, and two slugs struck the hovering botdrone. The sphere dropped to the floor, cracking the panel, and broke the chair before it finally landed on the floor.

Sara glanced through the doorway to see Scallion

standing there, his weapon raised. She smiled at him and then screamed out, but she was too late. The botdrone behind him fired and he fell. Retisen took out the botdrone before it could fire a further shot. Another of the flying spheres exploded on the far side of the room.

Sara surveyed the scene. The smoke was almost clear now. More than twenty neway lay dead or wounded on the floor or draped over panels and chairs. More had come through and were still coming through, using the curio-disc to reinforce their numbers. Of those still standing, it was apparent that the curio-armour had saved many of them as the clothing bore the scorch marks of blaster fire. Those without such armour hadn't been so fortunate, but Sara knew that none of them would have wanted to retreat or surrender. They would have fought until none of them remained. Retisen himself had told her that. They would all die if they needed to in order to complete Sara's plan.

Then it happened; the cone device behind Sara's ear connected to the station's crucial systems. Flow had succeeded, but not in a way she had imagined. The data stream that filled her head revealed information in a fraction of a moment that would have taken hours to understand and to have been able to be utilised by any other method.

The two flying botdrones in the room stopped firing and fell to the floor, where they became dormant. There was the sound of blasters being fired in the corridor outside the control room, and then silence fell.

"Lay down your weapons or be fired upon." The phrase was repeated several times in the corridor.

Demic was the first to stand. "Sara," she called. "Sara, where are you?"

The young woman walked from the small side room. She had hoped for no casualties, but bodies lay strewn everywhere. Dead, dying and injured neway littered the room. They had fulfilled their selfless act so that they might save their people from the human invaders, and many had given the ultimate sacrifice. To Sara, no matter what the outcome of all this, they had become exalted. Tears flowed down her cheeks, but her mind was already issuing orders to every botdrone in the station. No one, other than Peter, had known the origin of the term "botdrone". Bot referenced their autonomous programming that provided their systems instructions and parameters under which they operated. Drone referred to the fact that each or all could be piloted remotely. Sara now had complete control of every botdrone that operated inside the station, including the wall cannons and turret guns. She wasn't sure how she was able to operate the botdrones while still acting outwardly normal, but she did know for sure that it was related to her being a connected.

chapter sixteen

The Seed of Change

They had command of Station Six. The general population of both the grounders and the lofters knew nothing of the change in control. The majority of the station's elite had been stood down from the alert and told that the situation was under control. The few elite who were involved in the control room incident had been captured and subdued by their accompanying botdrones, and none of them had died or been injured. The controllers, too, had suffered no injuries during the fighting.

All those humans aware of what had happened were taken away and secured in the governor's guest quarters. They were locked in and guarded by botdrones, but they would be treated well.

Eleven neway, banished, had died. A dozen had been injured and had gone back via the curio-disc to be treated. Many were healed on the relic table by Lonlin.

Sky, Poppy and Jeb had used the disc to enter the station when it was deemed safe.

Scallion's dead body was found with Flow lying on his chest. The cat refused to leave him, digging in with her claws when anyone attempted to shift her, so they left her there until she moved off on her own accord.

Demic and Frisk were unscathed during the fighting, but Ninety-Six had taken more than one wound. Yet he remained strong and reluctantly, and only when pressured, did he agree to see Lonlin and get healed.

Governor Frisk took charge of the station's hierarchy, with Demic at his side as his bodyguard. He ordered the station closed down to all outside visitations, stating the reason as an unknown infectious illness that required the whole station to be quarantined. He dealt with the challenges thrown at them by the other stations and governors with typical political ambiguity, and no one attempted to visit.

Vereign had checked his comms device regularly since Sara had left until the expected communication arrived.

'I thought you had the girl, Sara, under control. She has overthrown Station Six and locked us out. You need to remedy this or we will be forced to act against you and all the vampires of your world. I want the girl, and the curio-cylinder, in my possession soon. This has all taken far too long. Get this done quickly, or you will suffer.'

Vereign replied: *'Consider it done. I will report when the situation is rectified.'*

about the author

Andy Sharp resides in Merseyside, UK, where he writes, paints art, and takes the occasional photo. More can be discovered on his webpage **www.penphotopaint.com**

This is his first book in the series - look out for more adventures.